THE OPPOSITE EFFECT

AN ALL MALE POV

SHANDI BOYES

COPYRIGHT

WANT TO STAY IN TOUCH?

Facebook: facebook.com/authorshandi

Instagram: instagram.com/authorshandi

Email: authorshandi@gmail.com

Reader's Group: bit.ly/ShandiBookBabes

Website: authorshandi.com

Newsletter: https://www.subscribepage.com/AuthorShandi

ALSO BY SHANDI BOYES

** Denotes Standalone Books*

<u>Perception Series</u>

<u>Saving Noah</u> *

<u>Fighting Jacob</u> *

<u>Taming Nick</u> *

<u>Redeeming Slater</u> *

<u>Saving Emily</u>

<u>Wrapped Up with Rise Up</u>

<u>Protecting Nicole</u> *

<u>Enigma</u>

<u>Enigma</u>

<u>Unraveling an Enigma</u>

<u>Enigma The Mystery Unmasked</u>

<u>Enigma: The Final Chapter</u>

<u>Beneath The Secrets</u>

<u>Beneath The Sheets</u>

<u>Spy Thy Neighbor</u> *

<u>The Opposite Effect</u> *

<u>I Married a Mob Boss</u> *

<u>Second Shot</u> *

<u>The Way We Are</u>

<u>The Way We Were</u>

<u>Sugar and Spice</u> *

<u>Lady In Waiting</u>

<u>Man in Queue</u>

<u>Couple on Hold</u>

<u>Enigma: The Wedding</u>

<u>Silent Vigilante</u>

<u>Hushed Guardian</u>

<u>Quiet Protector</u>

Enigma: An Isaac Retelling

<u>Twisted Lies</u> *

<u>Bound Series</u>

<u>Chains</u>

<u>Links</u>

<u>Bound</u>

<u>Restrain</u>

<u>The Misfits</u> *

Nanny Dispute *

<u>Russian Mob Chronicles</u>

<u>Nikolai: A Mafia Prince Romance</u>

<u>Nikolai: Taking Back What's Mine</u>

<u>Nikolai: What's Left of Me</u>

<u>Nikolai: Mine to Protect</u>
<u>Asher: My Russian Revenge</u> *
<u>Nikolai: Through the Devil's Eyes</u>
<u>Trey</u> *

The Italian Cartel

Dimitri
Roxanne
Reign
Mafia Ties (Novella)
Maddox
Demi
Ox
Rocco *
Clover *
Smith *

RomCom Standalones

Just Playin' *
<u>Ain't Happenin'</u> *
<u>The Drop Zone</u> *
Very Unlikely *
False Start *

Short Stories - Newsletter Downloads

Christmas Trio *

Falling For A Stranger *

One Night Only Series

Hotshot Boss *

Hotshot Neighbor *

The Bobrov Bratva Series

Wicked Intentions *

Sinful Intentions *

Devious Intentions *

Deadly Intentions *

PROLOGUE

Feet scuffling on a tiled floor steal my focus from my half-eaten cheesesteak sandwich. Even with me requesting they hold the relish, my hands are covered in the ghastly orange liquid that makes me gag just thinking about eating it.

When I lift my gaze from my partially dissected dinner, I spot Diesel standing in the lunchroom's doorway. His shoulder is propped against the doorjamb, his extensively tattooed arms are crossed in front of his broad chest, and a look of terror is stretched across his face.

After pushing back from the lunch table hidden out back, I dump my unsalvageable sandwich into the trash, then head to the sink to get cleaned up. Diesel is a cutthroat take-no-shit-from-anyone type of guy, so I'm surprised his cocky personality is a little off.

"What's up, man?" While washing my sticky hands in the kitchen sink, I mutter a string of profanities under my breath.

How the fuck can you mess up a cheesesteak sandwich?

Diesel waits for me to snag a dishcloth off the drying rack

before announcing, "Got a client out front requesting to speak to the manager." My lips quirk when he air quotes 'manager.' Although I've held the title for the past two years, it's rarely used by my crew.

Once I hang the damp towel onto a hook above the microwave, I gesture for Diesel to lead the way. Buzzing tattoo guns and the groans of idiot kids who walk through our doors the day they turn eighteen sounds through my ears when we stride through Inked Tattoo Shop.

When I spot Charity tattooing a Pokémon figure onto a kid who looks barely old enough to drive, let alone permanently mark his skin with the latest fad, I rake my fingers through my shoulder-length hair.

It will take a tattoo four times its size to cover up Pikachu or whatever the fuck Pokémon character that is. By the look on his face and the tears staining his cheeks, I'm confident having it covered won't be a walk in the park for neither him nor the tattoo artist assigned to the job.

When we reach the foyer out front, I scan the area, seeking the bozo who interrupted the 'manager' during his measly half-an-hour lunch break.

Upon failing to locate the irate face I regularly see when a client realizes their home-botched tattoo will cost over a grand to fix, I shift my eyes to Diesel. "Where is he?"

Diesel smiles a grin I only see when he's wrapping his arm around a bar bunny at the end of a Saturday night shift. "It isn't a he. It's a *she*."

Still grinning, he points to the far corner of the room. When I tilt my head, only just clearing Johnny's wide shoulders, I catch the quickest flurry of an enticing body. My heart rate kicks up a gear—*as does the pulse in my cock*—when I drink in the slender blonde sparring with Johnny like backyard brawls are a regular event on her schedule.

Her platinum locks roll past her shoulders like a satin waterfall, and her expensive threads showcase every curve of her fit body. Her face is fresh with only a slight sprinkling of makeup, and every strand on her faultless head has been meticulously placed.

Although I can't hear a word she's speaking, I know she's giving Johnny as good as she's getting. If the crossed arms under her ample breasts and stiffened stance aren't enough indication, her resting bitch face is a sure-fire sign.

This woman is two seconds from exploding.

Since I don't want a bomb detonated in my shop on a busy Saturday night, I pat Diesel on the back before heading for the attractive blonde. A rich floral scent with a hint of spice filters into my nose when I stand next to Johnny. I'm fairly sure the flowery scent is coming from the blonde, but I can't one hundred percent testify to that. Johnny is generous with the discount he offers female clientele. If the loss comes from his takings, I have no concerns about him accepting payments for services rendered in the form of extra-curricular activities.

"I'm pretty sure you're sitting at around two seconds," I interrupt when I overhear the blonde telling Johnny she's five seconds away from having his "moronic ass fired."

"Great." Her eyes snap to mine. They're as dazzling as the diamond bracelet circling her delicate wrist. "Another beast added to the mix. What is this, a poorly scripted rendition of *Beauty and the Beast?*"

Three females standing behind her break into an ear-piercing drunken cackle, but surprisingly, the blonde maintains eye contact. I'll give it to her. I'm impressed at her ability to keep her eyes on my face. Most women absorb my face before dropping to sample the rest of the package. It doesn't matter if they're screaming nothing but wealth like the princess standing before me, or they don't have a nickel to their name, the routine never alters. So yeah, I'll admit it, she gets credit where credit is due.

After propping my elbows onto the counter, I lean over it, which brings my six-foot-two height down to her at-a-guess five-foot-seven stature. "What can I do you for, Princess? Unlike you, some of us have to work for a living."

She rolls her eyes before saying in a snooty twang, "Not according to..." She gestures her hand to Johnny, sending a multi-hued shimmer of light across the cabinet from her diamond bracelet. "Him—"

"Johnny," I interrupt.

She rolls her eyes again. "Whatever you call him. No one cares. I came here to get a tattoo." She points to the tube light hanging from the shop's awning. "This is a tattoo parlor. But..." she snaps her eyes back to Johnny, "... *he* is refusing to serve me. I don't know about you, but in any other industry, that would call for instant dismissal."

I smirk, not shocked by her attitude but most definitely stunned by my positive response to it. Normally, I would toss out a berating client before giving them the chance to explain. Instead, I slot into the 'manager' role I'll never completely fill. "Lucky for Johnny, we aren't just any *other* industry." My voice has an edge of annoyance to it even with me being most entertained by the change-up in clientele. "If Johnny is refusing to tattoo you, it will be for a reason. So, what is it?"

With a huff, she digs her hand into the front pocket of her designer jeans that look like they cost more than my entire wardrobe. "Other than Johnny being a moron, I have no clue why he's refusing my request."

"It's beca—"

I slice my hand through the air, cutting Johnny off. His wife packed her bags and headed to Reno nine months ago, leaving him the sole guardian of their two children. He wouldn't refuse the chance to make a quick dollar without a legitimate reason. Just the blonde's overpriced shoes, designer handbag, and perfectly swept hair leave no doubt he could have charged her triple the regular hourly rate, and she'd have been none the wiser.

He'd never turn down an opportunity like this without a solid reason.

I lock my eyes with Johnny. "Why don't you head out back and work on those sketches you started last week? I'll man the counter. Next client who enters is yours."

Johnny nods before sauntering to the manager's office stationed next to his cubicle. Once he passes through the battered wooden door, I return my focus to the blonde. Victory is etched on her face, and the bitch pose she's already perfected escalates.

I stand from my slouched position, then shoot my eyes to a sign attached to the side wall of the foyer. "We have the right to refuse patrons under the influence of alcohol, drugs, or peer pressure." I tap my fingers on the big black letters scrawled across the sign. Even someone with their eyes as thinly slit as hers can still read it.

After speedreading the sign three times, she scoffs. "I'm not drunk," she denies while crossing her arms under her chest, hoisting her impressive rack higher.

It takes everything I have to drag my eyes away from her fantastic tits to peer at her intoxicated friends behind her, but I manage—somewhat. The blonde's snarky beast comment was delivered over five minutes ago, but her friends are still cackling like a bunch of overly botoxed biddies holding an annual meeting at a members-only country club.

My curved brow arches higher when I notice the only brunette in the trio is clasping an open bottle of champagne.

While running a hand over my jaw, which is marked with a few days of stubble, I shift my eyes back to the blonde. When I twist my lips, a deep rustle escapes her nose before she cranks her neck to her friends.

Even smacking them with a furious stink eye doesn't dampen their laughter.

If anything, her actions increases it.

Realizing her friends won't help me believe she isn't under the influence, she gestures to them that it's time to leave. Just before she emerges onto the sidewalk, she peers back at me and narrows her eyes. I smile and wink at her, more than happy to add a sprinkling of salt to her freshly opened wounds.

When a black town car slides up to the curb at the front of the shop, I swing my eyes to Diesel. "What was so hard about that?" My tone is dripping with cockiness. "You need to stop entertaining bar bunnies on your days off and wrestle a few rich chicks. They give a bit of lip, but since it's from the same mouth that will be screaming your name later that night, you put up with it."

After lifting my arms to protect my face, I throw a handful of rapid-fire jabs into Diesel's T-shirt-covered torso. A grin tugs on his fat lips before he spars up, priming for an impromptu spar in the foyer.

Usually, we box in an old gym at the back of the shopping complex in Ravenshoe. It's rundown, but the guy behind the rusty equipment is a brilliant trainer.

In just a few short weeks, Hank has switched Diesel from a backyard brawler to a low-ranking fighter.

Fighting isn't something I'm interested in, but I turn up every session to show my support to Diesel. Although I will admit, the energy boost after going a few rounds in the ring with Diesel has aided in my bedroom antics. I have stamina by the miles and more than a dozen bar bunnies willing to exhaust me of resources.

When Diesel uses my distraction of the shop's bells to his advantage, my neck snaps to the side, and my jaw pops under the force of his knuckles. After working my jaw side to side, I lock my furious eyes with Diesel's.

With a grin that announces he isn't sorry, he holds his hands in the air in a non-defensive manner. "Sorry." The shortness of his apology can't hide his laughter.

While rubbing my hand along my now throbbing jaw, I drift my eyes from Diesel to the door. "Welcome to Inked..." My greeting falls short when I'm confronted with the same pair of icy-blue eyes that stormed out of here mere minutes ago.

The bitch is back.

When the blonde completes her surveillance of the rest of my package, I wait for her eyes to return to my face before giving her a cocky wink. "Back for round two?"

My jeans tighten when she laughs. It's a dainty giggle full of poise and perfection—*just like its owner*.

"Unlikely." Her words are as cool as the color of her eyes. "I don't *wrestle* with Neanderthals."

Ouch. If my ego wasn't stroked by a pretty blonde out back thirty minutes ago—the same blonde who brought me my sandwich—this blonde's taunt may have bruised my ego.

Lucky for me, I have a gigantic shield protecting my even bigger ego from spoiled princesses with vindictive tongues.

"Unless your daddy found a cure for drunkenness, your *desires* will not be granted in this fine establishment this evening."

Her eyes narrow at the mention of her father, exposing her first flaw of the night.

"I'm *not* drunk." The crispness of her words adds strength to her statement.

Holding my gaze, she saunters closer, allowing me to see the frankness in her eyes. Her hardhearted eyes aren't truth-exposing.

It's the fact there isn't a single speck of life in her eyes, let alone the drunk shimmer most inebriated people get, exposing her sobriety. Her eyes replicate staring into an empty pit. They're void of any type of soul.

"I adhered to your rules by requesting my *tipsy* friends to leave. Now your *fine* establishment has no reason *not* to serve me." She tries to make her voice sound sincere. Her attempts are fruitless. I don't think she has a sincere bone in her body.

I grit my teeth, loathing that I'm about to overrule one of my guys, but just her take-no-shit stance exposes she won't leave until she gets what she came here for, so I may as well give it to her. "Do you have a design in mind, or are we going into this agreement freestyle?"

My dick knocks at the zipper in my jeans when she grins a traffic-stopping smile.

Yeah, not happening, buddy.

When she pulls out the sheet of paper she was clutching for dear life earlier, I only just hold in a swear word. She wants a man's name inked on her skin.

Don't ask me why, but the thought of *any* man's name on her skin that isn't mine pisses me off, and considering we've only just met and have spent most of our confrontation defusing her callousness, simply having a thought like that irritates me even more.

After running my eyes over the guy's name in thick black ink smack bang in the middle of the intricate design, I drop them to the blonde's left hand. Upon noticing it is void of a ring—engagement or wedding—I lock my eyes back on hers. "Is this your father's name?" I nudge my head to the tattoo design in my hand.

Lines indent her forehead before she shakes her head.

"Your grandfather? Brother? Deceased uncle? Any type of male relation?" When she shakes her head again, I say, "Sorry, Princess, I can't do your tattoo."

Her eyes slit more with every syllable I speak. "You just agreed to do it."

"Yeah, so?" I shrug like backtracking is on my resume. "That was before you showed me the design."

"What's wrong with the design?" She crosses her arms before arching a perfectly manicured brow. "Not *tacky* enough for you?"

"There's only one *tacky* person in this tattoo parlor, *Princess*." I draw out the word usually used as a term of endearment as if it is a derogative word instead. "It ain't me."

She huffs, her irritation growing by the second. She isn't the only one annoyed. My cock's thickness hasn't lessened from her feistiness. It stiffens with every snarl she hits me with.

"Look. I want to get this tattoo done. You're a tattoo artist. Do whatever you need to do to make this happen."

I nudge my head to the piece of paper. "Are you giving me permission to make alterations to this design as I see fit?"

"Yes!" She throws her arms into the air. "Can we just get this done, then I can get back to—"

"Prince Charming waiting for you in a crystal palace?" I turn my eyes to the clock on the wall displaying it is a little after eleven. "It's okay, Princess, you still have a good fifty minutes before you'll get turned back into poor, defenseless Cinderella."

She glares at me with shock all over her face.

Of course, a real-life princess wouldn't understand a fairy tale.

When I head to the drawing board to transfer her design onto tracing paper before adding the change I require to feel comfortable tattooing a lifetime commitment onto her no-doubt virgin skin, she stands to the side, glaring at me while swiveling her diamond tennis bracelet around her wrist.

Once I'm happy with the design, I amble back her way. "I've altered the design—"

"Yes, yes, whatever," she interrupts, her tone obnoxious.

With a tight jaw, I place the tattoo contract and a copy of the newly designed trace onto the glass cabinet in front of her. "If you're happy with the design, sign here, here, and here." I point to each section of the contract she's required to sign.

Snatching the pen out of my grasp, she signs each section in a frenzied hurry. After storing the contract in the locked drawer under the cash register, I gesture for her to follow me. As we walk through Inked, her eyes bounce in all directions, strengthening my assumption that this is her first tattoo.

The width of her pupils increases when we enter a private cubicle at the back of the shop. When she spots my tattoo gun sitting on a sterilized stainless-steel table, her face pales.

After closing the door behind me, I ask, "Where do you want your tattoo?"

Heat creeps across her cheeks before she points to her lower right hipbone.

"Then you're gonna need to remove your jeans," I advise before moving to the station to set up my instruments.

When her eyes snap to mine, wordlessly demanding clarification of my request, I nod.

I might be a fucking great tattoo artist, but I'm not a miracle worker.

She hesitates for a moment before doing as instructed. I'm not at all surprised to discover she's wearing a pair of panties I've only seen in the Victoria's Secret catalogs Charity peruses during her lunch break.

After ensuring my gear is in order, I nudge my head to my tattooing chair, silently demanding she sit. As she saunters across the room, I try to keep my eyes planted on her face. I miserably fail. Even with her bitchometer rocketing to the next galaxy, she has a tight, fit body that would only look better if she removed the massive chip off her shoulder.

After sitting in my swivel chair, I roll in close to her side. She stiffens when I lower the band of her panties to prep the area she wants inked. When our eyes briefly lock, her stern mask falters for the slightest second, exposing a side of her I'm confident she hasn't seen in years.

"First time being tattooed?" I query while placing the used alcohol prep pads into a bin at my side.

When she fails to answer my question, I lift my eyes from the stencil I've placed on the creamy skin covering her hip to her face.

Four simple words and her stern mask has slid firmly back into place.

"Do we have to do the small talk?"

"I'm just trying to be friendly."

"Well, I'd rather you didn't. You're *not* my friend. You will *never* be my friend. So, I'd prefer if you stayed *quiet* and did the *job* I'm paying you to do."

My back molars smash together before I grind out through clenched teeth, "Then let's do this, Princess." *Before you give me a motherfucking headache.*

It takes all my strength not to dig my tattoo gun into her delicate skin deeper than necessary. The only thing stopping me is my professional obligation. As much as my client is a malicious cow, my name will forever be associated with this piece of artwork on her body, which ensures I'll tattoo nothing but the best, even if I want to send her out in the world with a stick figure of me flipping her the bird.

Because of the intricate design she selected, the tattoo takes a little over two hours to complete. Princess Stuck-Up didn't speak a word the entire time. I won't lie. I loved the way her knuckles went white from her death grip hold on the armrest when I tattooed the skin near her hip bone.

"While it heals, it'll itch like a bitch, but if you keep applying the ointment as per these instructions, you shouldn't face too many issues." I hand her a pamphlet on taking care of freshly inked skin.

When she snatches it out of my hand, I drop my eyes to my newly created masterpiece. My lips purse. It is a sleek design, feminine with the inclusion of a tiger lily, but not overly girly. If it didn't have a name smack bang in the middle of it, it would have been a nice tattoo.

After wiping the excess ink off her hip, I wrap her tattoo with a protective covering and then assist the unnamed blonde from the chair.

A grin curls on my lips when a grimace crosses her face as she bends down to collect her handbag off the floor. "Run that while I get dressed."

Heavy grooves indent my forehead when she hands me an American Express Centurion card. I've heard rumors that this card costs a quarter of a million a year just to have it. I shouldn't expect anything less from a woman who looks like she uses Benjamin Franklins as toilet paper.

"It's a credit card. You've seen one before, haven't you?" she snarls, her tone condescending.

"Yes, madame," I reply while fighting the urge not to salute her pompous attitude with my middle finger. I jerk my head to the bathroom attached to my cubicle. "There's a full-length mirror in there if you want to check out your new tattoo." When she smirks a condescending grin, I mutter under my breath before slipping out the door, "I hope you like your new tattoo, Princess."

I've only just run her credit card through the terminal and placed the credit of her sale into Johnny's account when the blonde storms out of my cubicle. She barely notices a group of fraternity brothers getting matching tats wolf-whistling and catcalling at her as she charges across the room in nothing but a pair of cream panties and a long-sleeve shirt. Her face is red with anger, matching her vibrant lipstick, and her pupils are massive.

"You son of a bitch!" she yells while raising her hand in the air.

A chuckle topples from my lips when her wildly flung slap fails to connect with any part of my face or body since I took a step back, moving out of the firing zone.

When she preps for a second swing, I point to a sign hanging next to the one I read earlier. "We also have the right to remove any clientele deemed to be abusive to our staff or clients." My tone is as mocking as my expression. "If you try to strike me again, I'll have no other option than to place you on the curb." I lower my eyes to her scarcely covered body. "Panties and all."

The anger lining her face increases. "Where is the sign that says you can tattoo whatever the hell you see fit onto a person's body without first seeking their permission?"

The grin tugging on my lips breaks free. "In the top drawer." I point to the drawer I stored her contract in. "It's on the same contract *you* signed stating the design of your tattoo was left at the discretion of your tattoo artist. AKA... me."

I can see her scream work its way from her stomach to her lips. For every second that ticks by, the fury blackening her eyes grows significantly, but she detonates with only the slightest bit of carnage.

After releasing a window-shattering scream, she storms back to my cubicle, rambling incessantly under her breath about how she's going to sue me for every penny I have.

If I were a good man, I'd tell her I don't have many pennies.

Pity I'm not.

After redressing in her skin-tight designer jeans and four-inch stiletto boots, she saunters out of my cubicle, slamming the door behind her. Her nostrils flare when she snatches her credit card and receipt out of my hand, but she doesn't murmur a peep as she scrambles for the door.

"Have a wonderful day."

She slams the front glass door so harshly, the gust of its closure knocks the two signs I'd referenced earlier off the wall.

Upon hearing the commotion her abrupt exit caused, Ryder the owner of Inked, exits his office. "Everything all right?" His eyes bounce between the blonde standing at the curb shrieking into a cell phone and me.

I lift my chin. "It's all good."

Although I'm telling him everything is fine, I really need to start considering the consequences of my actions. If I knew I was going against a woman who has more money than sense, I may have considered taking a different route.

Oh, who am I kidding? Nothing would have changed.

Ryder nudges his head to the door. "So what's the deal? She didn't like the terms of your agreement?"

I laugh at the insinuation in his voice. "You know as well as I do, Elvis, nothing but money is exchanged for my services."

Ryder's heavy brow slants at my use of his infamous nickname. His son, Slater, let it slip a few months ago when he was here adding more ink to his already vast collection. I've been keeping it up my sleeve, waiting for a prime opportunity to use it. Tonight seems like the ideal time.

When the blonde curls into a black town car pulled to the curb in front of her, I shift my eyes to Ryder. "I may or may not have changed her boyfriend's name to Princess."

A lewd grin curves onto his lips before he shakes his head in disbelief. "Did you get her to sign the contract?"

"Do you think I got this handsome by lining up for brains? I cut that queue and went straight back to the looks department. Who needs smarts when you look like this?" I run my hand down the front of me while smiling a shit-eating grin.

Any humor in Ryder's face vanishes, replaced with nothing but pure anger.

"I'm joking, Ryder. Of course, I got her to sign the contract. I even stenciled her tattoo with the name adjustment included," I inform him while rocking on my heels. "She signed that too."

A chuckle escapes Ryder's no-longer stern lips. "Then we're all good."

"Yes, we are," I reply, grinning.

Although I have an inkling this won't be the last I'll hear from Ms. Clara McGregor.

The doorman at Vipers greets me with a fist pump before opening the large wrought iron door. Pricy leather, warm bodies, and the scent of alcohol filter into my nose when I enter the main section of the strip club.

My eyes divert from a pretty redhead with gold tassels on her breasts to the entryway bar when a distinctive throaty voice sounds through my ears. "Brax, it's been too long." Keke saunters around the bar to wrap her arms around my neck.

I return her embrace. "Hey, Keke, what are you doing over on this side of town? The prim and proper get too dull for you?"

She laughs before scraping her lengthened French tip nails down my forearm. "I'm always on the lookout," she purrs while skimming the full-to-the-brim club.

"For clientele or new staff members?"

Keke winks before she continues scanning the room. She is the manager of a very exclusive club on the other side of Ravenshoe. *Maison du Sexe* (French for House of Sex). Although she refers to her establishment as a bordello, every male on this side of Ravenshoe calls it a brothel. An incredibly high-priced, invited-members-only exclusive brothel. Though if you're friendly with the manager, even guys from my side of the tracks can dip their toes into the high-caliber services Keke offers.

Does that mean I've accepted the numerous offers she's bestowed upon me? No, it does not. Even though I only accept cash payments for my services, that doesn't mean I'm willing to cough up my hard-earned cash for services I can get without money exchanging hands.

Although with my dick on hiatus the past few weeks, I may need to consider other options.

Keke curls her arm around the crook of my elbow and leads me toward the main stage. She stops in front of a beautiful brunette doing an aerial ribbon routine with a set of black satin ribbons suspended from a bolt shackled to the ceiling. Her outfit selection, although skimpy, is more conservative than the clientele at Vipers is used to seeing. It could be deemed more as a gymnast's outfit than a stripper's ensemble.

My heart leaps out of my chest when the brunette rolls down the satin ribbon, her stomach-churning tumble only stopping a mere inch from the stage. One wrong move and she would have been splattered on the highly-polished wooden stage.

After loosening the satin material from her slender thighs, the brunette curtseys to the wolf-whistling crowd before the stage lights are switched off, plunging the entire area into blackness.

"Beautiful. Yes?" Keke questions, her fake French accent fully exploited.

Smirking, I nod. Even with the brunette having her god-gifted assets hidden from view, her routine was provocative and entertaining. No doubt a rare treat for any male clientele in a strip club.

"The clients at Maison's speak fondly of her very often, but no matter how much money I offer, she never accepts my proposition."

My shoulders lift into a shrug. "Showing your body for money is one thing. Selling it is entirely different."

When Keke scoffs, I turn my brown eyes to her and arch a brow. The longer I stare into her rich, chocolate eyes, the more her refined posture slackens. The persona she displays when working is a completely different Keke than the one you see behind closed doors. Keke is from Fredericksburg, Virginia. She rides horses bareback, drinks beer by the gallon, and when she comes, her voice reverts to its original country twang. *Y'all* included. How do I know this? We've messed around a few times in the past year.

Now don't take my admission the wrong way. Keke may be the manager of a brothel, but she has never once *worked* in that industry. Like the pretty brunette who just finished her ribbon performance, Keke refuses to sell her body for profit. Her firm stance on the issue ensures her staff at Maison's are treated with the utmost respect and dignity. For the industry she works in, that is no easy feat. Luckily for Keke and her staff, she's backed by an exceedingly notorious man—Mr. Henry Gottle, Sr.—mob boss of New York City.

"Have you thought about asking her to do a routine at Maison that excludes a bedroom?"

Keke's face brightens more with every word I speak. "Brax, you little devil. That could work. Get her in the door and convert her once she's signed on the dotted line."

"That wasn't what I meant."

Keke doesn't hear a word spilling from my lips. She simply smiles and presses a kiss on my cheek before sauntering to the roped-off backstage area. Once she enters through the dark red velvet curtains, I swing my eyes around the space, seeking Damon.

His rift with his big brother is the sole reason I've rocked up to a strip club at one in the morning on a Sunday.

While adding three hours to his back tattoo earlier today, Damon suggested we meet up for a few beers with his brother. Considering his brother is my best mate, I readily agreed. I had no clue at the time that his watering hole of choice was a strip club on the outskirts of town.

I will admit, though, my initial assessment of this establishment was a little off track. I thought it would be a seedy establishment with dingy lighting and cracked vinyl booths. It isn't. The owner has pumped some serious coin into this place, giving it a nightclub atmosphere.

The booths are high-end with varnished wood trim and black leather upholstery. The lighting setup is impressive, with it being incorporated into the music pumping out of the speakers shackled to the ceiling. From the caliber of staff I've seen serving clients and dancing, the standard is high. *Incredibly high.* It feels more like I've walked into the dressing room of a Miss Universe swimsuit competition than a seedy strip club.

My aimless wandering comes to a halt when I hear "Brax!" shouted by a profound voice in the distance.

Cranking my neck to the side, I spot Damon in a booth in the back corner. Surprisingly, he is alone. I dip my chin in greeting to numerous scantily clad women as I make my way across the room. The scent of sweat-slicked skin intensifies the closer I get to the back of the club. Damon stands from the booth and greets me with a slap on the back and a man hug.

He grimaces when I return his gesture.

"Sorry, still fresh?"

He nods. "I haven't drunk enough whiskey to lessen the sting of my new ink," he replies, laughing.

"Where's your brother?"

Just as the final syllable escapes my lips, I spot Ryan making his way through the throng of people mingling in the vast space. A smirk etches onto my lips when I see the disappointing glare Ryan is directing at Damon. Ryan and Damon are brothers cut from two entirely different cloths. Ryan was born and raised in Ravenshoe. The week after he graduated high school, he applied to join the police force. He was immediately accepted. He's spent the last nine years working at the Ravenshoe Police Department.

Damon was also born and raised in Ravenshoe, but unlike Ryan, he left the instant he turned eighteen. Although it's never been fully disclosed, there are rumors circulating that Damon and a certain member of the law enforcement office don't see eye to eye. That may be the reason this is Damon's first visit home in over eight years.

My brows lower when Ryan and Damon greet with a shake of hands. Anyone would swear they were strangers meeting for the first time, not brothers.

While issuing my greeting to Ryan, I mutter into his ear, "It's been eight years, man. Time to let bygones be bygones."

Ryan pulls back and peers into my eyes. "You know why he picked for us to meet here, don't you?"

I smile. "Yeah, I know. But there's nothing wrong with an off-duty detective spending his weekend looking at some fine ladies."

Damon picked this establishment as he knew Ryan would hesitate to show up here. Ryan works hard at keeping his reputation as an honest detective sparkling clean. It is a well-known fact that certain business entities in this area pay for the privilege of keeping their establishments off the local enforcement radar. I'm pretty sure this is one of the clubs that kept Ryan's dad's bank balance in the positive during his twenty-year stint with the Ravenshoe Police Department.

Within forty minutes, I've downed three overpriced whiskeys,

Ryan and Damon haven't spoken a word to each other, and Damon has secured himself not one but two lap dances.

I nudge Ryan with my shoulder. "What's the deal? Why is he back?" I gesture my head to Damon during my last question.

Although Damon and Ryan have personalities on opposite ends of the spectrum, their looks are nearly identical. Both have glacier blue eyes, cut facial features, and they're extremely popular with the ladies. I've never had any problems pulling in the ladies, but my looks are often referred to as laid-back compared to Ryan's. He has the cutthroat-businessman appearance, with his attire of choice being suits and polished shoes. My outfit selection rarely strays from ripped jeans and designer shirts.

Ryan tosses back a mouthful of the whiskey the waiter just sat in front of him before answering, "I don't know. He sent Ma a message a few days ago saying he might head back this way in a few months. He turns up on her doorstep the very next day."

My lips quirk. "You think he's running from something?" I query, noticing a mask of concern slipping over Ryan's face.

"Something or someone," Ryan mutters before taking another gulp of his drink. He runs the back of his hand over his mouth before locking his blue eyes with mine. "So what's the deal with you? I've seen you turn down three girls since I arrived. That's not the Brax I know."

After shaking my head in disgust, I down my entire nip of whiskey in one hit. "I think my cock is broken."

Ryan coughs, splattering the countertop with the whiskey he was in the process of swallowing. "What?"

I nudge my head to the gorgeous blonde prowling past our booth for the fourth time in the past three minutes. "Beautiful ass, a sinful body, and a rack I'd love to bury my face in." I drop my eyes to the crotch of my jeans. "Nothing. Nada. It's fucking broken."

Ryan throws back his head and laughs. I'm glad he can find amusement in my life-threatening situation. I've never faced this type of *issue* before. Normally, I'd just mumble the word 'pussy' and *schwing*! My cock is ready to pounce. But for the past two months, it's like my cock packed up and went on holiday, no notice given to me or my lust-riddled brain.

Ryan signals to the waiter for another round before aligning his eyes with mine. "Maybe things have just gotten too easy for you?" His voice is more sincere than his leering expression as he runs his eyes over my face and shoulder-length brown hair. "You need to mess up that pretty face of yours. Make it more of a challenge. Your dick has gotten bored with the ease of the game."

While rolling my eyes, I punch him in the arm. When he chuckles, I shake my head and turn my eyes back to the crowd to silently ponder. There are beautiful women as far as my eye can see, yet my cock feels nothing. Not a twinge. Not even a slight fucking throb. As much as Ryan thinks I'm joking, I truly believe my cock is broken.

But I'm twenty-eight for fuck's sake. I'm not even close to the age most men seek help with this type of situation.

Maybe Ryan is right? Maybe the game has gotten too easy?

My wallowing over my broken appendage stops when Ryan asks, "You still buying into Inked?"

I nod, happy to change the course of our conversation. "Yeah. With everything going on with Ryder's boy, he doesn't want to spend as much time at the shop. It's kind of a win-win situation. He gets time with his family. I get to dig my fingers into ownership."

Ryder's son, Slater, was admitted to rehab earlier this month. Slater's band, Rise Up, started smashing the charts late last year with two singles off their debut album. The week following the band's massive success, the band's lead singer, Noah Taylor, was involved in a traffic accident which resulted in him spending three months in a coma at a local private hospital. Ryder was worried about his boy, but Slater seemed to be handling the situation well... until his friend recovered. Then it all went downhill.

Ryder was suspicious a few weeks before Slater's best mate, Marcus, arrived at the shop, but he was giving his boy the benefit of the doubt. Once Ryder had solid proof Slater was dabbling in a wide variety of recreational drugs, he dragged his son's ass to rehab. After some heavy discussions with his missus, Ryder decided to put Inked on the market so he could spend more time with his family.

After losing their daughter a few years ago to leukemia, Ryder and Lucia weren't going to sit back and watch another illness claim the life of their child. Although I have enough coin saved to fully buy Ryder out, the fifty percent buy-in I suggested is a better situation for us both. Inked gets to keep Ryder's honorable name associated with it, and once Ryder's boy gets his head back in the game, Ryder will have Inked to fall back on if home life becomes too dull.

"So when will I make you a customer at Inked?"

Ryan smiles against the rim of his glass. "When you stop accepting cash only for services."

I laugh. "That will *never* happen."

"Then I guess I won't be under your inking gun any time soon."

I waggle my brows. "You keep talking like that, and it won't be an inking gun you'll need to be worried about."

Ryan chuckles. "Lucky I can handle myself," he replies, his tone full of cockiness. "Because I'm not just a good detective. I'm the best—"

"Fucking detective Ravenshoe has ever seen." I noogie his head, messing up his hundred-dollar haircut. "Better watch out.

Your head might not fit out the door with how fucking big it's getting."

He grins a smile that causes the girls fluttering around our booth to move in closer. He gestures his head to the crotch of my jeans. "You better watch out, or your severe case of blue balls might not fit in your jeans anymore."

When my eyes narrow in on a pair of rich chocolate eyes emerging from a set of dark velvet curtains, any concerns about my blue-ball status are on track to be decimated.

"I'll catch you around," I say to Ryan while lifting my chin in agreement with Keke's suggestive finger crook. "I've got some *business* to take care of."

Ryan stands from the booth to say goodbye in the same way he greeted me an hour ago. Upon noticing that Damon is indisposed with a pretty blonde, I issue him my farewell by paying for his tab before ambling to the door.

Keke interlocks her arm with mine when we emerge onto the bustling sidewalk outside the club. "My place or yours?"

My brisk pace falters.

"I'm just playing with you, Brax," she purrs, her voice quickly reverting from French madame to the Keke who only emerges behind closed doors. "I know you don't take girls back to your place." She spins on her heels and walks backward while undoing the buttons on her black trench coat. "Although, when you spot what I'm wearing underneath this coat, you may change your mind."

When she does the quickest flash, exposing inches of a baby pink lace teddy she's wearing under her coat, I snap my eyes closed and send a prayer to God for leading me to Keke tonight. Because not only did my eyes bulge when awarded with a visual of her naughty little ensemble, so did my cock.

It's back, baby! Primed and ready to go.

CHAPTER TWO

The annoying shrill of my cell phone wakes me from my slumbering state. Shifting my eyes to the alarm clock, a disgruntled groan rumbles from my parched lips.

Who the fuck is calling me at eight in the morning on a Monday?

Sundays and Mondays are the days Inked's doors remain closed. Although we could trade seven days a week, from the beginning, Ryder scheduled his staff on a five-day roster to ensure a good work-life balance.

After running my hand over my newly clipped hair, I snag my phone off the bedside table. My sleepy eyes pop open when I discover who was calling me.

Fuck, what has she done now?

I dial a number I know by heart before pressing my cell close to my ear.

"Caramine Care, Daniel Beckett speaking."

"Daniel, it's Brax Anderson. I just missed your call. Is everything okay?"

He sighs down the line. "We had a few *issues* occur this week that I'd like to discuss with you in person."

Great.

"All right." I swing my legs off the bed. "I'll be there in around forty minutes."

After disconnecting the call, I enter the bathroom to get ready while my brain tracks the events that transpired since the last time I received this same phone call.

Two hours later, I'm walking out of Daniel's office.

"I'll have a word with her before I leave, but I assure you the incident that occurred earlier this week won't happen again."

Daniel curtly nods before offering me his hand to shake. "She certainly keeps us on our toes. No one could ever accuse your grandmother of not having enough spirit."

Laughing, I spin on my heels and stride down the hall. A lack of spirit isn't something my grandma could ever be accused of having.

I'm not at all surprised when I walk into my grandma's room at the assisted living home she's a resident of to find her going toe-to-toe with an orderly unpacking her recently packed suitcase.

"You better not steal any of my panties. I've had those panties for four years and don't want some young grub like you stealing them."

She's aiming for her voice to be vicious, but I hear slight laughter in her words. The orderly—who would be in his mid-thirties—cranks his neck to my grandma. Shock and a slight bit of horror are marring his face.

"Don't look at me like that, young man. I know all about men and their weird fetishes these days. My navy-blue striped sailor boy legs vanished last month. Poof. Gone. Not seen hide nor hair of them in over a month." Her words come out with a husky lisp since she doesn't have her full set of dentures in place.

"Grandma, stop giving the staff a hard time. You know as well as I do that you've never owned a pair of boyleg panties."

She huffs, crosses her heavily wrinkled arms under her chest, then strays her rheumy gaze to the gardens outside her window. "I'd own a pair if they let me out of this hellhole," she mumbles under her breath.

Today has been my grandmother's fourth attempt to break out of her assisted living facility the past three months. She only moved into this facility as the staircase in my apartment became too much for her to handle. Although we considered moving to a more suitable location, with me buying a share in Inked and the housing market rocketing in this area, we both agreed there was no viable option other than her moving into an assisted living facility.

We visited numerous aged care facilities the four weeks following our decision. Caramine Care was the last facility we visited. With its approach on free living, a bustling social calendar, and the fact it isn't referred to as a facility for seniors, it seemed like the ideal residence for my grandma.

Obviously, we were wrong.

After gesturing to the orderly that I will finish unpacking the suitcase, I span the distance between my grandma and me. "What am I going to do with you, Grandma? Mr. Beckett said you nearly gave some of the other residents a coronary." I crouch in front of her and peer into her shimmering blue eyes. "He said it took over two hours to get Mr. Peter's heart rate back under control after the stunt you pulled earlier this week."

She rolls her eyes but maintains her resilient stance, her lips as tight as her silver ringlet hair.

"Mr. Beckett would like me to inform you that although the hydrotherapy pool is set to a warm eighty-two-degree setting, it is not a bath." I cough, clearing my throat. "Grandma, if you wish to remain living at Caramine Care, you must wear swimwear at all times while using the facilities."

I try to keep my voice serious, but when the corners of my grandma's red-painted lips curl into a cheeky smirk, any chances of me keeping this situation within chiding territory falters.

"If they don't want their residents using the bathing facilities for their intended design, they should have clear signs displayed throughout the premises for old girls like me."

Quirking my lips, I glare into her mischief-filled eyes. She tries to use her age as an excuse for her erratic behavior, but I know her better than that. She might have Daniel believing her seventy-eight-year-old brain thought the hydrotherapy pool was a bath, but I'm not at all convinced. Why? Because much to the horror of my neighbors, my grandma skinny-dipped in the pool in my apartment building in January last year. Her excuse was "If the twenty-something-year-old residents of your apartment building can do it, why can't I?"

"Besides. It wasn't Mr. Peter's heart that took two hours to control," my grandma mumbles under her breath.

Ignoring her snide comment for fear of it giving me nightmares, I say, "Even if you didn't realize the hydrotherapy pool required a swimsuit, what's the deal with packing your bags? I thought your escapee days were over?"

Although she's tried to escape three times previously, those attempts were during her first two weeks of *incarceration* at Caramine Care. For the past two months, she seemed to have settled in nicely, so I'm somewhat surprised by her sudden attempt to flee.

Before my grandma gets the chance to answer my questions, a

commotion at the door secures my attention. A pretty nurse in a tight white uniform and sheer black stockings stands in the entryway of my grandmother's room. She has platinum-blonde hair, peachy painted lips, and an enticingly curvy body.

The more the nurse's eyes wander over my face, the more her pupils dilate. A smirk tugs at my lips when her eyes lower to assess the entirety of my package.

The routine never alters.

Well, except that one time.

After the nurse finishes her avid assessment of my body, she aligns her green eyes with my grandmother. "I'm sorry, Mrs. Anderson, I didn't realize you had company. I'll come back later," she says before spinning on her heels.

Her quick departure is halted when my grandma says, "No. It's fine, Penny, come in and meet my grandson, Brax."

My brow arches, surprised at the chirpiness in my grandma's voice. She is an entirely different lady compared to the one sparring against the orderly mere minutes ago.

When Penny hesitates for several seconds, unsure if she's coming or going, my grandma kicks me in the shins and nudges her head Penny's way.

"Hi, I'm Brax, Grace's grandson," I greet before offering her my hand to shake.

Heat creeps across Penny's cheeks as she accepts my gesture. "Hi, Brax. It's a pleasure to meet you. Your grandmother has been telling me a lot about you the past two weeks."

"I'm sure she has."

I turn my gaze back to my grandma. Her excited eyes are bouncing between Penny and me. Air escapes my nostrils when the reasoning behind my grandma's sudden interest in escaping smacks into me.

For the past year, she's made it her mission to see me shacked up and married. I lost count of the number of times I arrived home from a shift at Inked to find a female in my living room lying in wait, ready to pounce.

My grandmother's tactics were so convincing, most of my *dates* believed I had personally invited them over.

No matter how often I tell my grandmother that it's not true in this day and age, she's convinced if I'm not married by the time I'm thirty, I'll live the remainder of my life as a childless bachelor.

Although she means well, her matchmaking is driving me crazy. It isn't her lack of taste that has my appreciation waning. The quality of the women she finds is excellent. It's the fact she lures my dates into my home with the promise of matrimony and a family. Considering neither of those items are on my agenda anytime soon, my newly acquired *friends* don't hang around for long after the initial greeting.

After a few more minutes of awkward silence, Penny checks my grandmother's blood pressure and temperature before excusing herself from the room.

The instant she slips into the corridor, I drift my eyes back to my grandma. "Stop trying to set me up with the nurses and doctors."

"Why? Penny seems lovely, and you need a smart girl in your life," she replies in the same tone she uses whenever we argue about her poor matchmaking techniques.

I arch my brow. "You're setting me up to fail."

"*Pfft*. I'm doing no such thing. Penny is single. You're single. How could that turn into failure?"

With a shake of my head to hide my smile, I say, "Grandma, you know as well as I do. Penny might be good for a bit of fun, but even if I were interested in something more than a few nights between the sheets, she will *never* take me home to meet her parents."

Grandma waves her hand in front of her face like she's shooing away a fly. "We're in the twenty-first century, Brax. Parental permission is no longer a necessity."

I shake my head to loosen the invisible noose she slung around my neck, but since I'm not willing to roll over without a fight, I say, "So when the fun is over with Penny, and she ends up broken-hearted, what do you think will happen to your secret candy stash the nursing staff knows about but ignores?"

Panic floods my grandma's eyes when she locks them with the top drawer, which is full to the brim with every candy bar you could imagine.

"Is meddling in your grandson's love life worth the risk of losing your beloved chocolate binge?"

Without hesitation, she shakes her head.

I crouch down so my eyes are level with hers. "I appreciate your effort, but my love life is fine as it is. Especially since I can take my dates to my place now that my grandmother isn't sleeping in the room next door."

My grandma tries to hold in her laughter, but the littlest giggle topples from her lips. She may be seventy-eight, but she has the dirty mind of a twenty-year-old male.

CHAPTER THREE

"Do you want me to head out or stay and see what card she's going to play?"

I shift my gaze from the blonde princess I tattooed three months ago, pacing the cracked sidewalk at the front of Inked to Diesel standing at my side. "Nah, man, you head out. I've got this," I assure him, my tone as unconvincing as my facial expression. "I'm locking up and heading out myself in a few, anyway."

Diesel snags his jacket from the counter and slings it over his shoulders. "She signed a contract, Brax. There's no coming back from that. No matter what her fancy lawyer told her," he reminds me after reading my concerned expression.

"Yeah, I know," I reply with a chin jerk. "But I'm still curious as to why she's been pacing out front for the past two hours."

Diesel bows his brow. "Maybe she's hoping to get you alone?" He waggles his brows. "Your tattoo might have convinced her she needs to sample your other gun. The more magic one."

I pick up a cash register roll at the side of the register and peg it at his head. A grin curves on my mouth when my fluke shot has perfect aim, hitting Diesel just above his left brow.

With a cheeky grin and while rubbing his brow, Diesel lifts his chin in farewell before striding to the door. Clara jumps in fright when the deep rumble of his Harley kicking over booms through her ears. Her eyes track Diesel as he executes a U-turn and rides past her.

Once he's no longer in eyesight, she runs her hand down the front of her jeans then saunters toward the entrance door of Inked. After dropping my eyes to her stilettos, I rake them up her body. Although she still screams of wealth and superiority, her outfit and jewelry selection aren't as elaborate as they were three months ago. Her fitted jeans cuddle the slender curves of her swinging hips, and her body-hugging jacket doesn't have a chance in hell of hiding assets most men would happily ignore her poor attitude to sample.

As the bells above the door ring into the front entrance, I stand from my slouched position and cross my arms over my chest, prepping for round three in our vicious battle. Clara's brisk pace falters when her eyes stop scanning the premises and connect with mine. A grin curls on my lips when she mumbles "Shit" under her breath before she continues her journey, acting like she isn't shocked to see me standing behind the counter.

When I tattooed her three months ago, I had long wavy brown hair that sat an inch below my shoulders, but after Ryan's little jab about my pretty-boy status, I had my hair clipped two weeks ago.

If I'm being totally forthright, it wasn't just Ryan's taunt that had me visiting the barber. It's the fact I've had the same haircut since I was a senior in high school. I was also hoping an update might inspire the same thing to happen between my bedsheets.

I'll do anything if it will fix my broken cock.

Did my plan work? No, not really. Unless you count Clara's

sudden arrival? She's only standing before me because the glare on the shop windows hides my new haircut. When she saw Diesel leave, I have no doubt she thought she was clear from running into anyone who'd remember her long-winded tirade the last time she visited the shop.

How fucking wrong was she?

"Did your lawyer stand you up?" I ask, believing that is the only reason she's been pacing out front for the past two hours this late at night.

She freezes like a statue before cranking her neck back. Upon failing to locate anyone behind her, she returns her eyes front and center. "Lawyer?"

I nod. "Yeah, to sue me for your tat. If I recall correctly, you were planning to take every penny I had," I say, quoting part of the rant she evoked the last time she was on these premises. "You signed an agreement, Princess. It is a binding contract—"

"I'm not here about my tattoo," she interrupts, her voice surprisingly strong. "I'm here about that." She points to a display in the shop window.

"You need to be a little more specific," I say when the direction of her finger points to numerous tattoo displays. "There are hundreds of tattoo designs in that window." Suddenly, I freeze, and my brows scrunch. "If you want another tattoo, I suggest you find another tattoo artist."

She shakes her head. "I don't want another tattoo." Locking her icy-blue eyes with mine, she mutters, "The one I have is *more* than enough."

I smirk, loving her edge of feistiness.

I've always appreciated a woman who calls it as she sees it.

After expelling a deep breath, Clara paces to the shop window. "I'm here about this." She pulls down the 'Help Wanted' sign that's been displayed in the window for the past six months. It is so old, the thick black ink has faded to a murky gray color. While spinning the sign around to face me, she says, "I'm here to apply for the position you have advertised."

I throw back my head and laugh. I'm not talking a slight chuckle. I'm talking a full belly-clenching, I-won't-need-to-do-a-sit-up-for-a-month laugh. Tears spring into my eyes, and my body slicks with sweat.

The only thing that dampens the intensity of my laughter is catching sight of Clara's furious glare. Her gaze is scorching, and her strong stance is even hotter than that.

I stop laughing and take a step backward.

She can't be fucking serious. Surely.

Confident I'm being pranked, I shoot my eyes around the deserted shop, fully anticipating one of the guys from my crew to be lying in wait because there's no way this shit is real.

When I fail to detect another body in our presence, I shift my eyes back to Clara. "You're serious?" Disbelief taints my words.

She strengthens her take-no-shit stance before nodding. "I need a job. You have a position advertised." She places her hand on her cocked hip. "Hire me, and it will be a win-win for us both."

I bite on the inside of my cheek, hoping it will hold back a second bout of laughter that's dying to break free.

It's a pointless effort.

The instant my lips tug higher, the grim expression on Clara's face firms. "Is this how you treat all your applicants?" she grumbles, clearly unimpressed.

Smirking, I shake my head. "But I've never had an applicant who looks like you."

Most women would take my reply as a compliment. Clara doesn't. The angry spark in her eyes brightens as the groove between her brows deepens.

Feeling playful, and since I have five minutes until I can officially close up the shop, I play along with her little game. "Can you tattoo?" I use the same tone I used when handling an inquiry from a junkie for the same position earlier today.

Clara's throat works hard to swallow before she shakes her head.

"Do you know how to sterilize tattoo equipment?"

"No," she replies, her tone as abrupt as her pose.

"Do you even know how to clean?"

I am no longer able to hold in my smile when she once again shakes her head. I'd never tell her this, but her honesty does rate her application one point higher than her earlier competitor. That guy couldn't lie straight in bed. Even with her outscoring previous applicants, not only does she not hold the skills necessary to fulfill the position, but I'm also not buying her story about why she's suddenly arrived at Inked.

Playing my part of manager, I connect my eyes with Clara. "As part of the management team at Inked Tattoo, I thank you for your interest in working with us, but unfortunately, you have been unsuccessful in acquiring the position advertised." I try to keep my tone neutral. My attempts are borderline.

Clara takes a step closer to the counter, engulfing my senses with her rich floral scent. "I may not know how to clean or tattoo, but I have no concerns maintaining a vigorous schedule, and I most certainly know how to handle money."

A ghost of a smile cracks my lips. "I'm sure you do, Princess, but we are not seeking a bookkeeper. We're after an all-rounder."

After snagging my keys from the glass display cabinet, I make my way around the counter. Clara balks when I curl my arm around her shoulders to guide her to the door.

I flip the sign to closed, open the front door of Inked, then gesture for Clara to leave. I'm not at all surprised to spot a steel gray Audi parked a few spots up from Inked.

Only a princess would apply for a minimum-wage job with a chariot idling at the curb.

"There's a tattoo shop two streets over called Gunned. I'm sure its owner, Tommy, would *love* to hire a woman of your caliber to count his money."

Tommy is a great tattoo artist—his shop is Inked's number one rival—but he is a fucking sleaze and an even bigger idiot. If anyone on this side of Ravenshoe will be fooled by Clara's sudden desire to get dirt under her French-tipped nails, it would be Tommy.

Clara's eyes bounce between mine. She appears to be considering citing an objection to my request for her to leave, so I'm somewhat surprised when she releases a quiet huff before stepping onto the concrete sidewalk.

After securing the deadbolt, I check that everything has been shut down in the shop, grab my jacket off the coatrack, then head out the back entrance of Inked.

With it being February, a nippy wind prickles my torso with goosebumps when I enter the poorly lit parking lot. I throw my arms into my jacket before locking the chained security door.

Happy everything is secure, I spin on my heels and walk to my custom Harley Davidson Fat Boy parked three spaces up.

My eyes roll skyward when clicking heels on concrete jingles through my ears. I don't need to shift my eyes to know who is shadowing me. The smell of expensive floral perfume and the way the hairs on my nape prickled is all the indication I need to know who is tailing me.

The bitch is back.

"I can keep things in the shop running, freeing up your precious time so you can... *doodle* on more people."

I stop walking to inhale a lung-filling breath of air. After calming down the mad beat of my heart, I turn around to face my newly acquired stalker. "Doodle?" I arch my brow as I glare into Clara's stormy eyes. "You think I *doodle* on people?"

Even though a pinch of fear clouds her impressively stern eyes, she ignores the grim expression on my face and nods.

"It's called art, Princess. It's not fucking doodling."

"Stop calling me that," she snaps, glaring at me with her well-worn bitch façade firmly in place.

"Why? Don't you like your name, *Princess?*"

She crosses her arms under her chest, hoisting her mouthwatering breasts higher in her tight, fitted shirt. "I'm not a princess, so why call me one?"

I shrug. "It's either Princess or Stuck-Up Bitch... The choice is yours."

The veins in her neck thrum as anger lines her face. "My name is Clara. Why don't you just refer to me as Clara?"

"I gave you your choices." My tone warns of my wavering constraint. I'm close to blowing my top.

Her mouth gapes, no doubt shell-shocked at my bluntness.

While scraping my hand over the stubble on my chin, I fight to rein in my anger. Although I've reached my quota of dealing with idiotic people for one week, Clara doesn't deserve to solely cop the wrath of my fury. She may have an icy personality, but my poor mood was lingering hours before she arrived on the doorstep of Inked.

"Look, you've had your fun, so can we please cut the shit? It's been a long-ass week, and I'm too fucking beat to be dealing with more crap right now." I try to keep my tone sincere, but when her eyes slit into thin lines, I realize she isn't buying my attempts at sincerity.

Deciding I'll never win a battle of words against a woman with a fierce tongue like Clara's, I issue my farewell with an emotionless smirk before continuing with my original endeavor.

I make it halfway to my bike before I hear, "What time do you want me to arrive on Monday?"

Fuck me, this woman is worse than a leech.

I don't bother turning around. "I'm not hiring you."

My hands shoot up to massage my throbbing temples when she asks, "Isn't it illegal to advertise under false pretenses?"

After exhaling a large puff of air, I spin around to face her. "What have I falsely advertised?"

"Your sign said you needed help." She stares into my eyes while running her hand down the front of her body. Even in my irate mood, I can't miss her budded nipples braced against her fitted shirt. "I'm here, willing to help, but you're refusing to hire me. I'm not a lawyer, but that sounds illegal to me."

While dragging my eyes away from her chest, I clench my fists into tight balls. It's the only defense I have to fight the urge to scream my frustration into the street. "You're not qualified for the position advertised. If you were, I'd hire you," I reply through gritted teeth.

"Then give me a chance to prove I'm qualified."

I arch my brow. "And how exactly can I do that?"

"Put me on a trial basis. Day-to-day agreement. No contracts. No paperwork." She impresses me with her on-the-spot negotiation skills.

I nearly take a minute to contemplate her recommendation before reality smacks into me. I don't owe her a damn thing. She should feel lucky I didn't have her ass thrown to the curb the instant she stepped foot into my shop after the less-than-stellar rant she unleashed during her last visit.

I lock my eyes with hers. "You're not qualified to work at Inked, but we thank you for taking the time to submit your application," I quote, giving her the same comment I've given every unqualified applicant before her.

She cocks her hip out and glares into my eyes. "You either hire me now, or I'll show up every day until you do."

After straddling my bike, I drift my eyes back to the teeming-with-sass blonde. "So no matter what I say, you're gonna rock up here Monday, ready to work?" When she smiles and nods, I inwardly chuckle. "All right. Good luck on Monday." When her plump lips lift into a broad grin, I realize my attempt at sarcasm was lost on her. "We aren't open on Mondays. If you had done your research on Inked before applying for the position we have advertised, you would have realized that."

Clara balks for the quickest second before stuttering, "Tuesday, then."

I scrub my hand over my clipped hair. "I get it, all right. You're on some soul-searching mission, hoping a few good deeds to those less fortunate will fix some of the fucked-up things you've done in your life, but you're barking up the wrong tree." I twist my body to the side and point down the street. "There is a women's shelter three blocks over. Go and offer them your charity."

She mumbles something under her breath, but she's so quiet, I missed what she said. After rolling her shoulders, she fixes her icy-blue eyes with my dark brown gaze. "I'm sorry for wasting your precious time. I hope you have a pleasant evening," she says before spinning on her heels and stalking back to the street.

A pleasant evening? Is she fucking serious? That proves she would have never survived working in a place like Inked. If the staff didn't scare her off, the clients soon would have.

Maybe I should have hired her and let my crew work their magic?

After snagging my helmet out of the saddle bag on my bike, my eyes scan the nearly pitch-black alleyway. Other than a couple of heavy-breasted bar bunnies bouncing around hoping to secure a warm bed for the night, the parking lot is empty, which isn't surprising considering it is well past midnight on a Saturday night.

The two heavy-breasted ladies' large smiles dampen when I dip my chin in farewell, denying their silent offerings. With Inked's regular schedule, the bunnies know the prime time to show up when they're after a night of adventure. Although their offer is tempting, after my run-in with Princess Stuck-Up, I'm not in the mood for the antics a pair of bunnies would bring to my weekend.

I also can't guarantee my dysfunctional cock will be up for the task.

The profound rumble of my bike echoes through the quiet night when I kick over the engine. After gliding it down the alleyway, I shift my eyes up and down the street, scanning for an opening in the dense flow of traffic that always clogs the streets of Ravenshoe. It doesn't matter if it is one in the morning or three in the afternoon, Ravenshoe's roads are always congested.

During my endeavor to find a break between vehicles, my eyes spot a flurry of blonde standing in the shadows of the bus shelter a few doors up from Inked.

What the fuck is she doing standing at the bus stop?

Unable to leash the moral compass my grandma embedded in me from a young age, I roll my bike away from the pavement and switch off the engine. After storing my helmet on the ape hangers of my bike, I stride to the bus shelter Clara is standing at. Although she frustrates the hell out of me, this side of town, at this time of night, is no place for any woman to be milling around unaccompanied.

"How far out is your ride?"

I rake my eyes along the street to seek the gray Audi I saw earlier.

It's nowhere to be found.

While finalizing the last few steps between us, I tug my jacket in tighter, blocking out the crisp breeze blowing through my thin long-sleeve shirt.

Clara's eyes stray from the street to me. Her pupils widen as a look of surprise washes over her face. "I'm not waiting on a car. I am taking the bus home."

"What?" I ask, certain I didn't hear her right. The roads are clogged with noisy motorists, so my hearing may be a little off.

"I'm waiting for the bus," Clara advises again, her voice stronger this time around.

"You're waiting on the *bus*?"

She huffs loudly. "Yes! The *bus*. You know that big metal thing on four wheels that clangs past here every twenty minutes or so. It's called a *bus*. That's what I'm waiting for."

She rolls her eyes before turning them back to the street. I stare at her in utter disbelief. She must be a fucking lunatic. It is well past midnight on a Saturday. She's decked out in designer threads and wearing more bling than the jewelry store three blocks over stocks, and she's planning on taking the bus. Clearly, she doesn't know this side of Ravenshoe after dark like I do. It isn't a place for anyone to be wandering alone, let alone a woman with the dick-twitching looks she has.

Upon noticing a bus approaching my right, my naturally engrained protective instincts kick in. "You don't need to take the bus. I'll give you a ride home." I nudge my head to the portion of my bike poking out of the alleyway.

"No."

Her abrupt response dumbfounds me.

"Excuse me?" Surprise is clear in my voice. "When someone offers you a ride, you're supposed to say, 'Thank you. That will be lovely.'"

Clara's eyes snap to mine. "Not when you don't want a lift. I'm happy to take the bus."

"You're not taking the fucking bus. Get your ass on my bike."

She steps closer to me as her thinly slit eyes bounce between mine. "Do you have a problem with your hearing? I said *no*."

I return her leering stare. "Do you think saying 'no' to a bunch of punks on the one a.m. express will stop them? You're swimming out of your depth here, Princess. This isn't fucking Kansas."

The smell of exhaust fumes filter into my nose when a rusted old bus marked with '57' on the side pulls in front of the bus shelter.

"I can take care of myself." Clara glares at me with the same fiery spark she wore three months ago. "If I can handle a *beast* of a man like you, I'm sure a couple of *punks* will be no hard feat."

After issuing me a final stink eye, she climbs aboard the bus, completely snubbing my request for her not to.

I stand frozen at the bus stop in absolute shock. I'm not just surprised by her stubbornness but astounded by how fucking hard her feistiness has made my cock.

I've never been so damn hard.

Yeah, not happening, buddy. You'd need a cool million in the bank to ever get the chance of unclamping those legs.

Clara's smug eyes glower into mine when the bus chugs down the road, leaving a throat-clogging puff of smoke in its wake. She thinks she can take care of herself, but she's swimming way out of her depth. But fuck it. If she wants to be stupid, so be it. It isn't my place to play babysitter to a spoiled little rich bitch who would cut off her nose to spite her face. Besides, although the bus company advises their drivers not to engage in any domestic situations, the moral obligation of any man would outweigh corporate propaganda, wouldn't it?

While cursing under my breath, I charge for my bike and throw my leg over it. The big rumble of my engine scares a group of feral cats out of the dumpster at the side when I kick over the motor. My heart beats double time when my departure from the alley has me narrowly missing a handful of motorists. When they honk their horns and yell obscenities out their windows, I flip the bird before pulling back on my throttle. My excessive speed has my front tire lifting off the pavement and the coolness of a late February wind pelting my chest.

Weaving my bike in and out of the heavy traffic, I locate bus 57 a mile out from Inked. When I pull my bike along the right-hand side of the bus, I scan the seats lining the edge, seeking any signs of Clara. When I fail to locate her, I lower my speed and slip my bike to the other side. A moment of reprieve pummels into me when I spot her sitting two seats behind the male driver.

At least she was smart enough to sit close to the driver.

Ignoring the absurdness of the situation, I continue to follow the bus as it makes its way across Ravenshoe. Even though she acts like she hasn't noticed my presence, I catch Clara occasionally glancing my way.

I'll admit, even pissed beyond hell that I've rode ten miles in the wrong direction and am wasting precious minutes of my days off tailing a lady who infuriates me more than any woman before her, the hardness of my cock hasn't lessened a smidge. If anything, her blatant refusal to acknowledge my presence has increased its thickness, not lessened it.

"What's wrong with you? You want some Grade-A pussy?" I mumble to myself while peering down at the crotch of my jeans.

My attention diverts from reprimanding my cock for its unattainable goals when I notice a group of gangbangers at the back of the bus have locked their sights on Clara. If I had to guess their ages, I'd say late teens, early twenties. I've seen them hanging around Inked a few times the past month, but we haven't officially met.

After doing a hand gesture with two of his pimple-faced

friends, the approximately six-foot boy with pasty skin and a red bandana wrapped around his grease-slicked hair moves down the aisle, his gangbanger swagger in full force. His wonky grin enlarges the closer he gets to Clara, as does his grip on his crotch.

Blood roars into my ears from the gleam in his eyes. I slam my hand on the bus's window, endeavoring to secure his attention. The glass rattles under the impact of my fist, but he doesn't look my way. My heart rate climbs into dangerous territory when I glance sideways to check my location.

Fuck!

I'm two seconds away from being splattered onto the back of a four-thousand-pound sedan.

Gritting my teeth, I release the throttle and pull back on the brake before veering my bike onto the sidewalk. A delivery driver stacking the morning papers on the curb squeals like a girl when I narrowly miss hitting him. Scraps of newspaper fly into the air, and the scent of fear filters into my nose as I zip past a newspaper stand.

Once the delivery driver gathers his scattered composure, he yells out a string of obscenities. His voice is as shaky as my hands.

I raise my arm into the air in silent apology before continuing with my original endeavor. A rutted grunt escapes my lips when my bike leaves the sidewalk with an almighty thud. I pull back the throttle and catch up with the bus, swerving in and out of the traffic like a mad man.

When I glide up next to the bus, my jaw muscle tenses. The young gangbanger is sitting in the seat behind Clara, twirling a lock of her glossy hair around his index finger.

I bang my fist on the glass once more. My thump is so hard, the glass wobbles under my force. Hearing my commotion, the gang-banger twists his neck to the side and eyes me curiously. His ostentatious grin amplifies when I stare him straight in the face while pointing to Clara.

After removing his hand from Clara's hair, he grabs his crotch while mouthing, "She's fine."

His cocky grin is wiped straight off his face when I use the same finger I pointed at Clara to make a throat-slitting gesture, wordlessly warning him if he touches another hair on her head, I will ruin him.

He balks as his eyes widen. He nudges his head to Clara as if to ask, "Is she yours, Brax?"

When I nod, he holds his hands out in front of his body like he didn't mean her any harm before he stumbles back to his original seat.

If I didn't arrive when I did, I'd hate to think of how far he was planning to take this. The good kids in Ravenshoe are slowly outweighing the bad, but there's still a bunch of rotten eggs tainting the batch.

The tick impinging my jaw lessens when the fear-faced teen returns to his original spot at the back of the bus. Although I've never been an overly violent man, I was born and raised in this area of Ravenshoe. That alone warrants me a fierce enough reputation that I'm not to be messed with.

When the gangbanger takes a seat next to his two male compadres, I swing my eyes back to Clara. For the first time in the past twelve miles, she isn't facing the front of the bus. Her eyes are locked on me, and all the smugness on her face has vanished, replaced with a look of a woman who is acutely aware of how close her stubbornness had her treading into shark-infested waters.

After issuing me a hesitant smirk, she returns her eyes front and center. Thankfully, the last ten minutes of her brush with the wild side is made without incident. I won't lie, a conceited grin curls on my lips when the young gangbangers bolt off the bus at the stop following our exchange.

Without a backward glance, they hightail it down the alleyway as quick as their quivering legs can take them. If Clara wasn't still sitting two seats behind the driver with a terrified gleam in her eyes, I would have had a good *talk* with them. But since my priorities remain with Clara, that *talk* is being held for a later date.

The instant the bus rolls into the good half of Ravenshoe, I could stop following Clara, but for some reason unbeknownst to me, I continue tailing her for the next five miles.

I've already come this far, so what's a few more miles?

When the bus comes to a halt in front of a fancy apartment building on the most expensive street in Ravenshoe, I pull my bike onto the curb behind it. I'm not at all surprised when Clara hops off the bus. Just seeing her in this expensive setting strengthens my belief that she was attempting to prank me earlier tonight.

Keeping her chin held high, she saunters toward the guarded doors. Just before she enters the heavily manned foyer, she spins around to face me. Her pupils are wide, exposing that she's rattled from her brief encounter with the rough side of Ravenshoe, but even frightened, she holds herself with a sense of dignity and class. She has the type of poise no etiquette class could teach. It is infused in her blood.

"Thank you."

A grin tugs on my lips. From the look on her face, you'd swear it was the first time she's ever said thank you.

I inwardly chuckle. *It probably is.*

"You shouldn't catch the bus at any time, let alone this late at night. It was a stupid thing to do."

Even though her lips thin in grimness, she nods. "I'll add it to my long list of things I'm unqualified to do." Her snarls reveal her stubbornness is still loitering in the shadows. "I've found out today I can't work at a tattoo parlor, a café, or even clean the gas station toilets on the outskirts of town." The hardness of her lips is firm. "Who would have thought you'd need a degree from Harvard to clean a washroom?"

My brows furrow. "You're that desperate for a job you're willing to clean toilets for a buck?"

With her gaze planted straight ahead, she briefly nods.

My heart freezes. I honestly hadn't expected her to say yes.

"Fingers crossed, biker bars and strip clubs aren't as demanding because at the rate I'm going, they'll be my only viable options," she mutters before spinning on her heels.

Strip clubs? Even knowing she's most likely goading me, and I don't know her from a bar of soap, I hate the thought of any woman working in a sleazy club just to make a dime. My momma did it, and I swore I'd never let any woman I know follow in her disastrous footsteps.

Going against my better judgment, I blurt out, "You start Tuesday at two," before my brain can compile a rejection.

Clara freezes halfway into the entrance of her building. Her shoulders rise as she gulps in a deep breath before her eyes snap to mine. "Really?"

When I nod, she smiles a heart-stopping grin that has my cock stiffening all over again.

Don't even think about it. She's way above your paygrade.

"You have a two-week trial to prove yourself. If you fuck it up or scare away any of my customers, your ass will be out on the curb faster than I can snap my fingers."

"I won't. I promise," she guarantees, her assuring eyes adding to the strength of her words.

I arch my brow. "And you're not to take the bus," I warn while glaring into her eyes. "This is not a negotiable term. If you turn up to Inked on the bus, turn around and get straight back on it because your ass will be fired."

Her face pales, and her breathing shallows. She looks more concerned now than she did when I began inking her virgin skin. "I don't have any money to put gas in my car," she mumbles, her quiet words relaying her embarrassment.

Jesus Christ! What the fuck am I getting myself into?

I dig my hand into the back pocket of my jeans to pull out my wallet and snag a twenty from the small selection of notes inside. I hold the note a few inches from my chest before locking my eyes with Clara.

If she wants my money, she'll have to come and get it.

A stretch of silence passes between us as her eyes dance between the crumpled note in my hand and my face. After exhaling a deep breath, she spans the distance between us, her steps shaky and reserved.

Just before she removes the twenty from my grasp, I pull it out of her reach. "This is not a loan. It's an advance. I'll be taking it out of your first paycheck."

She fights her hardest battle, endeavoring to keep her tears at bay before curtly nodding. "Okay. Good," she says, her voice stronger than the weakness in her eyes.

She removes the twenty from my hand, folds it up, then places it in the pocket of her jeans. "Thank you," she murmurs before walking into her apartment building, not once glancing back at me sitting on my Harley, shocked into silence.

Even though I could see the defeated look in her eyes when she accepted my money, I hope she just played me for a fool. No matter how much she irritates me, I'd rather have her pranking me than be so desperate for a job she turns up to Inked on Tuesday morning.

CHAPTER FOUR

Knocking distracts me from the tattoo I've been drawing for the past hour. It is a sleek design I've been working on for a long-time client. Although he doesn't have much prime real estate left on his torso for my artwork, this piece is just as important to him as the numerous other tats I've placed on his skin.

When I hear another knock, I slide the sheet of tracing paper to the side and check my watch. My lips quirk when I notice it is a little before one in the afternoon. Considering the shop doesn't open until two-thirty, I ignore the eager patron.

All my best-laid plans go straight to the gutter when the tapping grows louder and louder. Once it hits a point I'm no longer capable of ignoring, I push back from my desk and march to the door. I clasp the stainless-steel door handle, preparing to unleash a verbal tirade on the moron who can't read the hours displayed in thick red ink on the eye-level sign hanging from the door. My plan goes to shit for the second time in under a minute when I swing open the door and am smacked in the face with a rich floral scent.

"You really need to get your hearing tested. I've been knocking for ages," Clara says with her heat-scorching eyes blazing into mine. "Are you going to let me in?"

I nearly step to the side before reality pummels into me. This wasn't our plan. "What are you doing here?"

She freezes. "You said I have a two-week trial," she replies with her icy-blue eyes bouncing between mine.

"Yeah, Tuesday at two."

Her eyes roll skywards. "It *is* Tuesday, Brax."

I only just hold in my surprise that she knows my name. I shouldn't be shocked, though. I'm sure she spent her entire weekend digging for dirt on the guy she's playing tricks on.

"Yeah, it is Tuesday, *Princess,*" I say her nickname with the same disdain she said mine with. "But it isn't even one yet. You're way too early."

Her brows furrow. "My brother previously told me being early shows you appreciate the opportunity bestowed upon you." Her hands fist the fabric on her jacket before she stammers, "I appreciate the opportunity."

After leaning against the doorframe, I cross my arms in front of my chest. "First job?" My deep voice only just conceals my laughter. "How old are you?"

She smooths the crinkles her determined hold created in her jacket before locking her eyes with mine. "I'm twenty-five, and yes, it is my first job." Her tone is full of warning that this subject is not up for further discussion.

Deciding it is too early in the week to engage in World War III, I remark, "Arriving fifteen minutes before your shift will be more than adequate to show your appreciation."

Clara briefly nods before asking, "So can I come in?"

Her eyes narrow when I shake my head. "I'm assuming that's

yours?" I gesture my head to the white BMW convertible parked in prime position at the front of the shop.

A ghost of a smile creeps across her plump lipstick-covered lips. "Yes."

"Then you need to move it. There's an employee parking lot located at the back of the shop."

Her eyes rocket to mine. The gleam brightening her gaze from absorbing her expensive pride and joy dampens as the seconds tick by. "Is the parking lot secure?"

I throw my head back and laugh. "No, but it is where all *employees* park their vehicles."

"Then my car is fine where it is," she snaps out before crossing her arms under her ample chest.

"If you think your ride is safer parked in the street in clear view of thieving eyes than the parking lot, Princess, you've underestimated this side of Ravenshoe. No gangbanger will dare touch your *precious* pride and joy if it is parked at the back of Inked." She snarls, baring teeth, either hating my use of her nickname or me calling out her stupidity. Either way, I don't care. "If you're planning on walking into this premises as an employee, move your piece-of-shit car into the parking lot. If not, have a *pleasant* evening."

A winning grin stretches across my face when Clara rolls her arms in front of her body like she's curtseying the crowned Prince of Denmark before she walks backward. She just needs to remove the crown from her head and place it on mine, and her performance would be more realistic.

Smirking, I nod when she points to the alley at the side of the shop after unlocking her car doors. "Down the alley and around the back." She rolls her eyes at the arrogance of my reply.

"I'll meet you at the *employee* entrance," I add, rubbing more salt into her freshly cut wounds.

Not waiting for her to reply, I close and lock the door of Inked and head to the employee-only entrance at the back of the shop. I still can't believe Clara McGregor—Princess-Fucking-Socialite—wants to work at Inked. I took a bit of time the past two days running our prior confrontations through my mind. Other than hitting a late case of teen rebellion, I'm at a loss as to why someone like Clara would want to work at Inked, let alone anywhere. It honestly doesn't make any sense. Just her tennis bracelet alone is worth more than my annual salary, and her pride and joy I just insulted no doubt cost more than my apartment.

But even knowing she has more money than sense, I'll follow through with my pledge. Why? Because I'm a man of my word. I'll play along with Clara's little ruse for as long as she wants as I doubt she'll last a few hours, let alone a few days.

After snagging a spare key for the back door off the key rack, I push open the heavily weighted steel door at the back of Inked. Like a shadow I can't shake, Clara is standing under the rusted awning waiting for me.

"The lock can be a bit stiff, just jimmy the key a little, and it should pop right out," I instruct while pinching the key between my index finger and thumb.

Clara snatches the key out of my grasp and cocks her brow. "Why give me a key if you want me to jimmy the lock? Seems like a pointless task."

Ignoring her cattiness, I continue as if she never spoke. "You should also consider removing your bling. It doesn't fit in around here, and it will only lead to trouble." I clutch the diamond pendant dangling around her neck and hoist it into the air.

She snatches the pendant out of my grasp. "You should consider removing your attitude because it doesn't fit in around here," she snips under her breath.

I smirk. "Will it be like this the entire two weeks? I say something, and you fire back with a bitchy comment?"

"Depends," she replies with a shrug.

I glare into her stern eyes. "On what exactly?"

"On if you keep saying stupid things."

I back her into the outer wall of the shop and press my hands on each side of the brickwork next to her shoulders. The veins in her neck thrum, but she maintains my eye contact, trying to act as if my intimidating stance isn't affecting her. "If you want to work here, you need to lose the attitude. If you can't do that, I suggest you slide your pretty little ass back into your pretty little car and drive your stuck-up princess routine back to the pretty side of Ravenshoe. Because that side of town may see your hard-ball approach as determination, where I just see it as a spoiled little bitch hiding behind a pile of money."

Her lips thin into a hard, disapproving line. "I'm just giving as good as I'm getting, Brax," she replies after locking her challenging blue eyes with mine.

I'll give it to her. This time around, she's got me played. I've given her just as much attitude as she's been bestowing upon me. So much, I'm certain if my grandmother ever catches wind of my interactions with Clara, she'll have my head placed on the guillotine block.

She's quoted numerous times during the past twenty-eight years of my life that, "No matter if they're richer than a queen or poorer than a struggling artist, every woman has the right to be treated with dignity and respect."

But I can't help it. Clara riles me up. Not just my hackles but my cock as well. The first half of my weekend was filled trying to work out what her deal was. The second half was spent striving to release the stranglehold her feistiness placed on my cock.

Just like I came up stumped on why a socialite like Clara would want to work at Inked, nothing could ease the throb of my cock. Not even the pretty little blonde with icy-blue eyes I picked up last night.

For some strange, unknown reason, my cock has set his sights on a little temptress with a scornful mouth and even more sinful lips. I can't say I don't understand his fascination. Clara is so much of a sexpot she only needs to breathe to excite a red-blooded guy. Just the way she's staring up at me now, panting hard with her painted lips pursed, makes her so tempting all I want to do is wipe the sass right out of her mouth with my fucking tongue.

Knowing that will never happen, I drop one of my hands from the wall and scrub it over the few days of scruff on my chin. "I don't think this is a good idea. This agreement isn't going to work."

My cock is already aching to sink into her, and she's only been here for five seconds, so imagine how bad it will be in an hour?

Clara releases a long breath while crossing her arms in front of her chest. "I'm not going anywhere until my trial is over. I may not have signed an official employment document, but a verbal contract is just as binding as a written one. Believe me, I checked."

"Then I'll pay you two weeks of salary, and we'll call it a day."

After glaring at me, she slips under my arm and saunters into the shop like she owns the place. Her shoulders are straight, and her head is held high as she slings off her jacket and hangs it on the coat rack before heading to the foyer. For the first time in her three visits to the premises, she's standing on the opposite side of the counter. "Are you going to show me where everything is? Or am I going to figure it out on my own?"

I grit my teeth and take three steps toward her. "Did you hear anything I said? I'll pay you your two weeks owed."

"Yeah, I heard every word that spilled from your lips, *Brax.*" She spits my name out like it is a piece of trash. "Unlike you, I don't have any concerns about my hearing."

"Then why are you still standing in my foyer? I'm a man of my word. I'll follow through on my agreement. You'll get your money."

She places her hands on her hips and stares me straight in the eyes. "You *agreed* to give me a two-week trial. I'm here to begin my two-week trial. I'm *not* a charity case." Her words come out shaky during the last part of her statement. "Now, are you going to show me where everything is? Or am I going to figure it out on my own?" she requests again, glaring at me.

I stare at her, looking like a slack-jawed idiot. I've never had someone with enough gall to spar up against me on my turf before, let alone a woman my cock wants to wrestle with beneath the sheets. Even giving her a stare that would make most men cower, she doesn't yield the slightest. If anything, her determination strengthens. She came here to start her two-week trial, and she isn't leaving until that happens.

Realizing that arguing with a woman like Clara is utterly pointless, I eat humble pie before spending the next thirty minutes giving her a general rundown on how the shop operates. I explain how she will be left in charge of booking all the appointments, taking clients' payments, and pretty much doing anything the crew requests her to do.

She's quick, but I don't miss the tiniest flare of anxiety that crosses her face when I mention she has to do anything the crew demands.

"Other than Charity, the rest of the crew won't be overly demanding."

She nods as she follows me to the hallway.

"Charity can get a little handsy, but don't let it bother you. She's harmless." I stop talking and run my eyes over Clara's body. "Although, for you, she may be extra grabby."

The spark of worry tainting her face explodes into a full flare.

"If it gets more than you can handle, holla, and I'll have a quiet word with Charity."

Her throat works hard to swallow before she shakes her head. "It's okay. I can take care of myself." The shakiness of her words undermines the strength of her statement.

When we enter the manager's office, I take a seat behind my old scratched-up desk. "If you stay out of my hair, I'll stay out of yours. Then this arrangement might work out for both of us."

An uncharacteristic smile spreads across Clara's face. Although she looks out of place in my small, poorly furnished office, the careful consideration she paid while I explained her position shows she isn't walking into this job lightheartedly. Surprisingly, she appears as if she actually wants to be here. *Unsurprisingly, her smile has the front of my jeans tightening.*

My body's reaction to her pisses me off. Not because I'm ungrateful my cock appears to be back in working order but because the goal it is striving for is unattainable. I hardly know the woman standing before me, yet she already has me wanting to cross out the number one rule I swore I'd never break when I signed on as a partner at Inked.

Never mix business with pleasure.

The fact she already has me wanting to break my rules pisses me off more than the hardness in my jeans.

After she finishes absorbing the outdated office space, Clara connects her glistening eyes with mine. "Where's my desk?"

I laugh while pushing my chair away from my desk. "There's only one seat in this office, Princess. So you either take my knee, or..." My eyes stray to the faded red couch pushed up against the wall.

"The sofa it is," Clara fills in, moving toward the couch.

I have a feeling this will be the longest two weeks of my life.

———

CHAPTER FIVE

"Still can't believe you made Ms. Fancy Thing a member of the Inked family," Diesel says while walking into my office. "You gonna keep her around?"

I drift my eyes past his shoulder to Clara manning the front counter before lifting my shoulders into a shrug. "She seems to be doing all right."

Clara has slipped into her makeshift role at Inked surprisingly well. She's a little uptight, but the male clientele has had no complaints—they're too busy enjoying the view to be angry about her occasional smart mouth. The female customers, on the other hand... they're not as appreciative of the qualities Clara brings to Inked.

Thankfully, our male-to-female ratio at Inked sits at around seventy to thirty.

I turn my eyes back to Diesel. "Have any of the guys said anything? Got any concerns if we keep her on?"

He lowers himself onto the couch, crumpling the paperwork Clara has sprawled across her 'desk' before locking his eyes with mine. "I wasn't talking about keeping her around as an employee." He stares at me with a jeering grin etched on his face. "I was talking on a more *personal* level."

A whizz of air parts my nose. "The only reason Clara is standing behind that counter is because she's here for the dollars. Hell would freeze over before anything *personal* happens between us."

The mocking grin on Diesel's face enlarges. "Don't go acting like your cock hasn't stood to attention every time she greeted you with a bit of lip. You've always liked them with attitude. That's why you're always hiding out in your office the last two weeks... so your desk can conceal the stiffness in your jeans."

I smirk but don't refute his claim. Diesel and I have been friends since fifth grade, so he'd see through any ruse I dangled in front of him. I'm also not one for lying. Even with Clara giving me as good as I've been dishing the past two weeks, she just needs to nibble on the end of her pen, and my cock is paying careful attention to every move she makes.

I'm endeavoring to keep my head in the game—*the head on my shoulders, not the one between my legs*—which ensures our little tit-for-tat routine will never be anything more than an employee and employer having a difference of opinion. *Now I just need my cock to get the memo.*

Diesel cranks his neck to the side just as Clara bends over to gather a register roll from the lower shelf of the cabinet in the foyer. "Damn! I'd even take a bit of lip for an ass that fine."

I sink deeper into my chair. "You've got to get the bar bunnies out of your bed before you'll ever have the opportunity to get a woman of Clara's standards between your sheets. Besides, Inked has rules on the crew not messing around. When that happens, shit gets complicated."

Diesel chuckles. "Fuck the rules. We've never had a woman

like Clara work for us. If we did, the rules would have been broken years ago. And while I'm being totally fuckin' forthright, you would have been the first to break them. You had a fondness for bending the rules before you were out of diapers."

I smirk. What he's saying is true. Not just on my rule-breaking, but on the previous female employees of Inked. Other than Charity, none had Clara's sexpot beauty. They were interesting and had great personalities, but they were hired solely based on their credentials.

Does that mean I only hired Clara because she makes my dick twitch? No, not at all.

What? For someone who doesn't like lying, you're doing a mighty fine job of it, Brax.

In all honesty, at the start, Clara was offered a position solely because she's beautiful. But she remains a member of Inked because she has a strong work ethic. Her looks are merely an added bonus. What Clara said during her impromptu interview was true. This situation is a win-win for us both. By keeping our clients happy, they will return again and again.

The visual of Clara prancing around the shop in skintight designer dresses keeps my clients happy.

I scrub my hand over the few days of stubble on my chin while saying, "There's a difference between bending the rules and breaking them. Tapping Clara would be demolishing them."

"She'd be worth the hassle. You've always said it is the rich girls who are wilder in the bedroom. Clara is making me want to test your theory." Diesel's voice is a mix between playful and determined.

I glare into his hanker-filled eyes. "Are you gonna make a move on Clara?"

He rubs his hands together as his mocking grin switches to eagerness. "You got any objections if I do?"

The first thought to enter my mind is, *fuck yes, I mind*. The second is, *why do I even care?* Although I've been using the no-messing-with-the-crew clause as my excuse to stay away from Clara, it isn't set in stone for my crew. It's not in their employment contract, and it is not mentioned during the hiring process, so Diesel is well within his rights to ignore it. But even knowing this, I still don't want him touching Clara. She isn't mine, and she will most likely never be mine, but for some reason, unbeknownst to me, the thought of Diesel treating Clara like she's a bunny annoys the shit out of me.

Before I can reply to Diesel's question—or compile a reason as to why I object to his request—a flurry of blonde scurrying past my office door catches my attention.

After rolling my eyes at her imperfect timing, I say, "Come on in, Princess, you've never been concerned about knocking before, so what's changed now?"

Clara's red pumps enter the frame first, closely followed by the rest of her enticing body. "It's the first time I've ever seen a look of concentration on your face. I wasn't sure if you were holding a serious discussion or needing to use the bathroom."

Diesel's deep laughter fills the office.

"You'll be cleaning the bathroom if you don't watch it," I grumble, glaring at Diesel, my mood still edgy from his disclosure of interest in Clara.

"Un-fucking-likely," Diesel replies while sinking deeper into the couch.

After leaning back in my chair, I intertwine my fingers, striving to ignore the way Diesel's eyes roaming over the dark green dress clinging to the curves of Clara's body has caused a tick to impinge my jaw.

The clicking of heels bounces off the wall when Clara pushes off the doorjamb and ambles deeper into the space. "Charity has secured a walk-in, and Johnny has advised he will be *indisposed* for an hour." A ghost of a smile stretches across my face from the disgruntled cloud her eyes got when she referred to Johnny's unavailability. "The remainder of the crew don't have any clients arriving for another hour, so I'm going to grab a quick bite to eat."

My brow arches. "You're advising me that you're going to lunch?"

My eyes follow her hands when she runs them down the front of her dress before she nods.

"Why? You've never bothered the past two weeks, so what's changed today?" I question after dragging my eyes away from her petite frame. It's a hard-fought battle.

She stiffens. "I was just trying to be polite." Her brows stitch together tightly. "I guess it was imprudent of me to believe manners held any place in a tattoo parlor." With a sigh, she spins on her heels and saunters to the door. Just before she exits, she peers back at me. "You need to make a decision about converting my trial basis to a permanent position soon. It is highly unprofessional to leave such an imperative decision until the last minute." Although her words come out stern, the bitchy smear of her tone can't hide the desperation in her eyes.

"Actually, Diesel and I were just discussing your inclusion in the Inked family." I gesture my hand to Diesel, who hasn't taken his eyes off her ass since she entered my office.

Although my statement is slightly deceitful, it isn't a total lie. Before our conversation veered off course, Diesel and I were discussing the possibility of extending Clara's appointment at Inked.

Clara's breathing quickens, but she remains as quiet as a church mouse as her wide eyes shift between Diesel and me. "And?" she eventually squeaks out, unable to harbor her curiosity any longer.

I quirk my lips. "I haven't reached a decision yet. How about we extend your trial to a day-to-day basis until I've had time to decide?"

Anger spreads through Clara's veins, giving her skin a red hue. The veins in her neck pulse so furiously, they nearly burst. When she glares at me in disdain, I'm primed and ready to cop the wrath of her fury, so you can imagine my surprise when she holds back her usually bitchy retaliation and storms out of the office without a single word seeping from her lips.

I balk and turn my shocked eyes to Diesel. "What the fuck did I just miss?"

"A prime opportunity." Standing from the couch, he stretches his legs before striding to my open office door. After closing the door, he twists to face me. "She just gave you an in, and you shot her down like she has the clap."

I stare at him with bewilderment all over my face. "She didn't give me an in. She's just sucking up as she's worried about her position. Today is the last day of her trial."

Diesel throws his head back and laughs. "Yeah, right." He steps closer to my desk. "'I'm grabbing a quick bite to eat' is a bunny's way of saying, 'will you please fuck me over the lunch table?'"

I can't help the smirk that crosses my face at the way he changed his voice to mimic the women he usually spends his weekends with.

"Maybe for a bunny that might be true, but Clara isn't a bunny."

There's no way in hell Clara is a bunny. That name is solely reserved for girls who have no problems hopping from bed to bed. I may have called Clara a few choice names the past two weeks, but a bunny will never be one of them.

Diesel glares at me like I've grown a second head. "I knew you were off your game, man, but I had no clue it was this bad. Every woman is a bunny. Rich or not." He shifts his hazel eyes to mine, his expression changing from cheeky to serious in a nanosecond. "How long has it been since you graced a woman's womb with your seed?"

While glaring at him, I pretend I don't have a clue what he's referring to.

Not believing the phony look on my face, he continues, "I haven't seen you take home a bunny once the past two weeks. Not even one of the high-class ones I saw sniffing around last week."

"That's because the shit's gotten old. The game is overplayed," I interject with an edge to my voice. "My dysfunctional cock has nothing to do with the fine tail that just left this office. It's just tired of the game."

Diesel bows his brow. "The only shit that's gotten old is you, Brax. The game will never get old. Your dick gets cold, a bunny warms it. Your dick gets lonely, a bunny cuddles it. Your dick gets—"

"Yeah, yeah, I get it. A bunny on my cock is the answer for everything."

Diesel nods. "You've just got to decide if you want the high-class bunny your dick has set its radar on, or if you're going to settle for something a little less fancy but a shitload less complicated."

"My cock and its goals are no concern of yours."

He continues talking as if he didn't hear a word I said. "If you decide it isn't the latter, let me know, and I'll take a step back. But if a diamond-encrusted pussy isn't what you're chasing, step aside and let a real man show you how to seal the deal."

Not giving me a chance to reply, he strides into the corridor, closing my office door behind him.

CHAPTER SIX

"Charity, I'm heading out to grab some food," I advise while striding down the hallway at Inked.

Charity lifts her brown eyes from the lotus tattoo she's drawing on the shoulder of a long-time client and locks them with me. "Bring me back something sweet."

"If you want pussy on a platter, you should go visit Keke," I suggest with a cheeky wink.

Her pupils widen. "I've already tried to tap that, but for some reason, she's adamant her dinner dates must have dangling bits between their legs." She shrugs. "But, hey, I gave it my best shot."

I stop dead in my tracks. "I meant Keke's *establishment*. Not Keke herself."

Although the crew at Inked has no problems swapping bunnies, we draw the line at any other type of sharing. Since Keke isn't a bunny, I'm somewhat shocked by Charity's admission.

A bead of sweat forms on Charity's brow when she notices my surprised expression. "Oh, sorry, man. My bad?" Her eyes dance between mine. "I thought things between you and Keke had cooled since you've got Ms. Sweet Thing over there." She nudges her head to Clara standing behind the counter drinking some funky green concoction.

What is it with everyone assuming I'm knocking boots with Clara? I'm not knocking boots with anyone, let alone Clara, and my cock is not fucking happy about it.

Charity sighs loudly before drifting her eyes from Clara to me. "Why do all the beautiful women in this town only like cock?"

Any anger bubbling in my veins dampens from her assessment. Charity has the mouth of... well, a tattoo artist, but she's downright gorgeous—dark hair styled in an alluring short cut, rich brown eyes, and flawless skin accentuated with a collection of tattoos I designed specifically for her. She's proof not all the beautiful women in this town are solely cock lovers.

I shake my head, bringing my thoughts back to the present. "Something sweet?" I confirm, deciding Charity's attempts at seducing Keke aren't worth burning the solid bridge we've formed in the two years Charity has worked at Inked. Although Keke is a great girl, we both know our kinship isn't going any further than two sexually compatible companions sharing a bed for a few hours.

Charity grins a knockout smile as she nods.

"All right. I'll be back in a few."

Charity returns her focus to her client as I stride to the counter.

"You'll turn into a vegetable if you keep drinking that shit."

Clara lowers a glass of ghastly green liquid from her mouth. "There could be worse things I could turn into." Her icy-blue eyes lock with mine. "I could end up like you."

While smirking at her horrified expression, I say, "I walked straight into that one, didn't I?"

She screws up her nose before nodding. "Yeah, but you can't

win them all. Especially when you're fighting a battle you'll *never* win."

A breathy chuckle rumbles up my chest as I continue for the door. Just as I'm about to exit, Clara calls out my name, halting my fast escape. When I crank my neck, I balk. For the first time ever, she appears genuinely nervous.

"Have you given any more thought to extending my position here?"

The bells above the door chime when I close it and amble back to stand in front of her. Her stance is solid, but her eyes are giving away her real concern. She's petrified.

"Yeah, I have. Why don't we discuss it over dinner?"

Holy fuck! Did I just ask her on a date using her employment at Inked as leeway?

I'm so getting sued for workplace harassment.

Clara freezes. "I can't... I don't think that would be a good idea, Brax."

"Why not?"

Her refusal to dine with me has more impact on my gigantic ego than the time she tried to strike me months ago. Especially since I've caught sight of Diesel watching our exchange from the corner of the room. His face is laced with humor, and his whole demeanor screams of arrogance.

"I don't think we should mix business with pleasure," Clara replies, dragging my focus away from Diesel's smug face.

"It is a meal, Princess. There's nothing pleasurable about it." I rake my eyes over the curves I've been ignoring for weeks. "Unless certain *items* are on the menu?"

Yep, I'm definitely getting sued.

Clara's lips thin into a harsh line. "There's no chance of that *ever* happening."

When she glares at me through squinted eyes, hot anger

warms my blood. "Then it's lucky we're just grabbing a bite to eat, isn't it?"

My sudden decision to invite Clara to dinner has nothing to do with her employee contract and everything to do with Diesel's admission that he's interested in having her warm his sheets, but I can't help it. The instant Diesel shone his torch on Clara, it was like the possessive switch in my body was turned on. And now that it has been flicked on, I have no chance of turning it off.

Diesel has kept his distance from Clara the past week to give me the opportunity to decide on his suggestion. But he's eyeballing her now like she's a prime piece of steak he can't wait to sink his teeth into. To say my feeling of ownership kicked into overdrive would be an understatement. It's turned calamitous.

In my head, I know I don't have any claim to Clara, but it is like I've stepped back to my high school days, and I'm letting my competitive side overrule my rational-thinking head. I'm so far gone, I'm willing to make a fool out of myself in front of my crew simply to ensure I have the upper hand in the little black book competition Diesel and I have been running since our teen days.

Clara's eyes track me as I walk around the counter. Even though her stern gaze appears to be protesting, not a word spills from her lips when I curl my arm around her tiny waist, hoist her against my body, and guide her toward the front entrance of the shop.

I don't look back at my crew or Diesel to seek confirmation that I've secured their attention. I can feel their curious gazes burning a hole in the back of my head.

The hum of chatter filters into my ears when we merge onto the sidewalk. I swing my eyes to the left before drifting them to the right, seeking a suitable location I can take Clara to eat.

Upon realizing nothing on this side of Ravenshoe will be up to her impeccable standards, I make my way to Betty's Burgers two blocks over from Inked.

You can't go wrong with burgers and fries.

"You're nothing but a brute." Clara's words are barely audible over the scuffling of her stilettos on the concrete sidewalk. "You know I can walk, don't you? That's what legs were invented for. One foot in front of the other. I guess *beasts* like you might not understand the concept since you spend half of your day dragging your knuckles on the ground."

I stop walking and drop my eyes to hers. "If I release you, will you keep walking?"

When I spot the spark of rebellion brightening her light-blue eyes, I continue walking, dragging her along with me. Clara huffs when we enter Betty's Burgers, and her incoherent blubbering continues when I walk her to the booth at the back of the restaurant and place her on the cracked vinyl seat. I smirk when she shuffles across the plastic cladding to sit in the furthest corner of the booth. Her mouth is protesting that she wants to leave, but her actions are speaking louder than her words.

I greet Marnie—the regular waitress at Betty's—with a wink as I snag two menus from her grasp as she saunters past. "I'll be back to take your order soon, sugar," she mutters, her voice as sweet as the term of endearment she regularly calls me.

"Kale, poached salmon, carrot smoothies, or whatever other shit you usually eat isn't available here, but the burgers are good, and the cheese fries are even better," I advise while handing Clara a menu.

Her pupils widen more with every item she reads off the menu. "I can't eat anything here. My trainer, Pierre, would have a coronary." She lifts her eyes from scanning the menu to me. "Who eats a burger with four deep-fried beef patties? That's just asking for a heart attack."

"Are you kidding me? You're nothing but skin and bones. You could handle adding at least four of those burgers to your weekly diet."

That is a total lie. Clara is a slim build, but she has curves in all the right places. Her tits and ass have been the hot topic of many adult-only discussions in my tattoo chair the past three weeks. And I'm fairly certain she has been the source of many self-induced orgasmic experiences for the younger patrons of Inked. Even with her having perfected the princess-resting-bitch-face pose, her body is... *Jesus.*

I slide into the booth before every patron in the restaurant sees *exactly* what I think of Clara's desirable assets.

When a burning pain scorches my skull, I shift my eyes to Clara. Her face is lined with anger. "Did you just insult me?"

I shake my head. "No. Not at all."

Her brow arches. "I work my ass off in a gym for an hour every day before my shift at Inked. I watch every minute portion of food I eat, and I skip the dessert menu six nights a week, all to have a guy who shoves calories into his mouth like they're nothing but air tell me I look like a bag of bones."

"I didn't mean it like that."

"Then what did you mean, Brax? I'm not sure how you can mince words like that."

When she stands from the booth, her slit eyes silently demand that I move.

I don't budge an inch.

"Let me out," she snarls through gritted teeth.

When I shake my head, her anger hits an all-time high.

My cock is definitely broken. The instant her spikes hackled, it turned to stone.

"You honestly can't expect me to stay here after you insulted me! Only a fool would continue to associate with someone who ridicules them."

"That's sweet coming from the lady who has called me a beast on numerous occasions the past two weeks."

She crosses her arms in front of her chest. "If the name fits, use it."

I glare into her eyes. "Then sit the fuck down, *Princess*."

Her nostrils flare as the anger lining her face deepens. "Let. Me. Out. I'm not dining with you after you insulted me."

"I didn't insult you," I fire back, my loud voice gaining us a handful of spectators.

"Then what do you call it? You pretty much insinuated that you don't find me attractive."

Ignoring the dozen pairs of curious eyes bouncing between Clara and me, I lock my eyes with her and mutter, "Do you want to know the impact your hours of calorie counting and gym work-outs have on me?"

The tightness of her arms braced in front of her chest strengthens before she curtly nods.

"Then look down, Princess."

Her brows scrunch as confusion washes over her face. After delving her tongue out to replenish her dry lips, she drops her gaze. She inhales a sharp, quick breath when her eyes zoom in on the hardness my jeans don't have a hope in hell of hiding.

Feeling the heat of her furious gaze, the thickness of my cock grows.

Yep, it's definitely broken.

When Clara's massively dilated eyes return to mine, I say, "You need to stop acting so defensive. Not everyone is out to get you. Although I could have chosen better words, I didn't mean to insult you. If you look more deeply into what I said, it could be taken as a compliment."

When she huffs and rolls her eyes, I stand from the booth and move out, giving her a clear exit. "If you want to go, go. If not, let's sit down and have a meal together. No stipulations. No expectations. Just two friends enjoying each other's company."

Clara's eyes dance between mine for numerous heart-clutching seconds before she queries, "If I leave, will my position at Inked be on the line?"

My jaw muscle gains a quiver. "No. I may be a *beast*, but I'm still a man under this beastly disguise. I can't offer you a permanent placement at Inked as those positions are reserved for tattoo artists, but your current position is yours for as long as you want it on a casual basis. Take it a day at a time and see where this shit takes you. Once you've had your fill of Inked, just let me know you're ready to move on with a few days' notice."

For the first time ever, a genuine smile sneaks across her thinly slit lips. "Thank you."

I won't lie, my heart slithers into my gut when she slides out of the booth to stand next to me. "I like you, Brax, and I appreciate the opportunity you have bestowed on me, but we are not friends, and because we come from two entirely different lifestyles, we'll most likely never be friends. So why don't you stop pretending you actually like me and let me get back to the job you're paying me to do?"

She doesn't wait for me to reply.

She simply strides to the door and exits without a backward glance.

CHAPTER SEVEN

"How are you finding the move? I bet your boy is growing up fast?"

Hugo, one of my regular clients at Inked, smiles a beaming grin. "Yeah, Joel is..." He stops talking as his eyes sheen with moisture. "He's good. So much like his mother."

I pull my tattoo gun back from the rainbow rose I'm adding to his vast collection of tattoos on his right rib and inspect my work. "So what's the deal with this tat? Most of your pieces have some sort of connection to Ava, but this is the first time I've ever inked a flower on your body." My voice comes out shaky, hindered by a small bout of laughter dying to break free.

Nothing against Hugo. He's a tall brute of a man who could easily put any guy on his ass, but the majority of his torso is covered with a range of oddly chosen tattoos. Although his ink selection is one-of-a-kind, every one I've placed on his body has a significant meaning to his life before he moved to Ravenshoe. It didn't take a genius to realize his tattoos revolved around one woman.

If the hidden inclusion of the name Ava in most of his tattoos didn't give enough of a hint, the stories he shared while I added to his collection were a surefire indication. Tattoo artists are the male equivalent of hairdressers for women. The stories clients have shared while sitting in my tattoo chair could fill at least a hundred books.

After wiping the freshly-inked skin with my cloth, I lift my eyes to Hugo. He's grinning a smile I've only seen on his face once before—when I inked his son's name onto his chest. It sits just above his heart.

"I asked Ava to marry me," Hugo admits, his smile enlarging.

My lips curl into a broad grin. "Shit, man, you work fast," I jest. He only moved back to Rochdale three months ago.

He laughs. "That's only the beginning. We are having a baby at the end of the year."

I cock my brow. "Damn, you better watch out. You'll run out of skin to ink with all those memories you're creating." I nudge my head to the bathroom while pulling off my latex gloves. "Go tell me what you think. You'll have to switch off the light to see Ava's name since you went with the invisible ink again."

Hugo stands from my tattoo chair, filling my cubicle with his six-foot-five frame. I clean up my station while he checks out his newly inked piece in the bathroom attached to my cubicle.

He emerges thirty seconds later with a broad grin on his face.

"Good?" I query, already knowing his answer.

"Perfect." No more words are needed. His face tells the entire story.

Hugo throws his shirt over his head while shadowing me to the counter to ring up his purchase. I've worked at Inked for over ten years, and he is the only client I've agreed to tattoo a name on without seeing a wedding band wrapped around his finger. I didn't need to warn him about the lifetime commitment that comes with having a person's name inked onto your skin. His eyes relayed he was well aware of the commitment he was making. The fact he's getting married proves I didn't misread his loyalty to Ava.

My brisk pace to the cash register slows when "Brax" sounds from a pair of lips that can cause my dick and spikes to bristle at the same time.

Things between Clara and me the past three weeks have followed a similar path they did the weeks prior to my disastrous attempt at sharing a meal with her. Although she's a little stand-offish with both the staff and me, she does exactly what she's paid to do. And she does it well.

The only thing that has changed is our game of tit for tat. It came to a screeching halt the instant she exited the restaurant three weeks ago. I guess finding out your scornful tongue gives your boss a raging hard-on would dampen anyone's eagerness to take part in a bit of friendly banter.

Clara walks out of my office balancing a planner in one hand while twirling a pencil in the other. "Your seven o'clock appointment just canceled. Did you want me to bump up one of your following appointments? Or..." Her words stop when they lift from the leather-stitched planner to the enormity of Hugo standing beside me.

The longer her eyes roam Hugo, the more the raging tornado in her eyes grows. I can see her short temper flaring, dying to break free.

I'm not the only one who has noticed her blazing reaction to Hugo's presence. The buzzing of tattoo guns quiets down, and the usual hum of conversation dulls to barely a whisper.

The longer Clara glares at Hugo, the more attention she garners from her colleagues.

After sucking in a deep breath, Clara finally shifts her widened gaze to me. "You're busy. I'll come back."

I balk, staggered by her odd behavior.

She's never been concerned about interrupting me before, so what's changed now?

"No, let's do this shit now, Princess. The quicker I get these appointments over with, the quicker my weekend will start."

Her throat works hard to swallow before her narrowed gaze rockets back to Hugo. She stares at him as if she's daring him to say something while I bounce my confused eyes between them, trying to work out how they know each other. From the dazed expression on Clara's face and the shit-eating grin on Hugo's, it doesn't take a genius to realize they've met before.

My back molars smack together as my mind runs through various scenarios of how well they could know each other. All my skits follow along a similar path—Hugo and Clara naked together.

"Yeah, come on, *Princess*," Hugo says, his voice a thick drawl. "Brax hasn't got all day."

My brow cocks. Just from the contempt displayed in Hugo's words, I think my initial assumption of his friendliness with Clara may have been wrong. But even with having my unwarranted jealousy checked, my mood is still woeful. I've been working with a massive headache the past two hours.

Actually, make that weeks.

She's standing right in front of me.

The biggest fucking headache of my life.

Like my crippling headaches aren't irritating enough, my cock's stint in segregation has become even more severe since Clara arrived on the doorstep of Inked. Nothing kills a man's good mood quicker than losing his mojo.

Clara's narrowed eyes shift from glaring at Hugo to me. "We'll continue this later," she instructs, her tone smeared with superiority like the princess she is.

My eyes drift around the handful of the Inked crew watching

the exchange between Clara and me with eagle eyes. Charity's mouth is gaped, Johnny has his brows stitched, and Diesel is leaning against the doorjamb of my office with an amused grin etched on his face.

Not willing to let any member of my crew believe this type of behavior will be deemed acceptable at Inked, I sling my eyes back with Clara and order, "Do it now or collect your last paycheck."

She inhales a quick, jagged breath as her eyes dance between mine, no doubt seeking any deceit in my statement. Although I said the job was hers as long as she wanted it, I won't be disrespected in front of my crew.

I just hope she can't see the deceit in my eyes.

Unable to determine if my threat is idle, Clara swallows harshly before marching to the counter with her head held high. She snaps open the planner and drops her eyes to it. "I contacted Clancy. He's happy to take an earlier appointment, but he has some alterations he'd like to make to his design."

I adjust the tilt of my head, forcing her eyes to connect with mine. "Have Clancy's designs already been drawn up?"

After shifting her eyes from Hugo to me, Clara shakes her head.

"Then keep him at his original time. He's fanatical about the draw-up, and it can take hours to get him to agree to a design, so he'll hold up the appointments following him. What about Riley?" I suggest while pointing to my ten o'clock booking. "Call him and see if he can get here at seven, then slot Colby in after him."

"Okay. I'll make some phone calls. Once I have everyone scheduled, I will advise you of any changes," Clara informs, her voice still high-strung.

Once she snaps the planner shut, she diverts her focus to Hugo. "If you so much as breathe a word about me working here, I will ensure it is the last breath you take," she warns in a vicious snarl. "In fact, if you even mention you saw me in this dump, I'll do far worse than ending your pathetic life."

My eyes bulge, Charity's dropped jaw gains leverage as does the grin on Diesel's face, and Johnny... well, he's simply staring at Clara in complete awe.

It's not every day you see a princess sparring against a giant.

Upon hearing the shocked gasps of her work colleagues, Clara's eyes slowly filter around the shop. The fiery anger illuminating her face with a red hue fades when she realizes her tirade has gained her the attention of half of her co-workers and a dozen clients.

Snarling, she spins on her heels and darts down the corridor. I run my hand down my face as my brain tries to work out what the fuck just happened. This is the first time in the ten years I've been working at Inked that I've had to deal with a member of my crew verbally abusing the clients.

Usually, it's the other way around.

After gesturing for my crew to get back to work, I lock my eyes on Hugo. "Sorry about that. She's a little high-strung at times," I mutter, my voice hampered with frustration at being forced to apologize for the behavior of one of my crew, let alone a grown woman who should know better.

Hugo delves his hand into the back pocket of his jeans. "It's all good. It's nothing I haven't handled before."

When he passes me one of the many credit cards housed in his leather wallet, my brows furrow. "Since when did you stop paying cash?" I jest, saying anything to lessen the awkward tension plaguing the air.

"About as long as you've been picking up rich strays." Hugo waggles his brows.

I laugh, grateful he can see the humor in a difficult situation. "A dangerous endeavor for us both, no doubt?"

"You have no fucking clue," he mutters under his breath.

After seeing Hugo out, I walk down the corridor in search of Clara. Because of the size of the shop, it doesn't take me long to find her camped out in the supply closet. Although she appears to be busy working, the feistiness that radiates out of her in invisible waves is missing, clearly indicating she's in hiding.

"I need to talk to you in my office."

Clara places a bottle of blue tattoo ink onto the third shelf before hopping off the stepladder. "Okay. Let me just finish this—"

"Now, Clara," I interrupt, my voice conveying that this is not up for negotiation.

She places the ordering clipboard on the middle shelf and shifts on her feet to face me. When her icy-blue eyes lock with mine, my furious composure slips for the quickest second. She looks more concerned now than she did when I threatened for her to collect her last paycheck ten minutes ago. I guess this is the first time I've used her real name in the past six weeks.

I nudge my head to the hallway, wordlessly demanding that she follow me. Not waiting for her to reply, I spin on my heels and stride to my office. If her rich floral scent hadn't infused the air around me, I would have assumed she wasn't following me. She's so quiet, not even the clicking of her heels on the tiled floor sounds through my ears as we make our way down the corridor and into my office.

I move to my desk, prop my backside on the edge, then lift my eyes to the office door. Clara is standing in the open doorway, looking prepared to flee at any moment. Her pupils are wide, and her face is flushed.

This is the one part of my job I fucking hate. Just like I'm not a violent man, I also loathe confrontation, but Clara overstepped the mark tonight, and she must be reprimanded for it. I warned her when I offered her a trial at Inked that if she scared away any of my customers, she'd be out on her ass quicker than I could snap my fingers. Although it will take more than a spiteful threat to scare off a regular client like Hugo, she still shouldn't have said what she did.

When Clara remains standing halfway between the hallway and my office, I request, "Close the door."

Her throat struggles to swallow before she does as requested. Once the door is closed—blocking out the buzzing of tattoo guns—I gesture to the couch.

Her eyes follow mine before she timidly shakes her head. "I'm happy to stand," she informs me as her eyes stray from the couch to me. "If you're going to fire me, Brax, can you hurry up and get it over with?"

A deep sigh spills from my lips. "You don't have anything else to say? No pleading for clemency? No begging for forgiveness?"

"No," she replies with a brisk shake of her head.

I balk, utterly shocked.

"I did nothing wrong, so why would I feel the need to apologize?" she argues to my baffled expression.

I arch my brow. "Are you fucking kidding me? You did nothing wrong?" Pushing off the desk, I walk two steps closer to her. "You not only disrespected my business, my crew, and me with the little spectacle you unleashed, you disrespected yourself."

Her eyes bounce between mine, her confusion growing by the second.

"We're a family at Inked. The instant you agreed to work here, you became one of us. Anything said or done to a member of our family is done to the *whole* family, so when you ran your mouth about my business, you were running your mouth about yourself."

She inhales a sharp breath as the fiery spark in her eyes is smothered with shock.

I cross my arms in front of my chest. "I'd always wondered

why you chose to work at Inked instead of one of those fancy boutiques you buy your dresses from. Only now does it dawn on me why you showed up on this side of town. You didn't think anyone from your neck of the woods would turn up here."

Clara's tongue delves out to lick her parched lips, but she doesn't speak a peep.

"Well, I have news for you, Princess. Having tattoos doesn't make you trashy. I've *doodled* on judges, lawyers, doctors, and even stuck-up little *princesses* who have fancy-colored credit cards that cost a quarter-of-a-mil a year just to have."

The harshness of my words dulls when I spot a sheen of moisture forming in her eyes, but it doesn't completely stop my reprimand. "If your plan is to hide away from your country club friends in a place you won't be seen, the door is that fucking way." I point to the entrance of Inked. "As I guarantee you have just as much chance of being seen here as you would in some fancy dress shop on the other side of town."

After issuing my disappointment with my eyes instead of words, I walk around my desk and take a seat in my cracked leather chair. I secure a set of invoices off my desk and shuffle through them, needing something to distract my hands from the urge to take Clara over my knee and spank the sass right out of her.

Maybe that's half her problem? Perhaps her parents didn't discipline her enough?

My gaze lifts from the invoices in my hand when Clara whispers, "Am I fired?"

The roaring of blood in my ears slows as my gaze drifts between her remorse-filled eyes. "I said your position at Inked is yours for as long as you want it. I'm a man who keeps my word."

Relief swamps her eyes as she gently nods.

"But if you disrespect my crew or me again, I may reconsider."

She once again nods before pivoting on her heels and stalking to the door.

The furious twitch impinging my jaw lessens when the faintest murmur of, "I'm sorry, Brax," seeps from her lips before she slips out of my office as quietly as she entered.

CHAPTER EIGHT

tanding from my office chair, I down the glass of whiskey I've been nursing the past thirty minutes before snagging my jacket thrown over the edge of my desk. Considering it is a little after midnight on a Saturday, I don't bother checking if the premises are vacant. All the crew of Inked evacuates the instant the clock strikes midnight, more than eager to commence their two-day weekend. Clara included.

Ever since my run-in with Clara three weeks ago, things at Inked have changed. I'd like to say a majority of the change has been Clara's attitude, but unfortunately, that isn't entirely the case. Although she has toned down her prima-donna attitude, she's still coldhearted and standoffish.

You can't throw a princess into a pair of low-riding jeans and call her a cowgirl. At the end of the day, she will always be a princess. But instead of treating the crew at Inked as if they're a piece of chewed-up gum stuck under a bench seat, Clara has been treating them with more respect, as if they're members of her family instead of the enemy. It may be similar to an annoying little brother vibe, but it's better than the previous attitude she had.

After securing the deadbolts on the front door, I make my way to my Harley parked at the back of Inked. My eager steps lengthen when my eyes catch a flurry of blonde standing next to my bike.

I increase my stride as my eyes run over every inch of the fire-engine red dress clinging to the curves of the tempting female. The beat of my heart kicks up a gear as does the throb of my cock when my eyes are inundated with lavish curves on a knee-weakening body.

My excitement doesn't last long when the blonde notices my approach and twists her neck to the side to greet me. "Hey, Brax, you heading home?" asks Fallon, smiling a covetous grin that relays the question she really wants to ask, *Hey, Brax, you looking for company?*

Fallon is what I'd call a high-class bunny. With a body that brings mere mortals to their knees and the face of an angel, she could easily have her pick of any guy on the good side of Raven-shoe. Thankfully for the crew at Inked, she likes her men with a hint of roughness she can't get on her side of town. And the fact she's sprawled across my bike tells me she has her sights set on one member of the Inked crew tonight. Me.

While licking my parched lips, I run my eyes over her body for the second time. Red stiletto heels, lean runner legs, a smoking hot dress that hugs the curves of her more-than-tempting ass, and a decent rack I could easily be distracted by for hours.

Fuck it. My dick needs warmth.

After arching my brow, I stare into Fallon's bright green eyes. "You got any objections to fucking on a desk?"

"Not at all," she purrs while prancing toward me, not the slightest bit intimidated by the crudeness of my words.

<hr>

My sweaty hands strengthen their grip on Fallon's hips as her body quivers through her second orgasm since we entered my office thirty minutes ago. Thankfully, her cries of ecstasy are barely heard over the slapping of skin as I pound into her. My pumps are furious as my race to climax picks up speed.

I need to come.

I need the release.

I need to get *her* out of my fucking head.

Fallon's dress slides up her waist more when I adjust her position. After flattening her torso onto my desk, I pry her knees further apart with mine before slamming my cock back into her. She groans a long, quivering moan when I take my cock to the root before drawing it back out. Her pussy ripples around me, begging for me to stay immersed in her warmth, and sweat rolls down my glistening torso when I thrust my hips forward, slamming back into her.

"Ah, Christ, Brax," she pants breathlessly as I fuck her at a ferocious speed.

Her new position has her taking more of my cock than she was earlier while also increasing my sprint to climax.

"It feels so good, baby, so deep. So... oh..." Fallon purrs.

A familiar tingle races along my spine when her pussy clamps down on my cock, her third climax coming to fruition even more quickly than the first two. Unlike the lower-class bunnies, Fallon's climaxes are void of the usual ear-piercing screams I've come to expect. If it weren't for her pussy milking my cock and her slick wetness coating my balls, I'd be none the wiser that she's orgasming.

Once the violent shudders raking Fallon's body lessen, I close my eyes, trying to block her from my thoughts. It isn't that she doesn't have a body most men would take a stake to the heart for or that her pussy isn't milking my cock the way I like it, it is the fact my cock has some fucked-up ideas on what it classes as a fun time.

Tonight's event, unfortunately, has become a regular occurrence for me the past three months. My cock plays his part to a T. He shows up hard and primed to go, but no matter how close my chase to climax gets to the finish line, I've failed to cross the line every single time.

It's there, right in front of me, but the final push I need to get me over the line is missing.

Fuck, I hope I find my mojo soon, or I'm going to die of sexual deprivation.

My eyes sluggishly open when the door in my office creaks. Although shocked to see Clara, I'm not at all surprised when she walks in unannounced.

Princesses don't require permission to enter private premises.

She walks three steps into the sweat-infused space before her eyes lift from the cell phone in her hand. When she spots Fallon sprawled on my desk, one of her hands darts up to clutch her neck, stifling a scream, while the other yanks a set of earbuds out of her ears. As her eyes absorb the scandalous visual playing out in front of her, her pupils dilate to the size of dinner plates. Her lips part, and her cheeks turn a hue of pink.

Her flushed expression gives me the final push I need to cross the finish line. I close my eyes as the most intense orgasm I've ever experienced rockets through my body, shredding any concerns I had about dying of sexual deprivation. I come like I've never come before, a vision-hazing orgasm that utterly destroys me.

I'm so spent, I don't notice Clara slipping out of the room until the bells above Inked's entrance door chime into my office.

Fuck!

After pulling out of a delirious Fallon, I snag my jeans off the floor and take off after Clara. My abrupt departure has me accidentally stomping on Clara's expensive diamante-encrusted cell she left on the floor.

I drag my jeans up my thighs and tuck in my half-masted, condom-covered cock before staggering onto the sidewalk in front of Inked. My head cranks to the side when metal crunching together booms out of the alleyway. My heart thrashes against my ribs harder than it did when I was climaxing as I charge for the alley.

I take a step back when Clara's white convertible flies out of the narrow alley, missing me by the skin of my teeth. Tires squeal across the asphalt, and horns honk when she merges dangerously onto the street.

Any thoughts of jumping on my bike and chasing after her fade when my eyes lock in on my pride and joy lying on its side on the asphalt partway down the alley.

"Oh, baby, what did she do to you?" I mumble to myself as I bend down to collect the broken side mirror of my custom Harley Davidson Fat Boy.

"You owe me three grand," I declare while slapping the invoice from the panel beater who spent forty-eight hours of my weekend restoring my Harley back to her original condition onto the windscreen of Clara's BMW.

For the past hour, I've been lying in wait in the parking lot of Inked for Clara to show up. For the first time in the nine weeks she's worked here, she's arrived only ten minutes before opening.

I was getting worried I'd finally scared her off.

"I don't owe you shit," Clara replies before she opens her car door into my hip.

"Wow, Princess knows how to cuss. Did they teach you that in princess school?" My taunting words hide the grimace crossing my face from the sting her door made to my hip.

"Uh-huh. Along with how to avoid low-life scum." While glaring into my eyes, she curls out of her car all ladylike, her prim and proper composure not matching the malice of her words.

When she tries to sidestep me, I move into her path, foiling her quick getaway with my six-foot-two height.

Her nostrils flare as her icy eyes connect with mine. "If you don't move, you'll learn about another technique they taught me in *princess* school."

"Oh, yeah, like what?" I take a step closer to her, not the slightest bit intimidated by her threat.

When she takes a retreating step, her back splays against the driver's side door of her car. Like *carpe diem*, I seize the moment by taking another step forward. The pulse in Clara's neck thrums when my body pins her to her car. I try to ignore the way her nipples are budded and pressed against my chest, how her rich floral scent has my cock stiffening, and how I'd let her smash her BMW into my Harley again just for the chance of discovering if her lips taste as yummy as they look.

In case you didn't realize, my endeavors of being ignorant are fruitless. My body is acutely aware of every inch of her skin flattened against mine. And from Clara's wide-eyed and flushed expression, I'd say she's also mindful of my body's reaction to her closeness.

"This is workplace harassment." The hotness of her breath tickles my lips.

"If we were inside Inked, that might be the case, but since we haven't entered the premises yet, I'm perfectly within my rights to seek restitution for the damage you did to my property. Believe me.

I checked," I say, quoting some of the words she flung at me during our last tussle.

Everything I'm saying is a lie. I didn't check shit.

When Clara fights my hold, I lean in even deeper, nearly crushing her tiny frame under my two hundred pounds. My movements cause my cock to brush the tempting warmth between her legs. My girth swells when a breathless moan unexpectedly topples from Clara's O-formed mouth. Her pupils expand as she snaps her mouth shut, no doubt mortified at her body's response to my closeness.

Fighting the desire to request the restitution I'm owed in a non-monetary value, I repeat, "You owe me three thousand dollars," while peering into her arctic-blue eyes.

My blood heats from the cunning grin that curls onto her lips. "As I said earlier, I don't owe you shit. Your bike was like that when I exited the parking lot."

The throatiness of her voice makes me even harder, but even if I wanted to ignore the deceit her eyes are relaying, I can't ignore the massive streak of vivid black satin paint—the color of my bike—on the right front fender of her car.

Noticing the direction of my gaze, Clara huffs before she struggles against my hold, fighting to get free. I hold my ground, refusing to relinquish her from my grasp.

Realizing she has no chance of fleeing from a man my size, she sighs. "It was an accident! I didn't mean to hit your bike." Her words come out in a hiss as she strains them through her clenched teeth.

"You didn't mean to hit it?" I quote, moving my head into her line of sight, demanding the attention of her bouncing eyes. "You dragged it halfway down the alley."

"It was an accident!" Her chest heaves against mine. "Because I was blinded by an image I'd give anything to forget, I *accidentally* clipped your bike with my car. Believe me, I was just as mortified as you were."

I don't know if the last part of her statement is referring to the damage done to my bike or the scene she witnessed in my office. While I strive to unravel the mystery of Clara, I return her determined stare. I've said previously her eyes were soulless, but the small sparks of life that have grown in them the nine weeks she has worked at Inked display she's telling the truth. So, ignoring the screaming protest of my cock, I take a step back, not only unpinning her from her car but also moving away from the warmth my cock wants to delve into.

The instant I step away, Clara runs her hands down her dress, smoothing the crinkles I caused to the material. My mind goes straight to working out a way I can get that dress creased on my bedroom floor.

What the fuck? I don't take girls back to my place.

Correction. I don't take bunnies back to my place. Since Clara isn't a bunny, technically, she doesn't count. But either way, I shouldn't be having those types of thoughts about a member of my crew.

"What were you doing at Inked at that time of the night?" I ask, endeavoring to return my thoughts to less deviant grounds.

I racked my brain the majority of the weekend trying to work out why Clara would be entering my office a little after one in the morning. Not one plausible reason was found.

"I could ask you the same thing. Haven't you heard of a bed?" She fakes a gag.

I smirk, loving not only her feistiness but the glint of jealousy firing her icy eyes. It's rare to spark a reaction out of her, so I'll take it for all it's worth. I'm not sure which look I prefer the most on Clara—the feisty little temptress or the jealous scorned woman. Both are as enthralling as the other.

"When you have an itch that needs to be scratched, you scratch it."

The rise and fall of her chest grow the longer I bounce my hankering gaze between her wide eyes. Even knowing I'm playing a game I shouldn't participate in, I add more chess pieces to the already overstacked board.

"Have you got an itch, Princess?" I mutter, no longer able to harness my curiosity on what has caused the glint of lust in her eyes.

The zipper of my jeans dig agonizingly into my cock when she murmurs, "Uh-huh," in a soft, throaty moan.

The pinch of pain turns into a full throb when she takes a step closer to me. She stands so close, the minty freshness of her recently brushed teeth fans my hungry lips.

"I have a *really* bad itch," she purrs, her voice the most provocative thing I've ever fucking heard. "It's just one a *beast* of a man like you wouldn't know how to scratch."

My conceit surges into unchartered territory. "Is that so?" I mutter, dropping my eyes to the generous swell of her curvy breasts. "Your tits are telling me a different story, Princess." I raise my eyes from her heaving chest to her face. Believe me, it's no easy feat. "They're telling me you not only want me to scratch your itch, but you also want me to fuck you hard and fast on my desk like I did to the little bunny Friday night."

Any concerns about my grandma having me lynched are left for dust when Clara's knee catches my groin unaware. Hot lava seers through my lungs as the air is violently removed from my body. I stumble backward and curl over, fighting through a torrent of pain I've never experienced before.

No grown man should ever experience this type of pain.

There are no doubts about it. Clara McGregor—Princess-Fucking-Socialite—has officially broken my cock.

"Jesus Christ, Clara. You could have just said no," I wheeze out.

"Oh. Could I? I once had someone tell me little punks don't understand the word no. So I figured I'd try a new tactic. I think it's safe to say my new ploy worked." Her words are vicious and add to the pain crippling me.

I cough, feeling my balls gargling in the back of my throat. "Yeah, it's safe."

My balls have barely returned to my stomach—let alone my sack—when Clara mutters, "Just in case the knee to the balls wasn't convincing enough, I'll spell it out for you, Brax." She spits my name out like venom. "The odds of me paying your three-thousand-dollar repair bill are nearly as good as your chances of scratching my itch."

The hot air of her breath flutters my earlobe when she snarls, "Pigs will fly before either of those things will happen."

She saunters away with her head held high and her hips swinging.

Even hunched over and nursing a set of crushed balls, my fucked-up brain tries to invent a way to get pigs to fly.

CHAPTER NINE

Did I get an apology from Clara for my balls being crushed beyond recognition? No.

Has Clara coughed up a dime of the three thousand she owes me? No.

Do I care? In all honesty, no, I don't.

Clara set me in my place, but I deserved it. I pushed, she pushed back harder.

Although we have spoken since the incident in the parking lot two weeks ago, we've never discussed what led to our heated exchange. If she's happy to forget I suggested fucking her like a bunny on my desk, I'll happily forget she crashed her BMW into my Harley before she crippled my balls with the same amount of intensity. Seems like a fair compromise.

I'm totally fucking pussy-whipped.

Ignoring the thoughts that would have Diesel paying out on me for weeks, I wander aimlessly around Inked. Not wanting another *incident* marked in my ledger, I now check that Inked is void of any living thing before I lock up each night.

Happy that the premises are lacking human contact, I amble to my bike. A grin curls on my lips when I enter the thick six-foot steel enclosure my bike is now protected behind. I had it installed three days following Clara's *accidental* collision with my bike.

The look on Clara's face when her BMW rounded the corner the morning it was installed was priceless. She looked a cross between amused and mortified. I've been loving all the new expressions she's been experimenting with for the past two weeks.

I squint my eyes when flashing orange lights impede my vision as I glide my bike down the side alley of Inked. Even with my vision hindered by bright lights, I can't miss the panicked expression on Clara's face as she pleads with a gentleman wearing a pair of grease-stained overalls.

I park my bike next to a tow truck that has Clara's BMW sitting on the tray and switch off the ignition. Clara's panic hits an all-time high when the second man with inky black hair clamps a set of safety chains onto the tires of her pride and joy.

Since Clara is so immersed in pleading with the middle-aged gentleman, she fails to notice me approaching. "I sent a check yesterday, I swear," she says, her begging eyes locked onto a man who has 'Jim' stitched on the upper left side of his overalls. "If they just waited a day or two, this whole situation could have been avoided."

"I'm sorry, sweetheart, I don't make the rules. I just enforce them," Jim replies while flicking the ash from his lit cigarette onto the ground. With a nudge of his head, Jim gestures for his employee to hop into the cab of the truck. "If you're going to rack up thousands of dollars in credit and cannot make a payment, you have to be prepared for the repercussions," Jim reprimands Clara while tearing out a sheet of paper from his extensively used tow slip pad. "If you can come up with the payment they're requesting by Monday, call the number at the bottom of the slip. If not, your car will be auctioned."

Jim gives Clara an apologetic smirk before he climbs into the cabin of his tow truck and drives down the street. Clara's chest thrusts up and down as she watches her beloved car become nothing but a speck on the horizon.

An ear-shattering scream expels from her lips when she spins and crashes into my chest. Snapping her eyes shut, she inhales a large breath as her hands scan the ridges of my chest and stomach.

A few inches lower and she'd discover the knee to the balls she struck me with two weeks ago didn't sustain me any permanent damage.

"How long have you been standing here, Brax?" she questions with her eyes still shut as tight as a bank vault.

I smirk. "You can tell it is me just from feeling me up?"

Quicker than a flash of lightning brightening a blackened sky, her eyes pop open. "I was not feeling you up."

"Yeah, you are." I nudge my head to her hands still plastered across the ridges of my stomach.

She freezes for a second in shock before she yanks her hands away as if scorched by an open flame. The tears glistening in her eyes prevent me from issuing a smart-ass remark to her absurd reaction. *She was touching my stomach, not my cock, for crying out loud.*

After running her sweat-slicked hands down the front of her designer dress, she turns her wide eyes to mine. "Have a pleasant evening." She cringes at her poor choice of words before she storms down the sidewalk.

It takes a minute for the reality of the situation to dawn on me.

After clenching my fists into firm balls, I hotfoot after her. "My warning still holds credit. If you get on a bus, your ass will be fired," I state.

Clara's quick strides to the bus shelter come to a dead halt halfway down the sidewalk. Her shoulders rise and fall as she inhales a large breath before she spins around to face me. "You just saw my car towed away, right?"

I nod.

"Then you know I have no other way to get home than to take the bus," she continues before crossing her arms over her chest.

The nod of my head converts to a shake. "You don't need to catch the bus. I'll take you home."

Her lips quirk as her perfectly etched brow curves high. "Do you have another mode of transportation that has more than two wheels?"

I crack a smile at the sassiness in her voice. "No," I reply with a brisk shake of my head.

Her brow arches even higher. "Then I'm taking the bus."

"Like fucking hell you are," I shoot back, my words flying out of my mouth like daggers.

All the high-spiritedness in her face drains, making way for the well-worn angry mask Clara usually wears. "You may be my *boss* when we're inside those walls," she spits out while pointing to the doors of Inked behind my shoulder. "But you have no power over me on this sidewalk."

The stern mask she's wearing slips for the quickest second when I take a step closer to her. "Are you sure about that, Princess?"

She squares her shoulders and looks me dead in the eyes. "Certain."

Not thinking of the repercussions my actions could cause to my business, I seize her elbow and drag her toward my bike. The clicking of her heels drowns out a small portion of her incessant rant on my beastly demeanor.

The angry sneer in her tone changes to panic when I snag my

helmet out of the saddlebag and place it on her head. When squealing brakes shriek over her blubbering, Clara cranks her head to the side in just enough time to see bus 57 pulling away from the curb.

Realizing the next bus doesn't arrive for another forty minutes, she swings her eyes back to me. Her pupils are massive, nearly swamping her entire cornea. "I can't, Brax... oh God. I can't," she mumbles with her eyes fixated on my bike.

She shakes like a leaf when I ignore her continued protests by lifting her in my arms and plopping her onto my seat. She looks prepared to flee, but her panic has rendered her motionless. I open my mouth, planning to deliver some reassurance to the dark cloud of fear forming in her eyes, but my words fail when my eyes zoom in on the indecent amount of her smooth thighs her new straddled position has exposed. I don't think I've ever seen anything as provocative as a princess on the back of a Harley—*my Harley.*

After dragging my eyes away from the mouthwatering visual I have no right to be perusing, I climb on my bike. "If you don't want to fall off, you better hold on tight," I warn.

Any objections spilling from her lips are drowned out by the loud rumble of my engine when I kick over the motor. As I pull into the heavy flow of traffic, Clara plasters her torso to my back and wraps her arms around my waist. It should feel wrong to have her sitting on the back of my bike—*very, very wrong*—but this feels right.

Actually, it feels fucking great.

Clara remains quiet the entire twenty-mile trip to her apartment building. There isn't much chance of holding a conversation between the warm May wind whipping past us and motorists honking their horns as I glide my bike through the densely populated roads.

When I pull into the driveway of Clara's apartment building

on Hyde, she wastes no time scampering off my bike. "Are you a goddamn lunatic!" she screams after yanking my helmet off her head.

I slide down the kickstand, then dismount my bike. "I did the speed limit... just," I reply with a chuckle.

A winded grunt escapes my lips when Clara shoves my helmet into my chest with brutal force. "You could have killed me."

"I've been riding these streets for years, Princess. I know them like the back of my hand."

"You could have killed me, Brax!" she screams again, her eyes teeming with tears.

Although I've imagined for weeks what she'd sound like screaming my name, I don't want to hear it like this. "I'd never..." When her eyes stray to the ground, I grip the top of her arms, forcing her to lock her eyes with mine. "I would *never* let anything happen to you, Clara." I stare into her eyes, ensuring she can see the truth in mine. "I shouldn't have forced you onto my bike, and I'm sorry if I scared you, but I promise you, you were safer on the back of my bike than on the bus."

Gritting her teeth, she yanks out of my embrace and storms into her apartment building. I run my hand over the top of my head, vainly trying to gather some of my scattered composure. It's a fruitless effort considering the reasoning behind my skittish demeanor just stormed away from me.

After gesturing to the valet that I'll be back in a few, I take off after Clara. I only just make it into the elevator before the doors snap shut. Clara maintains a quiet front, but I can tell she has noticed my presence. Not only did she intake a sharp breath when I first entered the cramped elevator car, but her scorching eyes also haven't left mine for the past ten floors.

For each floor the elevator rises, the number of occupants dwindles. Once we reach the thirtieth floor, Clara and I are the only remaining riders. When I take a step toward her, she spears me in place with her furious gaze. Even with her composure screaming annoyance, her pupils are massive, exposing her earlier panic is still firmly clutching her throat.

"Clara—"

My words halt when the elevator dings, announcing we've arrived on the penthouse floor. My strides out of the elevator car come to a dead stop when Clara suddenly spins around to face me. "I can take it from here," she mutters, her words shaking as badly as her composure.

"I just want to make sure you don't pass out in the hallway." My tone relays the honesty of my statement. She looks beyond rattled that I don't feel comfortable leaving her unattended.

Her wide eyes bounce between mine, but not a word escapes her hard-lined mouth.

"I've come this far. What's a few more steps?" I gesture my head to a set of double doors a measly few feet from us.

Clara's eyes follow mine before she faintly whispers, "Okay, but you're only walking me to my door. You can't come in."

I gesture with my hand for her to lead the way. Although annoyed at the bitterness of her tone, I'm also grateful she's lowering some of the impenetrable walls she has placed between us.

My thankfulness is short-lived.

Any panic left on Clara's face from the ride on the back of my bike turns to absolute fury when her eyes drink in the eviction notice taped to her apartment door. After snatching the document off the polished hardwood door, her eyes speed-read the notice. "You bitch!"

Her hair smacks me in the face when she abruptly storms to a door directly across from her apartment. Her abrupt movements infuse the corridor with her rich floral scent. Loud bangs on a wooden door bellow through my ears when Clara whacks her fists on her neighbor's door. Her pounding is so hard, I won't be shocked if she turns up to Inked on Tuesday with busted knuckles.

Clara stumbles forward when the door is suddenly yanked open. I grab the top of her arms, ensuring she doesn't kiss the pristine marble foyer of her neighbor's entrance.

After gathering her footing, Clara pulls out of my embrace and locks her angry eyes with the blonde who just opened the door.

When I follow Clara's irate gaze, my eyes bulge. *Damn! I'm living in the wrong neighborhood.* With long, wavy platinum-blonde hair, fierce green eyes, and a body any man would happily spend hours exploring, Clara's neighbor is a knockout, an easy ten out of ten.

"You can't do this." Clara shoves the piece of paper she snatched off her door into the chest of her neighbor. "I still have another two months remaining on my lease."

The blonde grins a ball-clenching smile that *nearly* has the same effect on my cock as Clara's feistiness. "Chapter 83 of the Florida State landlord statutes clearly state Isaac is acting within his rights by issuing you an eviction notice," she replies, her words as strong as her stance.

Clara takes a retreating step, bewilderment evident all over her face. She isn't the only one surprised. The last time I was confronted with the name Isaac was when Clara wanted it inked on her skin nearly six months ago.

"Isaac approved this?" Clara queries, her voice hindered with shakiness.

The blonde crosses her arms under her impressive rack. "Isaac is a businessman, Clara. His priorities remain focused on his empire, leaving me the task of ensuring the trash is placed on the curb."

"Trash?"

"Yeah. *Trash*," her neighbor replies, drawing out the derogatory word in a long hiss. "You are nothing but a vindictive little bitch who is about to be taught a precious lesson."

Ouch! Even my ego got slapped by that catty remark.

Though she copped a low blow, in true Clara style, she straightens her spine and gives as good as she's getting. "Well, I have news for you, *sweetheart...*"

I grin, loving that she used a term of endearment as if it is an offensive word.

"The only person going to be taught a valuable lesson is you. You can act all high and mighty in your designer pantsuits, sipping expensive wine from a crystal flute in your fancy top-floor penthouse, but at the end of the day, you're no better than me." Clara takes a step closer to her neighbor, meeting her eye to eye. "Enjoy it while it lasts, Regan, because when Isaac finds out about the *special guest* you've been *entertaining* the past two months, it's all going to come tumbling down, one Chanel suit at a time."

After flashing a sly grin, Clara enters her apartment without a backward glance. I remain motionless, standing in the foyer with my mouth gaped open and my cock as hard as stone.

There's nothing as compelling as a feisty princess standing her ground.

I'm not the only one rendered into silence by Clara's gutsy tirade. Her neighbor stands just as muted as me.

Several seconds of dense awkwardness pass before Regan shifts her eyes to me. "You should be cautious about messing with a woman like Clara," she warns, her tone not as snarky as the one she used while tussling with Clara.

A grin tugs my lips higher. "I could say the same to you."

Regan doesn't attempt to refute my statement because you can't deny the truth.

CHAPTER TEN

I jerk my chin up in greeting to Penny—the nurse my grandma tried to set me up with three months ago—before I continue striding down the corridor of Caramine Care.

Although Penny has the naughty-nurse getup down pat, I'm glad I steered clear of her tempting offer. I've got enough on my plate with a certain feisty princess to be adding any more into the mix.

I knocked on Clara's door for a good ten minutes last night, only to be asked to leave through a crack the width of an inch. I only left when she guaranteed me she wouldn't take the bus to work on Tuesday. Even though she agreed to my demand, I have an inkling she won't adhere to my advice.

She better, or she will find out the hard way that I'm a man of my word.

Just as I'm about to enter my grandmother's room, the quickest glimpse of a profile stops me in my tracks. Clara just exited a door a few spots down from my grandma's room. She stops halfway down the corridor to chat with a man in a navy-blue suit and a white doctor's coat.

A woman of Clara's caliber could never be referred to as dowdy, but with her pale face and red rims around her eyes, her usually bright appearance is a little more tarnished than normal. Even tired, her beauty can't deter her male companion's longing glance at her backside as she saunters away from him.

Clara's composure is so off-kilter, she doesn't notice me gawking at her as she strides down the narrow hallway. Even stepping into her path doesn't slow her brisk pace.

"Sorry," she mumbles, her voice barely recognizable as she sidesteps me and continues for the door.

Her brisk pace only falters when I ask, "Why are you in such a hurry, Princess?"

Her hands dart up to rub her face before she slowly spins to face me. I take a step back, uneased by the look on her face. Bitchy, hormonal women I can handle, but a crying one? Not so much.

Acting purely on impulse, I draw her into my chest and guide her into my grandma's room. Thankfully, the room is empty. Clara stiffens like a board the instant I curl my arms around her shoulders, but surprisingly, she doesn't fight against my hold. I expected her to shove me away or yell at me to "get my filthy beast hands off her." But she does nothing. She just accepts my comfort without a single qualm spilling from her lips.

Hell must have frozen over.

I'm confident she can hear my heart hammering my ribs, but I don't care. I continue to hold her in as tightly to my body as I can, relishing a moment of reprieve from the bickering we've endured the past three months.

My bliss doesn't last long.

"Let me just grab my coat then... oh, hello, Brax," my grandma greets me with her rheumy eyes bouncing between mine before they lower to Clara plastered against my torso.

Clara freezes before pulling away from my embrace. Her red-rimmed eyes stare into mine for numerous heart-clutching seconds before she swings them to my grandma standing in the doorway. The whiteness of her face grows when her eyes absorb my grandma's flushed cheeks and gaping mouth. "I'm sorry."

Not waiting for a reply, she bolts for the door.

"You don't need to leave, dear," my grandma advises Clara's quickly retreating frame.

Either not hearing a word my grandmother spoke or choosing to ignore it, Clara continues for the door.

"Clara!" I shout when she flees into the corridor without a backward glance.

By the time I make it to the hallway, being extra attentive not to bump into my grandma, Clara has already exited the automatic double doors of Caramine Care and climbed into the back seat of a taxi idling at the curb. Although I'm grateful she was smart enough not to take the bus, I'm not sure how her bank balance will handle the forty-mile cab fare from here to her apartment building.

Once Clara's taxi disappears from my view, I walk back into my grandmother's room. She has seen Mrs. Porter off and is sitting on the edge of her pale blue bedspread-covered bed. Her face looks as shocked as Clara's did when I told her she had secured a two-week trial at Inked.

"I didn't realize you knew the McGregors."

While rubbing the back of my neck, I take a seat on the recliner next to my grandma. "Yeah, Clara's been working with me for the past few months."

My grandma's eyes rocket to mine. "Clara works at Inked?" Her voice is smeared with uncertainty, and she looks the most dumbfounded I've ever seen her.

"Yeah." I nod my head. "Don't look so shocked, Grandma. We aren't all tattoo-covered Neanderthals."

My grandma slices her hand through the air. "It's not that, Brax. I'm proud of you and the crew at Inked. They're my family. I'm just surprised a sweet young thing like Clara would be seen over that side of town, let alone need a job."

"You're not the only one surprised. I've been asking myself the same question for the past three months." I scoot across the leather seat and rest my elbows on my knees. "Do you know who Clara was here visiting?" My voice is shaky, hampered by the guilt I feel for prying into Clara's personal life.

My grandma locks her glistening baby blues with mine. "When she wants you to know, Brax, she will tell you."

I sink deeper into my chair before running my hand down my tired face. I shouldn't have expected a different response from my grandma. She's never seen politeness in snooping.

After giving myself a few minutes to gather my strewn composure, I ask, "Do you know if Clara has any family out this way?" When my grandma's eyes thin, I add, "I'm not prying into her personal life, Grandma. I'm just trying to keep an eye on her. She had her car towed last night, and when I drove her home, there was an eviction notice taped to her front door."

The concern in my grandma's eyes intensifies with every word I speak. "Oh, Brax, you've got to help her," she requests, her words pleading.

"I'm trying, but she's the most guarded woman I've ever handled. Unlike you, she holds in her inner dialogue and protects her secrets with an iron fist... *or knee.*"

I confessed my prior run-ins with Clara to my grandma the Sunday following the knee-to-my-balls incident. It wasn't that I felt forthcoming. It was the fact I couldn't walk without grimacing that had me spilling the beans. It was only my crippled status that stopped my grandmother from issuing her own form of justice.

My grandma's lips tug into a wry grin, but the concern in her eyes doesn't dampen the slightest from my witty comment. "The McGregors were based in Hopeton up until a few years ago. When Clara's momma got sick, they moved her to a superior care facility in New York City. Since most of the children were young, they moved right along with her."

A niggle hits my chest. "Is her momma still sick?" Concern for finding out Clara's mother is unwell is evident in my voice.

My grandma nods. "There's no cure for dementia, Brax. No matter how much money you throw at the fancy doctors."

The niggle in my chest turns into a full stab. "How old is her momma?"

Clara is only twenty-five, so even if her mom had her late in life, she'd still only be mid-fifties to sixties now.

"I'm not sure, but way too young to be dealing with dementia. Some days she recognized her kids. Others, she couldn't tell them apart from the nursing staff."

I run my hand over my recently clipped hair. "Tough break."

My grandma connects her sorrow-filled eyes with mine. "Yeah, especially after everything Clara has been through. She needed her momma, but unfortunately, her momma needed her more."

The pain in my chest turns catastrophic.

As sweat rolls down my back, my head cranks to the side in super slow motion. My teeth smacking together shrill into my ears as I plummet to the ground. While I was distracted by my conversation with my grandmother yesterday, Diesel's right-swung fist connected with my left jaw. He knocked my jaw into the next century, right along with my ego.

I spit out my mouth guard before running the back of my hand across my mouth, removing a smear of blood his hit produced. Diesel stands in the corner of the ring as instructed by Hank. His grin is smug, but his eyes show his correct response—regret.

Hank, Diesel's trainer, squats down in front of me. His nearly black eyes assess my face as he runs his thumbs along the edge of my jaw. "Nothing appears broken, although you may end up with a nasty bruise in a few days," he advises.

He stands from his crouched position and offers me his hand. His strong yank on my arm has my feet lifting from the ground. For an older guy, Hank is ripped and extremely fit. He has dark afro hair clipped close to his scalp, his mocha skin is covered with a collection of tattoos Ryder inked on him, and his eyes are the darkest I've ever seen.

Hank's son, Derrick, was not only a customer of mine, but he was also a longtime friend. I was devastated when I was informed he was gunned down four years ago as he and Hank left a boxing tournament. It's one of those moments I will never forget. Derrick was set for greatness, all to have it snatched away by a man who couldn't grasp defeat. It was a truly senseless tragedy.

I'm ashamed to admit before Diesel started training with Hank, I hadn't seen him since the day of Derrick's funeral. It wasn't that I didn't want to. I just didn't know what to say to Hank. Derrick was Hank's world, and no measly words I could have offered him would have changed that fact. Although now, while scanning my eyes over the old, desolate gym we are working out at, I wish I'd taken the time to make sure Hank was doing okay.

Four years ago, this gym was the number one spot for wannabe fighters. Hank's training services were in high demand. Now, the equipment is outdated, the gym is devoid of clients, and Hank's once full-of-life eyes are bleak. I had heard his marriage was on the rocks after Derrick's passing, but I didn't realize things had gotten this bad.

My attention diverts from staring at the boxing mat when Hank cranks his neck to Diesel and asks, "Did Brax go and get himself a weak spot?"

Diesel's smug grin turns massive before he nods. I bounce my bleary eyes between Diesel and Hank, trying to work out what the fuck they're on about. They eyeball me with a glint of amusement sparking their eyes, but they fail to ease my curiosity.

Ignoring the two grown men glaring at me like imbeciles, I mumble a curse word under my breath before untying the laces of my boxing gloves with my teeth.

After pulling apart the boxing ring ropes for Hank to exit, Diesel comes and stands next to me. "I don't need to ask who has your mind, but I'm willing to play along."

Arching my brow, I stare into his hazel eyes. "I don't have the faintest fucking clue what you're referring to." My words are rough like I dragged them over a gravel road before spitting them out.

Diesel smirks. "I know boxing isn't your thing, Brax, but even you're off your game today. My first guess was you had an issue with your grandma but considering you wouldn't be here if it were a problem with Grace, I'm going to say it is a woman who has you kissing the pavement... a certain blonde member of the Inked family."

The smugness he's been wearing most of the morning increases when I attempt to shrug off his insinuation. I don't know why I bother trying to deceive him. He knows me well enough to know where my mind has wandered to.

"What makes you say it's a personal problem? You catching me in a moment of weakness might have something to do with work," I reply while running a white towel over my head to absorb the mountain of sweat running down my face.

Hank has always been a hard-assed trainer. Nothing's changed.

Diesel takes a seat on the boxing mat to unlace his shoes. "Inked is your baby, Brax, but it isn't your first love. It might keep your bank balance in the positive, but it doesn't keep the blood pumping to your chest."

I grin but don't refute his statement. Inked is my business, but at the end of the day, it is nothing but a pile of bricks and mortar. It is family and friends who keep my blood pumping. And if I'm being totally forthright, it has been pumping a little faster since my run-in with Clara yesterday.

Clara can spar with the best of them, and she can dish out scornful words like grenades, but I hated seeing her upset. Every tear shed from her eyes cut me deeper than I ever anticipated.

Even though she's icier than any woman I've ever handled, there's something about her I'm drawn to. Call it a case of macho-ism, but I want to wrap her up in cotton wool and protect her from the world. And if that isn't a shocking enough confession, my desire to protect her has nothing to do with my cock's fascination with her. I don't know if this revelation should have me running for the hills or running to Clara to seek confirmation on what the fuck she's doing to me. Yes, I've always been a sucker for helping a woman in distress, but it's never been this profound.

When Diesel spots the expression on my face, he smirks. "It's not just your cock she's gone and twisted up, is it?"

"What are you, a psycho? Get out of my fucking head," I mutter, throwing my sweat-soaked towel into his mocking face.

"It's called 'psychic,'" he replies while yanking my towel off his head. "But I don't need to be a psychic to recognize that glimmer in your eyes. You got it bad, man. You've let her get under your skin. I just hope you know what you're doing. There's no way to predict how chasing a woman like Clara will go. You've just got to work out if she's worth the risk of having your heart decimated."

I scoff. "Fuck, Diesel, no one is talking long-term commitment. It's all about a bit of fun. A few hours between the sheets. Nothing permanent." I keep my words strong, vying to undermine the seriousness of our conversation. My efforts are less than stellar as deceit has never been a game I can play for long. "Besides, I can't mess with a member of my crew. A few hours of fun wouldn't be worth the legal complications."

Diesel etches his brow high into his sweat-slicked hair, but he doesn't need to speak. His skeptical gaze speaks volumes without a peep spilling from his lips. He knows as well as I do that bedding a woman like Clara would be worth any hassle.

"Well, I wish you luck, brother, because you're going to need it."

Not giving me the chance to reply, he darts between the boxing ropes and hotfoots it to the outdated locker rooms at the side of the gym.

I'm straddling my bike, recalling the conversation I had with Diesel yesterday when Clara enters my peripheral vision. I was so immersed in wading my way through the massive mess of confusion muddling my mind that I hadn't noticed her exiting her apartment building and walking down the street until she stopped directly in front of me.

"What are you doing here, Brax?" she questions while shoving her hands into the front pockets of her mid-length skirt to conceal their shake. "If it's about Sunday, I can assure you I'm fine. You just caught me during a weak moment. It won't happen again." Her words are stronger than the pain in her eyes.

"It's not about Sunday."

She stares at me in shock.

"I just want to make sure you get to work safely." I keep my tone low, not wanting to spark another Jerry Springer-inspired battle between us.

Her eyes widen as she sucks in a lung-filling gulp of air. "I can't get on the back of your bike again... I-I can't."

"I know." I stop her retreating steps. "But I still want to make sure your travels are done safely."

The feared expression on her face morphs into confusion. When bus 57 pulls into the curb in front of us, I gesture my head to it. "You can ride the bus to Inked, but only when I'm following you."

Her eyes snap to mine. "You rode all the way to this side of town just to follow me to work?"

Nodding, I reply, "Yep," without a smidge of hesitation.

"Why?"

I shrug my shoulders. "Why not? You're my friend. I want to help you out."

Call me pussy-whipped or any other name you like, but this is the only solution I could come up with for Clara's predicament. Although she may be a smart-mouthed lady when she wants to be, that doesn't mean she shouldn't have someone looking out for her. Considering no one appears willing to fill that role, I've stepped up to the plate.

When Clara remains quiet, I stare into her confused eyes, wordlessly advising that my offer comes with no strings attached. It is nothing more than a friend helping another friend. No matter how much she makes my cock ache, I'm not here trying to find a way into her panties. I'm just looking out for her.

"If you don't hurry, your chariot will leave without you, Princess." I nudge my head to the bus driver, who's glaring at her as he impatiently waits for her to board.

Clara's massively dilated eyes bounce between the Asian bus driver and me for numerous heart-clenching seconds. Her pulse is throbbing through her veins so furiously, the entire left side of her neck is twitching. I don't know if her freaked-out expression is about her upcoming bus trip or at my sudden attempt to call a truce between us. Either way, she needs to board the bus before it leaves her stranded on the sidewalk.

My heart thrashes my ribs when she snatches my helmet resting on my thigh, throws it on her head, then hooks her leg over my bike. Even though I hoped this outcome might be a possibility, I honestly didn't believe it would actually happen. Don't get me wrong, I'm beyond stoked. I'm just shocked as well.

Clara plasters her torso as close to my back as possible before muttering, "Go before I change my mind."

I tighten her grip around my waist before kicking over my bike. Even the deep rumble of my engine can't overtake the mad beat of her heart pulverizing my back. Not wanting to scare her, I keep well under the speed limit and leave a good three car spaces between the motorist in front and me. Although I can't see her, I'm fairly sure her eyes are snapped shut as tightly as her arms are curled around my waist.

Twenty miles later, the loud boom of my engine bellowing down the alley secures the attention of Charity and Diesel as they make their way from the parking lot to the employee's entrance of Inked.

When Charity notices Clara on the back of my bike, she smiles a broad grin and playfully winks. Even though Diesel bowed out on his endeavor of pursuing Clara months ago, he still looks like a kid who had his lunch money stolen. If I were as respectful as him in our little black book game we've been playing since our school years, I could inform him that his assessment of the situation is misguided. But unfortunately for Diesel, I have no intention of doing that.

If he fails to see the true meaning of my relationship with Clara, so be it. Nothing against him—he's a great employee and an even better friend—but I'm not an idiot. I'll do anything I can to ensure his greasy mitts stay off Clara. Even going as far as pretending I've sealed the deal when I haven't and have no intention of doing so.

CHAPTER ELEVEN

"Hey," Clara greets, her voice a throaty purr.

I jerk up my chin in greeting before handing her the black helmet I purchased especially for her to use when she rides with me. Her face pales as she places the helmet onto her head and climbs onto my bike. Even though she's been riding with me the past three weeks, the panicked expression that crosses her face hasn't once altered.

The only thing that has changed is her clothing selection. She no longer wears designer dresses and fancy skirts, opting instead for black trousers or the occasional pair of jeans. Although her clothing choices are more suitable for riding on a motorbike, I'd be lying if I said I don't miss watching her strut around Inked in her figure-hugging dresses.

Actually, come to think of it, I'm not the only one complaining. A handful of male customers have cited objections the past three weeks. Some even went as far as stating I should make it mandatory for Clara to wear a dress as her uniform.

I may have dug my tattoo gun in a little deeper those days.

Things between Clara and me have been following along the same path that started when she began working at Inked, although she's a lot less bitchy now. Don't take my admission the wrong way. She doesn't hesitate to whip out her fiery tongue when needed. She can argue with the finest, but instead of unleashing a torrent of malicious words with no just cause, she reserves them for more compelling moments.

Take last week, for example. Johnny was happily accepting part of his tattooing payment in a non-monetary way. Stupidly, he decided to do the exchange in the supply closet of Inked. When Clara walked in on them, let me just say, Johnny was lucky he walked away with only a slight limp. The bunny he was entertaining... she'll think twice before she calls Clara a skanky bitch again.

When we arrive at Inked, Clara climbs off my bike and hands me her helmet. "Thanks for the ride. It should only be a few more days until my car is returned. It was all just a *huge* misunderstanding."

I nod, pretending I haven't heard the same declaration twice a day for the past three weeks. It eats away at me not knowing what's going on with her life, but no matter how badly I want to know why her car was towed the same night she got served an eviction notice, I won't force her to share. Clara is only just coming out of her shell, so I won't do anything that will risk her taking a step backward. It is also not my place to demand an explanation of her private life. Although our relationship has veered more toward the friend zone the past few weeks, I'm still her boss, so it wouldn't be appropriate for me to demand anything from her.

"Are you listening?" I mumble to my cock while shadowing Clara into the back entrance of Inked.

I'd like to say my cock's interest in Clara has waned as the weeks rolled by, but unfortunately, that isn't the case. Whether she's giving me lip or whining about the outdated computer in my office, my cock's attention has never wavered. I may not have any claim to her, but if you asked my cock the same question, I'm confident he'd tell you Clara owns his ass. He doesn't care about protocol or morals. He just wants Clara.

Clara's brisk pace slows to the speed of a tortoise when the crew of Inked breaks into a poorly serenaded version of "Happy Birthday" the instant they spot her sauntering down the hallway. She stiffens before her wide eyes bounce between her work companions and me. When she notices the triple-layered chocolate cake I asked Ryder's missus to bake for her, a single tear escapes her eye and rolls down her ashen cheek.

"I can't," she mutters under her breath as she barges past Charity, nearly sending her and her birthday cake toppling to the ground.

The crew stops singing as they follow Clara's swift bolt down the corridor leading to my office. After slipping inside, she closes the door so harshly, I'm sure the patrons dining at Betty's Burgers felt the ripple effect.

I turn my eyes toward Diesel. "Open up the shop and tell my first client I'll be out in a few."

He nods before instructing the rest of the crew to get ready for a normal workday.

Charity smiles a tense grin as she hands me Clara's birthday cake. "She's still trying to find her place in this family, Brax."

Nodding, I reply, "I know." But I'm still shocked by Clara's reaction. I shouldn't be, though. Nothing about her has ever been simple.

After placing the cake on the break room table, I stride to my office. Clara's head lifts from a barrage of paperwork on her makeshift desk on the couch when the creak of the door's old hinges announces my arrival. Even though she puts on a brave front, I can't miss the tears staining her blemished cheeks.

"We weren't going to force you to eat it," I jest, saying anything to ease the thick tension suffocating the room. "The guys just wanted to get you something for your birthday."

From her silence, you'd assume she didn't hear a thing I said, but from the way her chin is quivering, I know she heard every word.

I gather documents from the couch before taking the seat next to her. When she fails to acknowledge my presence, I place my index finger under her chin and lift her head. Her glistening glacier-blue eyes appear to be staring straight at me, but they're looking right through me.

"What's the deal? Don't the rich celebrate birthdays?"

Now her eyes are focused on me, and they're fierce enough they could cut through glass. "Does a card showing up a week after your birthday count?" she mutters ever so quietly.

I shrug. "Depends on what's in the card? A check with a million bucks, I'd happily accept years later."

Her lips twitch as she battles to hold in her smile, but she maintains her silent stance. I continue with my endeavor to force a smile on her face. Even if she can get my hackles up quicker than any woman before her, I hate seeing the dejected look her eyes are carrying, even more so since it's her birthday.

"If you thought their singing was bad, wait until you see the wilted bunch of daisies waiting for you on the counter. Oh, and don't be surprised when you open your box of chocolates to discover it's half-empty. They're an impatient bunch, but Johnny promised he saved you all the good flavors."

The heaviness on my chest lessens when the quickest smirk stretches across Clara's face. "They brought me gifts?" she murmurs ever so softly.

Her smirk turns into a full smile when I nod. "Nothing fancy, but they purchased them themselves. Well, except the flowers. Johnny stole them from his neighbor's garden."

Clara's smile enlarges even more.

I wait for it to fade before saying, "I have one final thing to give you. It was a little hard to wrap, so I didn't bother."

Her surprised eyes bounce between mine when I delve my hand into my pocket and pull out a key. The longer she stares at the car key, the more her pupils dilate.

"It's nothing like your old car, but it will get you from point A to point B safely," I advise her shocked expression.

Her lips quiver as she begins to speak. "I can't accept it, Brax. It's too much."

"You can accept it, and you will." My voice is sterner than I expected. "This isn't a gift, Clara. It is a payment for all those late nights you worked your first eight weeks at Inked."

Her eyes snap to mine. Shock is all over her face as I stare into her eyes while nodding my head, silently advising I'm aware of the work she put into the shop after hours. I only discovered her strong work ethic after going through the surveillance tapes the day following our incident in the parking lot of Inked.

For the first eight weeks of her employment, Clara stayed back a minimum of an hour every night, restocking the supply closet and preparing the invoices for the following day. She even went as far as donning a pair of fur-lined pink gloves to tackle the male staff bathroom a handful of times. I could tell from the determination in her eyes those first few weeks that she'd do anything to secure a permanent position at Inked, but I didn't realize her need for employment was so dire she was willing to scrub a urinal.

"I really needed the job," she murmurs under her breath, confirming what I already suspected.

I gently pinch her chin and lift her eyes back to mine. "I know. But you didn't need to break your back for it. Your work ethic during the opening hours already earned you your place in the Inked family." After setting the key for the piece-of-shit car the crew of Inked chipped in for into her palm, I nudge my head to the door. "Your new ride is in the lot. Take the rest of the day off and go spend your birthday with your friends. It will be a hard feat, but I will hold down the fort tonight."

Clara's teeth graze over her bottom lip. "Thanks for the offer, but I don't have anywhere to go."

"Sure you do." My eyes dart between hers. "There are at least a dozen restaurants in Ravenshoe that will happily serve vegetable scraps as if they're a main course."

A rare and genuine smile etches onto her plump lips. If that isn't rewarding enough, the little giggle that spills with her smile is worth spending my days off scouring the used car lots searching for the perfect car for her. This is the first time I've heard her real laugh. I hope it isn't the last.

When her laughter dies down, she locks her eyes with mine. "It isn't that I don't have a place to dine. I just don't have anyone to go with me." The last half of her sentence comes out in a faint whisper as her eyes stray to the floor.

My brows furrow. "What about your drunk chook-cackling friends? Surely, they would have a spare hour to help celebrate your birthday?"

Since I know Clara's momma had dementia, I forgo mentioning her family, not wanting to upset her on her birthday any more than I already have.

Clara's eyes lift from the floor and connect with mine. Confusion and another expression I can't read mars her face.

"The friends you showed up with the night you got your tattoo," I explain to her puzzled expression.

I swallow the brick in my throat when her eyes narrow into

thin slits at the mention of her tattoo. *Apparently, she hasn't gotten over our first tussle in the ring yet.*

"I know who you are referring to," she replies, her tone bitter. "Unfortunately, they're too... *busy* to socialize with me today."

I scoff. "It's your birthday. Tell them to get un-busy."

She rolls her eyes before rising from the couch. "It's fine, Brax, honestly. I'd prefer to stay here anyway. Wasn't it you who said Inked is my family now? Shouldn't I spend my birthday with my family?"

Even though she's asking a question, she doesn't wait for me to reply. She just moves to my desk to gather a pile of unpaid invoices from the top.

I glare at her in a shocked, disbelieving type of way. "You'd rather stay here than hang out with your friends?" When she nods, I say, "I'm sorry, Princess, but I'm calling bullshit."

She cranks her neck to the side. "Lucky for me, your opinion doesn't bother me in the slightest."

I push off the couch and step closer to her. "What's really going on, Clara? The princess who walked in here demanding a job three months ago would never turn down the opportunity to live it up on the good side of the tracks."

Her shoulders square as she murmurs something under her breath. She's so quiet, I miss every word she speaks.

"You need to speak up. I've been told on a few occasions I have a problem with my hearing." Even though I was aiming for witty, my comment comes out a little snarky.

When Clara ignores me, I grasp the top of her arms and force her to face me. I'm taken aback when her eyes lift to mine. Gone is the vibrant spark that typically alights her fiery gaze replaced with a pair of eyes that look lost. I'd even go as far as saying haunted.

Fear grips my heart when she snaps her eyes shut, battling to hold in her tears.

Fuck, I hope she doesn't cry. The tears she shed weeks ago in my grandmother's room still haunt me.

"Clara—"

My words stop when the plumpest set of lips brush against mine. I freeze, not to give myself time to assess the situation but to investigate the unique taste of her mouth—minty-cool freshness with a hint of sweetness and warmth.

Only a woman as complicated as Clara could have her lips described as warm and cold at the same time.

Forgetting the seriousness of our conversation, I run my tongue along the seam of her lips, daring her to open her mouth for me. My hang-ups about not messing with a member of my crew are left in the dust when her lips part, giving me full access to her mouth. My cock pulses against the zipper of my jeans as one of my hands moves to her nape, securing her mouth to mine, while the other drops to the curve of her back to pull her closer.

Although I keep my lips sealed over hers, I don't take the kiss any further than an innocent game of tonsil hockey in the janitor's closet at my local high school. If she wants this kiss to go further, she'll need to make all the moves. This way, I won't fall into the trap of sexually harassing my staff. If anything, she's assaulting me, and I'll love every goddamn motherfucking minute of it.

A rough groan tears from my throat when Clara delves her tongue inside my mouth in a long, tantalizing stroke. Her kiss is robust and determined—just like her personality—but warm and enticing. For a woman whose heart appears to be carved from ice, her kiss causes a roasting fervor of excitement to scorch my veins. I shouldn't be surprised she knows how to kiss. She's no ordinary woman. Her kisses are no different.

The skin on my torso prickles with goosebumps when she slips her hands under my shirt to rake her nails against the skin of my lower back. I'm certain she can feel the effect her touch has on my body, but I don't fucking care. If she wants to touch me, I sure as hell ain't going to stop her. The only thing I'm stopping is my desire to ravish her on my desk. Why? Because Clara isn't a bunny, so I won't treat her as if she is one.

When I pull my lips away from hers and she whimpers, my strength is pushed to its absolute limit. I skim my lips along the edge of her jaw and down her delicate neck before stopping at the collar of her shirt. Just knowing my lips are near an area of her skin I've never seen has my cock throbbing furiously and my restraint faltering. It's a thrilling and torturous experience at the same time.

The throaty moans toppling from Clara's throat while I nibble on her neck have an edge of danger to them—a clear warning I'm stepping over the line of what is acceptable for an employer and his staff. But, in all honesty, I don't give a flying fuck. My cock... No. Correct that. *I've* wanted this for months.

From the very moment I laid my eyes on her going toe-to-toe with Johnny in the foyer of Inked, I've been dying to find out if her feisty personality holds the same level of intensity in the bedroom. From the way her nails are raking my back and the warmth between her legs two layers of jeans can't conceal, I'll say my answer is an unequivocal and resounding yes.

My poorly wavering constraint gets harnessed when the creak of my office door sounds through my ears, closely followed by a deep voice. "Your three o'clock is getting snarky."

My eyes shift to Diesel at the exact moment Clara pulls away from me so abruptly, a blast of warm air smacks me in the face. Pretending there isn't a massive elephant of awkwardness sitting in the room, Clara peruses the invoices on my desk while muttering, "I'll be sure to get these paid right away." She lifts her lust-filled eyes to me. "Was there anything else you needed me to do?"

She puts on a good act of being unaffected, but her blemished cheeks and wide eyes are giving away her true composure. She looks exactly how I want her to look—like a woman in the process of being claimed.

Clara's head rockets to the side when I instruct Diesel to tell my client I'll be there when I'm good and ready. His hooded gaze bounces between Clara and me for numerous seconds, his face expressing the words his mouth fails to produce. *I knew you'd be the first to break Inked's no fraternization policy, Brax.*

I glare at him, silently warning that the rules won't be the only thing I'll be breaking if he doesn't leave. With a shit-eating grin, he cockily winks and exits my office, closing the door behind him.

I wait until I hear the stomping of his feet on the tiled floor before I turn my eyes to Clara. She continues rifling through the invoices on my desk, seemingly unmoved from our heart-stopping kiss. I stand motionless in my office, unsure whether I should take the slap to my ego like a man or kiss the living hell out of her again just to ensure she's aware a kiss like the one we just shared could never be forgotten.

But even if she wants to pretend her flushed expression is from the warmth of a late May afternoon, she sure as hell can't come up with a reason for the marks on her neck the stubble on my chin created, let alone her kiss-swollen lips. Although I have no right to admit this, I fucking love seeing her body marked because of me. If I weren't concerned about my business and my crew, I'd strip her naked and mark every inch of her from the top of her disheveled locks to the tips of her expensive designer shoes, stopping only to pay careful attention to the needier regions of her body.

Shaking my head to remove the thoughts that could have me breaking another rule I swore I'd never break—fucking Clara on my desk like a bunny—I lock my eyes with her and ask, "We good?"

Clara licks her kiss-swollen lips before nodding.

"All right. I'll be finished up here by ten. We'll discuss this more then."

I canceled my last two appointments three days ago when I discovered today was Clara's birthday. Clara was so quiet about her upcoming birthday that if I weren't in the process of working out how to have her signed at Inked as a full-time employee, I would have never discovered today is her twenty-sixth birthday. I have an inkling she was hoping the day would pass with no celebration. Although I'm not a fan of getting older, I'm all for celebrating life milestones, birthdays included.

Clara's brows stitch as she stares at me in shock. "*This?*"

"Yeah, *this.*" I gesture my hand between us.

Her brows become lost in her blonde hair. "There's no *this,* Brax." Her face looks stern, but her words are unsteady.

When she veers her confused gaze back to the documents in her hand, I curl my hand around her elbow. Unlike thirty seconds ago, she repels from my grasp instead of melting into it.

Here comes the pounding headache that's been plaguing me for the past four months.

"I don't know how many times I need to tell you, Brax. *This...*" she gestures her hand between us, "... is *never* going to happen." For the first time since I've known her, she keeps her voice sincere. Almost regretful.

I connect my eyes with her. "Well, I've got news for you, Princess. *This* is fucking happening."

Her eyes narrow and glare into mine. I swear I can hear her teeth grinding together. "Why? Because *beasts* just take what they want?" Her tone has reverted back to the bitchy sneer she hasn't used in weeks.

I smirk while shaking my head. "No. It has nothing to do with that."

"Then what is it?" She places her hand on her cocked hip.

"Because you're loving this game of chase just as fucking much as I am."

Clara's pupils widen to the size of dinner plates as her cheeks go even pinker, but she remains as quiet as a graveyard at midnight, abundantly proving what I said is true.

I fucking knew it.

"So, as I said earlier, we'll continue our *discussion* at ten."

I stride toward my office door, needing to exit before I kiss the shocked look right off her face.

CHAPTER TWELVE

On the night of her birthday, I wasn't at all surprised to discover Clara had left Inked at precisely 9:55 p.m. You can't be chased if you aren't running. What I said to her that night wasn't just to soften the blow my ego took from her blunt dismissal of me, it was to prove a point. I'd like to say my point was proven beyond a reasonable doubt when she failed to deny my accusation that she's loving this game of chase we've been playing the last few months. Unfortunately, her denials came in hard and fast the following day. From her reaction, anyone would swear it was *me* who made the moves on *her* in my office that day.

I'm not going to lie, even playing in a game I swore I'd never field, my ego still got a little bitch-slapped. Not because I believed a single lie spilling from her lips, but because I've never had a woman blow me off the way Clara has. Call me conceited, but usually, I'd just flash a quick smirk to the woman I was interested in, and she'd be purring at my feet moments later.

I know half of my interest in Clara is because she will never be the type to kneel before me, so she's a challenge any guy would love to conquer. But the other half... I'm at a complete fucking loss. I seriously don't know what is happening to me.

Now don't get me wrong, Clara is no doubt beautiful. She's one of the most ravishing women I've ever laid my eyes on, and the feisty girls have always been a lot of fun between the sheets. But this little game I'm playing with Clara feels different. It isn't your standard game of cat and mouse. It's... it's... I don't know *what the fuck* it is.

It's a fucking minefield I should be retreating from, not encroaching, but no matter how much I try to pull the pin, I can't. Even though Clara denied having any interest in me, she still treats me in the same manner she did in the weeks leading to our kiss. She gives me lip, has no trouble putting me in my place, and if my whole flirting radar hasn't completely blown off-kilter, she's been laying down some solid groundwork on a bit of sexual flirting.

Every time she has entered my cubicle the last two weeks, I've had to fight the urge to pull her into my lap and resample her lips. Why? Because without fail, every time she's in my eyesight, she has something in her mouth. Just watching her slowly chew on one of the chocolates the crew gave her for her birthday had my tongue dying to discover if her mouth took on the raspberry flavor.

If that wasn't bad enough, more times than I can count, when she advised me of my next appointment, she nibbled on the end of the pencil. I swear to God, I've jabbed my tattoo gun into my thigh at least a dozen times this week alone just to keep myself seated in the swivel chair. If I didn't, her little teases would have forced her lips to become acquainted with the one part of my body she's kept firm a minimum of ten hours a day for the past two weeks. Considering I'm endeavoring not to treat her as a bunny, I refuse to have her kneel in front of me, no matter how badly my cock wants to be surrounded by her lips.

I have no doubt Clara knows the effect she has on me. If the smug grin etched on her face isn't enough proof, the glimmer of lust sparking in her eyes is a surefire indication. Thankfully, even with all the blood in my body rushing to the lower half, I can still tattoo. Don't get me wrong, it is no easy feat, but the fact all my clients over the past two weeks have been male has been a lifesaver.

I adjust the crotch of my jeans as a faint cough sounds at the door. Glancing up from the sketch in front of me, I run my eyes over the enticing physique of Clara standing in my office door-frame. Because she's driven herself to work the past two weeks, she's reverted to wearing the body-hugging dresses she used to wear. Today's dress is a fitted-to-every-single-mouthwatering-curve-of-her-body ensemble. I struggle to ignore my cock's response to her most days, but today is by far the hardest day I've had. She doesn't merely look downright gorgeous, she looks positively edible. And since I've tasted her lips, I know without a doubt her lips taste even better than the sexiness of her dress—one hundred percent.

I drag my eyes away from her cock-twitching body when she questions, "Hey, Brax, can I ask a favor?"

"Sure. What's up?"

"Is it all right if I head home a few hours early today?" she asks, her voice hesitant. "I know it is Saturday night, but we're not as busy as—"

"It's fine, Princess," I interrupt, not requiring further explanation. "I have no problem with you leaving a few hours early."

I won't lie, even saying I have no concerns, a stabbing pain is hitting me right in the chest. Even though it should have never been turned on, I can't flick off the possessive switch Diesel's interest in Clara instigated. Believe me, I've tried. Nothing works. I just really fucking hope her reasoning for leaving early has nothing to with a member of the opposite sex.

"Is everything all right?" I strive to keep my tone neutral. My attempts are borderline.

Clara grins a soft smile while nodding. "Yeah, I'm just moving into a new apartment tomorrow. That's the reason I need to leave early. I have some loose ends to tie up at my penthouse."

My brows hit my hairline. The last I heard of Clara's living situation was that she fought the eviction notice and was staying put in her luxury penthouse on Hyde, so to say I'm shocked by her revelation would be an understatement.

"My new apartment is close to work so it will save me the commute," she blabbers out, saying anything to ease the staggered expression on my face.

I slouch deeper into my chair, battling the urge to force her to open up to me.

My fight doesn't last long.

"Who's helping you move into your new pad?" I ask, deciding to start my meddling with a less nosy question before I move on to the big hitters.

Clara's throat works hard to swallow before she faintly murmurs. "Umm... me."

I drop my pencil onto my sketching pad and arch my brow, silently demanding the attention of her fleeing eyes. "Princess," I grumble, my word as grating as my jaw is clenched.

With a huff, she turns her hard-set eyes to mine. "I don't have much stuff to move... I'll be fine," she assures me.

Her firm stance weakens the more I glare at her, but she maintains her calm approach. Not willing to holster our conversation, I push away from my desk and stand from my chair. The throb of the pulse in her neck speeds up when I stride around my desk to stand in front of her.

"What time is your moving truck arriving tomorrow?" I narrow my eyes into thin slits when a cloud of deceit filters over her eyes. "Only someone who is planning on lying takes time to contemplate a response," I remark, quoting something she's said to Johnny many times in the past four months.

"Ten o'clock," she whispers, finally grasping she's waging a battle she'll never win.

"I'll be at your penthouse at eight."

Not giving her the chance to reply, I head back to my desk to work on a set of sketches I've been designing for the past six weeks.

A grin tugs my lips higher when the faint murmur of "Thanks, Brax," sounds through my ears before my office door closes.

CHAPTER THIRTEEN

"Are you fucking kidding me?" I murmur to myself.

After yanking my sunglasses off my face, I snag my cell phone out of my pocket and check the address Clara texted me earlier. The tick of my jaw increases when I discover the graffiti scrawled on the wall of the derelict apartment building matches the address Clara texted.

My fear that this rundown block of apartments is Clara's new residence surges when her little beat-up Ford Focus pulls to the curb behind my bike. I grit my teeth together, barely swallowing the string of illicit cuss words dying to break free from my mouth. Not only is Clara's new crash pad closer to Inked, but it is also in the seediest part of Ravenshoe.

Although Ravenshoe has seen a massive growth in the past three years, the money being pumped into the good half hasn't spanned this far yet. Broken beer bottles line the gutter, tennis shoes dangle off the power lines, and the sounds of sirens wail in the distance. And don't even get me started on the condition of the hideously ugly apartment building. If there wasn't a steel gray

Audi parked a few spots up, I would have said Clara was the only thing of value on this entire street.

Clara curls out of her car and saunters to stand next to me. Sheltering her face from the mid-afternoon sun with her hand, her eyes run over the rundown apartment building. Her lips quirk and the scent of fear plagues the air between us. She keeps her shoulders high, endeavoring to ensure me she isn't rattled by the ghastly sight standing before us.

While spinning a set of keys around her finger, she strolls up the cracked concrete sidewalk, her steps shaky and slow.

I hop off my bike and follow her. "You're *not* staying here."

If my abrupt statement wasn't greeted with a glaring stare, I would have assumed Clara didn't hear me over the blaring music pumping from an apartment three stories above. Clara's furious gaze silently warns me she's on the verge of snapping, but I don't care if she's about to blow her top. She can call me a brute, beast, or any other name on her wish list, but I'm not budging an inch. I wouldn't let the feral cats living in the dumpster at the back of Inked stay in a joint like this, let alone the woman my cock is infatuated with. And although I've said earlier my status as Clara's employer gives me no rights over her personal life, I don't give a flying fuck. Even if we didn't share a kiss two weeks ago and hadn't been flirting like it is going out of fashion, there's no way in hell I'd let a member of my crew stay in a dump like this. Male or female. No fucking chance.

"Call the delivery truck driver and get your furniture taken to the storage sheds on Traeter. Once we find you a new apartment, we'll have your furniture shipped there."

Acting like she didn't hear a word come out of my mouth, Clara shoves a key into a door that is hanging by a thread and enters the dimly lit apartment. Growling at her ignorance, I shadow her inside. The deepness of my growl intensifies when I walk into the mildew-scented living area.

"It's not too bad," Clara mutters while roaming her eyes around the paint-peeled walls and heavily stained carpet. "Nothing a bit of elbow grease won't fix."

"Elbow grease?" I arch my brow into my hairline. "The only thing that could fix this place is a gallon of fuel and a match."

Clara rolls her eyes before moving to the front window. Dust particles riddle the air when she draws open the mold-covered curtain. I crunch my teeth together. Adding sunlight hasn't helped the situation. This place is a fucking dump.

"You're *not* staying here," I advise again.

Seizing her elbow, I drag her to the door we only just entered. She tries to pull out of my embrace, but I stay holding on tight, refusing to relinquish her. She can dig her claws into my arm all she likes, sue me for harassment, or knee me in the balls, but I'm not leaving her here.

My quick strides only stop when Clara whispers, "It is the only apartment available in my price range."

Even knowing she has never lied to me, I can't hold in my retaliation. "Come on, Princess, cut the bullshit. Even if you weren't dripping in wealth in your thousand-dollar dresses and shoes, I know what you get paid since I'm the man who pays you."

I don't mean to snap at her, but my mind is spiraling, unable to adapt to what is going on in her life. First, her car was towed, then she got an eviction notice, and now she's moving into an apartment that is smaller than the storage closet at Inked. I don't know if this is all some fucked-up rich-person joke, but I ain't laughing. I'm all for branching out and trying new things, but this is taking it a step too far. She's not only experimenting with a new lifestyle, she's risking her safety, and that's something I won't stand for.

Clara takes on her fighting stance. Her hand is splayed on her cocked hip, her eyes narrowed. "You may pay me, Brax, but you don't pay my bills." Her words come out like hot lava spilling from a volcano. "I know what I can and can't afford." She nudges her head to the shoebox apartment we just vacated. "That is all I can afford."

"Then I'll give you a fucking pay rise," I snap back.

Anger envelops Clara's entire body, flushing her skin with a red hue. "I'm not a *charity* case," she snarls through gritted teeth, her words rickety, hampered by a sob she's barely holding back.

I scrub my hand over the stubble on my chin, giving myself some time to calm down before I say something I'll later regret. "I'm not saying you're a charity case, but you won't be *anything* if you live in this area of Ravenshoe. It isn't safe, Clara."

The anger lining her face softens when I use her real name. She knows I only ever use it in dire situations. *This is a dire situation.*

Her hand slips off her hip as the harshness in her eyes fades. "I appreciate your concern, but I can take care of myself," she replies, her words not as callous as earlier.

I ball my hands into tight, white-knuckled fists when she ambles back into the rat-infested apartment. It's the only defense I have to fight the urge to scream my frustration into the street.

I want to drag her away from here kicking and screaming, but instead, I stay standing on the graffiti-painted path. I need a few minutes to contemplate her predicament. I'll never win an argument with a woman who is as stubborn as Clara, but I have to do something.

Call me a chauvinistic pig, but just like she was wrong about catching the one a.m. express, she's wrong to believe she can look after herself in this part of Ravenshoe, and no amount of arguing will change that fact.

After a few moments of silent pondering, an idea formulates in my overworked brain. Instead of dragging Clara to a safer location, I'll bring the safety to her. With a grin, I yank my cell phone out of my pocket and call in a favor with a long-time client.

Forty-five minutes later, Hunter Kane pulls his security van onto the curb at the front of Clara's apartment building.

"Brax," he greets me, slapping his hand into mine before leaning in for a man hug. "What the hell are you doing in a dump like this?"

"Long fucking story," I mutter while returning his embrace.

Hunter's eyes assess the apartment in great detail when I gesture for him to enter before me. "What type of security system are you after?" he queries, intuiting why I requested his help this afternoon.

It wouldn't take a genius.

"The best you have." I walk over to close the door of the main bedroom.

When I saw Hunter's security van pull down the street, I suggested that Clara start unpacking her boxes of designer clothes and shoes. For the first time ever, she did as requested without a single qualm escaping her lips. I'm not hiding her away as I don't want her to meet Hunter. It's the fact I know she will put up a fight when she discovers the amount of coin I'm going to hand Hunter to have her apartment wired with the world's most advanced security system. Considering there's no chance of me budging on this term to feel comfortable having her live here, I'd rather keep our argument on the back burner until Hunter leaves.

The fewer witnesses to my pussy-whipping, the better.

After running his hand over his scruffy beard, Hunter shifts on his feet to face me. "I've got a new system I've just designed that will be ideal for a place like this. Motion sensors, burglar alarm, sirens, voice command, but it will cost you a pretty penny. I'm happy to give you wholesale prices, but the equipment itself is expensive."

"I don't care how much it costs." I shrug. "All I care about is when can you get it done?"

Hunter smiles a broad grin. "How free is your tattooing chair this month?"

"As free as you need it to be."

His smile widens. "Then I'll have this wrapped up before the sun goes down."

The heaviness that's been sitting on my chest for the past hour lessens. "That will be great. Call out if you need any help."

Hunter nods before making his way to his van parked out front to gather some equipment while I head to Clara.

The smell of damp, moldy carpet filters into my nose when I prop my shoulder against the wall of the main bedroom. Since she is sorting through boxes of shoes, she doesn't notice my presence straightaway.

I stay quiet, relishing seeing a side to her I rarely get to see— her outside the walls of Inked.

There's no doubt Clara is a girly type of girl. If the cute dresses, high-altitude shoes, and glossy hair aren't enough of an indication, her fascination with color coordinating her shoes is a surefire sign.

I give myself a few more minutes to quietly absorb her before pushing off the wall and stepping deeper into the room. "Not enough room in your closet?" I ask when I notice she has several boxes of shoes and garment bags sprawled across her queen-size bed. Because her apartment is so small, the movers were in and out in under thirty minutes.

She screws her nose up. "Not exactly." I follow her gaze to the half-empty closet. "I was considering giving them to the women's shelter three blocks down from Inked."

My lips purse, not only shocked by her generosity but also wondering if couture dresses would be suitable for homeless women. It seems pretty pointless. I've worked in the soup kitchen numerous times over the past three years. From what I've seen, the women and children who live there only want food in their bellies and warm clothing. They don't need designer dresses worth thousands of dollars.

"But I've decided to sell them instead," Clara continues, lifting her wintry-blue eyes to me. "Half the money I make from the sale will be donated to the shelter. The other half will be put toward the security system *you're* getting installed in *my* apartment."

I balk, faking innocence.

She doesn't buy my woeful attempt at candor. Not in the slightest.

"You heard that?" I gesture my head to the living room of her apartment.

"Yeah," she replies with a nod. "Just like I knew you were stalking me for the past ten minutes."

I give her a cocky wink. "So that's why you kept bending over to reach the shoes in the furthest corner."

A hearty chuckle scuttles through my lips when she picks up one of the shoes off her bed and pegs it at my head. You can laugh. You haven't seen the size of the heels she wears. They could kill a man.

After picking up the stiletto that airport security would class as a lethal weapon, I step closer to Clara. I'm shocked when she doesn't cite an objection to me having a security system installed. My surprise only lasts as long as it takes for me to see the width of her pupils. Although she's putting on a brave front, she's just as petrified as I am about her staying here.

Nothing typically scares me, but the idea of her being hurt scares the shit out of me.

CHAPTER FOURTEEN

My brisk pace into the break room slows when my eyes are inundated with a set of curves I have no chance of ignoring. Clara has one arm braced against the refrigerator while the other is propped on her hip. The top half of her body is hidden as she seeks something in the sparsely filled refrigerator. The figure-hugging fire-engine red dress she's wearing displays every perfect curve the clients at Inked won't stop raving about—inches of luscious, soft skin, a mouthwatering ass, and a pair of legs that go on for miles. And let's not get me started on the regions of her body I can't see.

The inviting image of a bent-over Clara has a particular area of my body springing to life.

Sensing a presence in the compact lunchroom, Clara tilts her torso out of the refrigerator. The hardness of my cock turns fatal when my eyes zoom in on her painted red lips wrapped around the end of a whole carrot. Illicit thoughts slam into me on more appropriate things her plump lips could wrap around.

Just like the intense bout of flirting we'd been undertaking the two weeks prior to her move, nothing has changed. If anything, our playfulness is venturing into new territory since a few hours of our time together have been spent outside of Inked's walls.

Clara will never admit her new surroundings daunt her, but the fact she has invited me to her place for a late supper each night this week is all the sign I need to know she hates being alone in her dingy, cramped apartment even more than I hate her living there.

Don't take my admission the wrong way. Our flirting has never crossed the path it did in my office three weeks ago, but we've been cutting it close. Although I'd love nothing more than to sample her lips again, I'll never make the first move. I have a massive ego and confidence in the bucketloads, but in the back of my mind, I know a woman like Clara is way out of my league. *Hell, she's way out of my universe.* But by waiting for her to make the first move, I know she isn't being coerced into doing something—*or someone*—she doesn't want to do.

Shaking off the thoughts that will have my good mood sin-binned, I make my way to the coffee percolator in the corner of the room. Clara's eyes track me as I step toward her.

"Did you enjoy my salmon, Brax?" Her tone is a unique mix of bitchy and playful. "Probably the first time a guy of your standards has sampled something so refined."

I lift the coffee pot from the base and pour myself a generous helping before turning around to face Clara. "Salmon? What salmon?" I brace my back against the counter.

She arches one of her perfectly manicured brows high into her hairline. "I saw *my* empty container on *your* desk." Her eyes drop to a stain on the top left-hand corner of my white shirt. "Not only can I smell the garlic lemon sauce that was drizzled on my salmon leaching from your pores, but you also stained your shirt with it."

I roll my eyes. "I didn't eat your salmon, Princess. That's a toothpaste stain."

That's a total lie. When I first saw a fancy takeaway container in the refrigerator with Clara's name on it, I had planned on jabbing my finger into her food just to mess with her, but when the delicious aroma swamped my senses, my initial plan went to shit.

Although I've never eaten pink fish before, it was quite tasty.

Clara glares at me, not believing a single word seeping from my lips. I return her leering glare while taking a large gulp of my unsweetened coffee. Black liquid comes spraying out of my mouth, dousing the lunch table and my jeans when my taste buds recoil at the disgusting flavor besieging them.

I lift my shirt and run the cotton material over my tongue, doing anything to lessen the ghastly taste that has my stomach heaving. Although Clara is quick, I don't miss her eyes dropping to absorb the exposed skin of my lower stomach.

Glad to see I'm not the only one having a hard time keeping my eyes above the belt.

While running my now thickened tongue under the tap water, I spot a nearly empty box of Epsom salt sitting next to the percolator.

No fucking way. Is she pranking me?

Although the crew and I have pranked Clara numerous times during the past four months, not once has she gotten us back. If she's pranking me, this will expose a side of her I've never witnessed before.

Clutching the box in my hand, I shift on my feet to face her. Her amused eyes lock with mine as she takes a big bite out of the tip of her carrot. Even knowing it is only a carrot, my cock scampers away, frightened by the determined look in her eyes.

"Don't touch my food, Brax," she warns, glaring into my eyes. "Or things will get a lot more... *complicated.*"

After issuing me a knee-clattering stink eye, she saunters out of the room, her hips swinging even more provocatively than normal.

Even though I won't taste anything for a week, I have the biggest grin stretched across my face. Not only did Clara return my prank, she did it without a single drop of blood being shed.

Finally, after four long months, the real Clara is emerging from the shadows, and I can't wait to share the experience with her.

***

My head lifts to the clock hanging on the wall on my right when the buzz of my cell phone clatters through my ears. Since my last client's tattoo didn't take as long as expected, I headed down to a fancy deli a few miles away from Inked to replace Clara's salmon I ate. Call me pussy- whipped, but I hate the thought of her only eating a carrot for supper because I couldn't calm my stomach's cravings.

After wiping my sweat-slicked hand down my jeans, I yank my cell out of the front pocket. My lips quirk when I peer down at the screen and notice it is a call from Inked's landline.

"Fucking hopeless," I mutter under my breath.

I only left Inked twenty minutes ago, and they're already interrupting me. Unfortunately, this is nothing new. It wouldn't matter if I were gone for five minutes or fifty, I field calls from my crew the instant I step out of the premises.

God forbid I ever have a vacation day.

I swipe my finger across the screen and press the phone into my ear. "What's up?" I try to keep my annoyance at the interruption out of my voice. My effort is fruitless.

"Hey, sorry to disturb you." Johnny's deep tone is more jittery than normal. "But some shit went down out back I thought you'd want to know about."

I grit my teeth. Probably another bunch of gangbangers brawling in the side alley. Unfortunately, that's a regular occurrence at Inked, even more so since it is Saturday night. Standing from my seat in the waiting area of the deli, I head to the far corner of the room to ensure I can hear Johnny over the hum of patrons enjoying their overpriced meals.

My head cranks to the side when the restaurant hostess calls my name. Jennifer—the bunny who stuffed up my order of a cheesesteak months ago—jingles Clara's order of salmon in her hand. I lift my chin in thanks before pointing to my ear, advising her I'll be right there after my call. She nods before sauntering into the kitchen at the back of the deli. Her hips sway even faster than her words did when she thought I'd rocked up tonight for a replay of our rendezvous in the supply closet at Inked six months ago.

I swear I let her down as gently as possible, but I'll still be checking Clara's salmon for spit before I serve it to her. No girl likes being told they'll never take the leap from cocksucker to sheet-warmer—no matter how polite you say it. Nothing against Jennifer, she's a nice girl and gives great head, but the instant she lost the interest of my cock, she also lost me.

I shift my focus back to Johnny. "Has Diesel got it handled? Or do you need me to call in Ryan?"

"Ryan's already on his way." Johnny's tone is still off-kilter. "Diesel said you'd usually want to keep this type of thing in-house, but considering Clara was involved, he told me you'd want the authorities called in..."

Although he continues speaking, I don't hear a fucking word he's saying. His deep voice is nothing but white noise as I sling open the restaurant door and barrel onto the sidewalk. "I'm on my way."

Not giving him the chance to reply, I disconnect the call and house my cell back into my jeans. Since it is early on a Saturday night, the sidewalks are populated with heavy foot traffic. My heart thrashes against my chest as I weave through a throng of people completely oblivious to the anger blackening my blood. Just the thought of any woman being hurt makes me furious, but since it is Clara, my anger is reaching levels I've never experienced.

Upon reaching my bike parked half a block down, I throw my leg over it and shoot out of the car park not even thirty seconds later. Within minutes, I've reached Inked. My fists are balled, my jaw is clenched, and red-hot fury is seething through my veins, but nothing can slow me down—not even the close call with death I had on the way here. I'm running on pure adrenaline.

As I guide my bike down the alleyway, I dart my eyes in all directions, both assessing the situation and seeking Clara. Diesel is on my left talking to three teens. Charity has her shoulder braced against the brickwork near the dumpster, and Johnny is manning the back door.

I park my bike to the side, dismount, and make my way to Diesel. My furious pace slows when, in the corner of my eye, I spot a flurry of blonde. Clara is huddled on the stained concrete ground shaking like a leaf. The furious heat scorching my veins intensifies when my eyes run over her bloody, scraped knees.

"Why the fuck is she still sitting in the alleyway?" I ask Charity, who is two steps up from Clara.

"She won't let anyone touch her." Charity's voice is as shaky as Clara's composure. "I think she's in shock."

I crouch down in front of Clara and lift her downcast face. The fiery spark that usually brightens her eyes has been snuffed, replaced with a haunted glint. Her lips are cracked and quivering, and her cheeks are stained with tears. Her defeated pose angers me even further.

"What happened?" I shift my gaze to Charity.

She shrugs. "I didn't get the full story, but from the marks on her neck and wrist and the fact all her jewelry is missing, I'm assuming she got jumped."

"Fucking hell. I told her to take that shit off," I mumble under my breath.

Even though my declaration was only meant for me, Clara must hear it as a painful whimper escapes her lips while a new flood of tears rolls down her cheeks.

Riddled with guilt at placing unwarranted blame on her shoulders, I seize Clara's wrists and pull her into my arms. She must be suffering from shock as she doesn't put up a single protest.

I stand from my crouched position, draw her in close to my chest, and amble to the back entrance of Inked. "When Ryan arrives, send him into my office," I demand, not once taking my eyes off Clara gathered in my arms, staring up at me with a pair of bleak eyes.

By the time Johnny announces Ryan's arrival, Clara's tears have created two large wet patches on my shirt. She hasn't spoken a word for the past ten minutes, but the earth-shattering shakes havocking her body have simmered to a dull vibration.

Ryan smirks an uneasy grin as he strides into my office. After removing a pile of invoices from the couch, he takes the spare seat next to Clara and me. When he locks his eyes with mine, I'm not shocked to see they're clouded with anger. He's witnessed some bad shit no man should ever see. Unfortunately, not all of it has been from his service in the police force.

It takes a bit of effort on Ryan's part to get Clara to open up, but the cocky statement he made at the strip club months ago rings true. He is a great detective, one of the best I've ever known, so with a little encouragement, he eventually gets Clara talking about what happened.

I will not lie. Over the past thirty minutes, I formulated at least a dozen ways to kill a man with my bare hands. The desire grew even more potent when Clara mentioned her assailants were carrying guns. If it weren't bad enough she got jumped in the alleyway by three men while taking out the trash, two of them were wielding weapons.

I've never been more ashamed of this part of Ravenshoe than I am right now.

"Did any of the jewelry have distinguishable markings?" Ryan queries, his eyes lifting from the notepad in his hand to Clara.

She runs a tissue under her nose before gently nodding. "My necklace pendant has an inscription on the back." Fresh tears prick in her eyes before she quietly mutters, "To C, Happy 18th Birthday, Love Remy."

Ryan snags a few extra tissues out of the tissue box on my desk and hands them to Clara. "That's all I need for now, but if you recall anything you believe may help my investigation, Brax has my number."

Clara nods while accepting the tissues.

When Ryan gestures his head to the corridor, I turn my eyes down to Clara, who is still sitting on my lap. "Will you be all right if I talk to Ryan for a minute?"

Her massively dilated eyes bounce between mine for several heart-pounding seconds before she gently nods. I stand from the couch, taking her with me. It takes all my strength to pivot around and place her back on the sofa. The only reason I do is because I want to know who is responsible for doing this to her.

"I'll be back in a minute," I advise Clara. I wait for her to acknowledge that she has heard me before stepping into the hallway.

Ryan's mouth opens, but I begin speaking before he gets the chance to say anything. "Was it the teens Diesel was talking to when I showed up who did this?"

Ryan shakes his head. "No. They saw the assailants running out of the alley. When they discovered Clara, they were the ones who sounded the alarm."

His answer removes three names from my hit list.

"Give me a chance to do my job before you step in, Brax," Ryan requests, sensing I'm on the verge of dishing out my own form of punishment.

Mine won't be as pleasant as Ryan's. Guaranteed.

"She's a member of *my* fucking crew, jumped in the alley of *my* fucking shop." My loud voice bellows down the hall. "You know I can't be disrespected like this without issuing some type of punishment. If I let it slide, you'd have to add Inked to your nightly drive-by schedule as we'd become a mockery to the community."

"She's a *member* of your crew..." His words come out a little hazy like he doesn't fully believe my anger is solely based on Clara being a team member of Inked. "So if you're genuinely worried about her well-being, the best thing you can do is take a step back from this investigation and look after her. She's in shock, Brax. You need to convince her to let the medics look at her."

I shake my head. Ryan suggested the same thing to Clara at the start of their interview. She blatantly refused his request. "She feels violated enough as it is. She doesn't want any more people prodding her."

Ryan runs the back of his hand over his tired eyes before nodding. He's been dealing with so much shit the past six months, his exhaustion can be physically seen. His eyes are plagued with dark circles, his skin is blotchy, and his hundred-dollar haircut is well overdue for a trim. "I get that. I do. But she can't be left alone like she is."

I nod. "I know. I'll look after her."

Deep down in my soul, I know Ryan won't rest until he finds

out who did this to Clara. He doesn't understand the word *defeat*, but it doesn't lessen the fervent rage pumping through my veins that someone messed with a member of my crew on my watch. Let alone someone as important to me as Clara.

"I'll give you twenty-four hours, but if one of my guys finds them before you do, I can't guarantee they will call in the authorities."

"Fuck, Brax, you can't say shit like that to me," Ryan replies, his eyes drifting up and down the corridor, ensuring none of his fellow officers are listening. Happy we haven't caught the attention of any unwanted ears, he pulls me deeper down the hallway. "I'm asking friend to friend. Give me forty-eight hours before you send out your guys."

I shake my head. "That's forty-eight hours she will stay panicked like that." I hook my thumb to Clara. "I can't erase what happened to her, but I can ease her fear that the men who did this to her aren't still walking the streets."

Ryan peers over my shoulder to look at Clara. His composure alludes to the general confidence he exudes in bucketloads, but his eyes are giving away his true feelings. He's as angry as I am. "Thirty-six hours and I'll give you ten minutes with them when I bring them in," he negotiates, drifting his eyes away from Clara and locking them with me. "Alone."

I take a moment to consider his request. Although I'm sure Diesel and Johnny will locate the men responsible for jumping Clara, there's no guarantee it will happen within thirty-six hours, and although I hate entrusting the care of my crew to an outsider, I've known Ryan most of my life. He's like family to me, so I can trust he has me and my crew's best interests at heart.

While exhaling a deep breath, I hold out my hand. "I'll still send my guys out. If they find them first, I'll instruct them to call you."

Ryan looks like he wants to push the issue further, but thankfully, he leaves it as it is and accepts my handshake. "In her condition, please don't put her on the back of your bike," is the only request he makes as I walk him to the front door.

"I may have skipped the line for brains, but even I'm not that stupid." I wrap my arms around his shoulders and pull him in for a brief hug.

"When you're out seeking your revenge, stop and think about who will keep an eye on Clara when you're rotting in jail for defending her," he mutters in my ear before pulling away and strolling down the sidewalk.

I should have known he wouldn't leave the conversation as it was. Not only does he love having the last word, but he also knows how to play my weaknesses. My biggest weakness is the people left behind to fend for themselves.

After taking a few moments to ponder Ryan's statement, I return to my position on the couch next to Clara. Not thinking, I pull her back into my arms.

She doesn't protest.

She doesn't cry.

She doesn't do a damn thing.

And that worries me even more than her frightened expression.

CHAPTER FIFTEEN

"**I**f you need anything, I'm only a phone call away," Charity offers from her crouched-down position in front of Clara. After giving Clara's forearm a final rub, she heads to the door.

"Wait up. I'll walk you out," I shout, not wanting another incident on my conscience.

Usually, one of the crew walks Charity to her car each night. Considering I'm the only remaining male member of Inked here, it's my responsibility to ensure she arrives at her car safely.

Diesel and Johnny left not long after Ryan and the rest of my crew dwindled out of Inked the past thirty minutes. Although none of them are to blame for what happened to Clara, their shoulders were still weighed down with guilt. What I said to Clara weeks ago is true. What happens to one of us happens to all of us. We're family. And whether she likes it or not, Clara is now one of us.

Clara's massively dilated eyes lift to mine before she gently nods, acknowledging my silent question if she's okay with me walking Charity to her car.

"I'll be back in a minute."

Standing from the couch, I place her down. It isn't any easier the second time.

A humid mid-June wind greets us when we exit the back entrance of Inked. Surprisingly, the parking lot is void of the bunnies who usually frequent the space this time on a Saturday night. *Perhaps they heard of the earlier incident?*

My lengthened strides slow when Charity mutters, "Diesel called an hour ago. He's got a solid lead on the guys who jumped Clara."

I arch my brow, wordlessly demanding why I'm only being informed of this now.

"We figured if you were the only one left to watch Clara, you might actually stay put," she mutters as her skittish eyes dart around the lot.

Her eyes snap to mine when a furious growl rumbles from my throat. "We?"

"Diesel, Johnny, and I." She turns her eyes to the back door of Inked. "She's not from this side of town, Brax. But even if she were, this still wouldn't have been a pleasurable experience. You need to focus on Clara and let the boys have your back for a change."

The anger bubbling my blood with furious heat simmers to a slow boil. Not only is everything Charity is saying true, but I also need to remember my advice. Clara is just as much family to Diesel and Johnny as she is to me. This ensures they will handle this situation to the same degree I would.

"Did Diesel call Ryan?" My words aren't as scratchy as earlier.

Charity shakes her head. "He said he would, just not until after he has a *talk* with them."

My right shoulder lifts into a shrug. "Fair enough."

I rub a kink in the back of my neck as my earlier conversation with Ryan runs through my head. Fuck, why did I give him my word?

Because you're a soft cock when it comes to Ryan, that's why.

"Can you do me a favor and call Diesel? If he hasn't already had a solid word with them, request that he lower the severity and contact Ryan. I gave Ryan my word I'd call him if we found them in the first thirty-six hours. Considering it's only been a few hours, I don't want to break my word."

Charity nods. "All right. I'll call Diesel on my way home." She wraps one of her tiny arms around my torso and squeezes me tight. "Look after Clara for me."

A brief chuckle spills from my lips, spurred on by the hidden innuendo laced in her words.

I wait for Charity's taillights to become a blur in the heavy flow of traffic before making my way back to Clara. I'm surprised to find her standing near the window of my office. From behind, you wouldn't have a clue about the seriousness of the situation she just went through. She looks the same as she has every other day. She's stared out that window the past four months. It is only when she spins around does the reality of the situation slam back into me. She smiles to put on a brave front, but her eyes show she's still sitting in an incredibly deep, dark pit.

"Is everyone gone?"

I nod while striding deeper into the space. Before I can comprehend what is happening, Clara jumps. One of her hands pushes me hard in the chest, sending me sprawling onto the two-seater couch, while the other moves to the buckle on my belt.

"Whoa, Princess. What the fuck are you doing?" I don't mean to yell at her, but I'm so beyond shocked by her reaction that my first response is anger.

Her icy-blue eyes rocket to mine. "What does it look like I'm doing, Brax?"

"It looks like you're about to suck my cock."

She winks before muttering, "Bingo."

What the fuck?

I stop her frantic movements with my hands. If I weren't a man who liked my women feisty, the fierce glare she scorches me with would have made quick work of the hard-on her eagerness has triggered.

"People handle shock differently, but sucking my cock isn't the way to go."

"How do you know? Have you actually tried it?"

"No, I haven't, but sucking cock isn't really my thing, so I've got nothing to go off." I keep my tone cheeky, hoping to diffuse the seriousness of our confrontation with humor.

My optimism doesn't last long. A heaviness slams into my chest when Clara slumps to the floor and bursts into tears.

Fuck!

Crouching down, I scoop her into my arms and flop back on the couch. I run my hand down her back as the heavy shaking hampering her body earlier returns full force, as do the wet patches on my shirt.

"It's okay, Princess. You're okay. Nothing like this will ever happen to you again. I promise you," I assure her.

"You can't guarantee that." She hiccups through tears.

"Like hell I can't."

She lifts her tear-stained face off my chest before her watering eyes bounce between mine. "How?"

I remove a strand of hair stuck to her tear-drenched cheek before locking my eyes with hers. "By never letting you out of my sight. That's how."

Clara inhales a sharp, quick breath but remains as quiet as a sleeping baby. I draw her in close to my body and stand from the couch. After gathering her purse from the filing cabinet at the side of my office, I head to the back door of Inked.

Clara's eyes drift between mine as I stride down the hallway, but not a word spills from her lips. By the time we make it into the parking lot, the tears flooding from her eyes have dampened to a slight trickle, and her shakes have dulled.

I adjust her position so she's being held by one arm, before digging my hand into her purse to search for her keys. A growl of frustration rolls up my chest when I fail to find them. My excavation is hampered by the massive amount of makeup and girly shit she carries in her oversized purse.

The heaviness weighing down my chest the past two hours lightens when a giggle spills from Clara's lips before she snatches her purse out of my hand and delves her hand inside. I roll my eyes when she produces a set of keys in under two point five seconds.

Once I locate the car key I gave her four weeks ago, I jab it into the passenger side door and unlock her car. Clara's gleaming eyes lift to mine when I gently lower her into the passenger seat before securing her seat belt. After closing the door, I race around her car and glide into the driver's seat. Her second giggle of the night topples from her lips when my knees become trapped behind the steering wheel.

"What the hell? How can you drive sitting so close to the steering wheel?" I grumble, yanking on the seat mechanism.

Clara giggles again.

She must still be in shock. I've never heard her laugh so much.

After pushing the seat back as far as possible, I prod the key into the ignition and fire up the engine. The only noise heard in the cabin of Clara's car for the first two miles is the small pants of her breath.

Another mile out, I shift my eyes from the road to Clara.

Although she doesn't appear as rattled as earlier, her pupils are still filling her cornea, and her face is stained with tears. When another mile clicks over, the expression on her face surges from confused to concerned.

"Where are we going?" she queries as I pull her car into the underground parking lot of my apartment building.

I park her car in my assigned parking bay and switch off the ignition. "My place," I reply before yanking open the driver's side door and stepping onto the concrete.

Any words she might speak are drowned out by the loud echo of the driver's side door slamming shut. Not giving her a chance to protest, I run around the car, swing open her door, and pull her into my arms. I'm shocked as hell when I walk through the deserted parking garage, and she clings to my chest. I expected some type of response—at the very least, a gripe about how she can walk and doesn't need to be carried—but she doesn't say a thing until I place her on her feet at my apartment door.

"Why am I here?" she asks as her eyes aimlessly float around the empty corridor.

Her eyes rocket to mine when I answer, "Because you're in shock."

Her confused gaze stops bouncing between mine when my apartment door gives out a slight creak when I swing it open. I lean in and flick on the lights, illuminating my modest but well-decorated loft apartment.

Clara takes two steps inside before stopping dead in her tracks. She stands frozen in the entryway I finished refitting six months ago. After my grandmother moved into Caramine Care, I downgraded from a two-bedroom apartment to the loft on the top floor. Although I lost the bonus of a guest bedroom, I have the same floor space and the new addition of a rooftop patio.

I track Clara's eyes as she absorbs my apartment in great

detail. A double-size living room with two suede sofas sits to her right, a manly black kitchen adeptly stocked with all the latest appliances is on her left, and a four-seater dining table is directly in front of her. Her eyes circle when she takes in the black wrought iron and wooden spiral staircase that leads to my bedroom floating above the living space. The thrum of the pulse in her neck quickens when her eyes run along the wood-lined pitched roof.

Once she has surveyed every inch of my apartment, she locks her eyes with mine. "Why am I here?"

"Because you're in shock," I repeat. I curl my arm around her shoulders and guide her deeper into the space. "You're shaking and shit. I can't leave you alone like this."

To be honest, I don't know if the new shakes hammering her body are from the mugging or because she's just realized I only have one bedroom. Either way, I'm not leaving her alone in this condition.

When her shakes increase, I say, "Unless you can give me the address of a friend or family member I can take you to, you're staying here." I move to stand in front of her. "Can you give me an address?"

Fresh tears spring in her eyes before she shakes her head.

"Then you're staying here."

Her eyes continue to absorb my apartment as she shadows me up the staircase. While her eyes drink in the king-size bed in the middle of the room, I walk to a set of drawers on my left.

After yanking out a dark blue T-shirt, I pivot to face Clara. "Do you want to shower before you go to bed?" She licks her dry lips before shaking her head. "All right, then put this on and jump into bed." I hand her my shirt then nudge my head to my bed.

Her pupils enlarge to the size of dinner plates as shock makes itself known on her face. "Can you turn around?"

I arch my brow. "You were just about to suck my cock, but now you're acting all shy."

Quicker than the flash of a camera bulb, Clara grasps the hem of her dress and whips it over her head.

Holy fuck!

I knew her body would be dynamite, but mother-fucking-lord it's even better than I expected. Perky round breasts only just concealed by a hot pink fancy lace bra I've only seen on the runway, a smooth, flat stomach, and lusciously long legs spread far enough apart, her sheer panties award me the slightest peek of a pussy I have no doubt tastes sweeter than honey.

Staring me straight in the eyes, Clara drops my shirt beside her feet before sauntering to my bed. The hardness of my cock turns deadly when she slips between the sheets wearing nothing but a lace bra and a tiny pair of panties.

The rise and fall of her chest increases when I grab the collar of my shirt to drag it over my head before lowering the zipper of my jeans. Her soft pants quicken when my jeans are kicked aside two seconds later.

Just like I couldn't take my eyes off her during her provocative striptease, her eyes drink in every inch of me as I stand before her in nothing but a pair of white briefs.

"Calvin Klein?" she queries with her brow bowed high.

I shrug. "What? They're comfy," I reply before slipping into the opposite side of the bed.

I freeze, and a curse word seeps from my lips when a warm hand grips my crotch, instantly turning my cock to stone. It takes a few moments for my brain to register what's going on, but when it does, it takes all my strength—and then some—to stop Clara from stroking me through my briefs.

"Nope. Not happening." My words are rough, relaying the moral struggle I'm trudging through.

"Why?" Clara snaps back. "If this isn't what you brought me here for, why the hell am I here?"

"Because... *you're in shock!*" I hiss through clenched teeth. "And when I take you... and don't have any doubt, Princess, that is a when, not an if... it won't be while you're in shock. I made a mistake once letting you kiss me when you were rattled. It ain't happening again." Leaning over, I switch off the lights. "Now roll onto your hip, so I can spoon you."

Clara gasps in a sharp breath, astonished by my demand. She isn't the only one surprised. I don't spoon. I've never fucking spooned. But I'll spoon her if it guarantees the parts of her body I want to explore the most are facing away from me.

While grumbling under her breath, Clara rolls on her opposite hip. I splay my hand across the smooth planes of her stomach and draw her back.

What? If I'm going to do this, I'm going to do it right.

My lips quirk. This spooning shit isn't too bad. My cock is nestled between the crack of her ass and halfway up her back, my torso is being warmed by the heat of her body, and the scent of her recently shampooed hair is penetrating my nostrils. It isn't half bad. I could get used to this.

A few minutes pass in silence as I run my hand up and down Clara's forearm. If her breathing pattern had leveled out, I might have believed she was asleep, but I know she's awake, even with not seeing her face.

After another stint of quiet, Clara does a one-eighty. The moonlight sneaking into the room from the roof window illuminates half of her face. Even though I can only see half of her beautiful features I've studied in great depth the past six months, I can see enough to tell she's struggling to emerge from the dark pit her attack pushed her into.

The warmth of her breath flutters my lips when she quietly murmurs, "Why am I here, Brax?"

I run the back of my hand down her face, removing a tear that sneakily escaped her eye. "This may be a little hard for you to believe, but you're here because I actually like you, Princess. I want to take care of you." When she gasps, feigning shock, I chuckle. "Is my revelation really that shocking?"

She sighs. "Depends. If you really knew me—"

"I know you," I interrupt.

"The real me, Brax. The before-Inked Clara," she interjects, her voice shaky and low. "If you knew *that* Clara, your opinion of me might change."

"Un-fucking-likely," I reply without the slightest hint of hesitation.

Another stretch of silence passes between us. It isn't awkward but necessary. Clara needs time to compose herself, and I need time to get over the shock I brought a woman to my apartment, and I'm not freaked out about it.

An uneasiness settles in the bottom of my gut when Clara asks, "What are the chances of my necklace being found?"

"I don't know," I reply honestly. "Depends on the value. If it's worth a lot, the chances are low." A heaviness slams into my chest when a stream of tears rolls down her cheeks. "Was it worth a lot?"

Clara shakes her head. "No." She draws herself into my torso. "It's not even valuable, but it's all I have left." Her lips quiver against my bare chest as she cries and cries until her eyes have no tears left, then she falls asleep in my arms.

CHAPTER SIXTEEN

My already brisk pace down the spiral staircase of my loft increases when three quick taps hit the front door of my apartment. I finish buttoning my jeans before swinging open the door. Diesel greets me with a broad grin and the key for my bike dangling from his index finger. "Thought you might need these," he says before attempting to enter my apartment.

I step into his path, blocking his entrance. "Clara is still sleeping," I advise him, my voice rough from just waking up. "She's not appropriately dressed for guests."

Diesel's bawdy grin turns huge. "So a shit night transformed into a good one?" He waggles his brows before curling his arm around my neck to noogie the top of my head.

I punch him in the ribs, winding him. "Not exactly, asshole. She didn't have any other place to go."

He takes a step back and peers into my eyes. "You still playing with that overstacked deck?"

I scoff. "Only as long as it takes for her shock to wear off." My tone has a smear of annoyance attached to it. "Wouldn't be much of a man if I took advantage of her while she was in shock."

Diesel's lips purse before he curtly nods. "True. Didn't think about that."

"You don't really think about anything," I quip.

His smile enlarges. "True." He props his shoulder onto the doorjamb of my entryway. "We found two of the guys who jumped Clara last night."

My eyes drop to his knuckles. I'm not at all surprised to see they're busted. "Did you call Ryan?"

Diesel bites his lip. "Yeah... after I had a quiet word with them."

"Were they locals?"

He shakes his head. I'm not shocked by this revelation either. Inked has had a not-to-be-messed-with stigma attached to it from the day Ryder opened the doors. There's also the fact most of the crew who work there are born and bred Ravenshoe residents.

Ravenshoe locals protect their own.

"Did they have any of Clara's jewelry on them?"

My heart stops beating as I wait for Diesel to reply. It feels like I'm sucker-punched when he briefly shakes his head. "I checked. They had nothing on them. For how well they kept their mouth shut, I think they're nothing but bottom feeders. When we snag the main guy, we might have a better chance of getting her stuff back." He pushes off the doorjamb. "Anyway, I'll let you get back to it. Just wanted to let you know Johnny and I are handling everything." He flicks his eyes up to my loft bedroom. "You look after her."

Nodding, I shadow him down the corridor.

"I parked your bike half a block down because I didn't know

the code for the underground garage," he advises when he reaches the peak of the staircase.

I run my hand across my tired eyes. "Thanks. I'll move it into the garage later."

Diesel's brows shoot up into his hairline when I hold out my hand for him to shake. "Since when have you been a shaking-hands type of man?" he jests before wrapping his arms around my shoulders and drawing me in for a man hug. A chuckle escapes from my lips when he adds to Charity's request last night. "Take care of Clara for me. If not, step aside and let a real man show you how it's done."

He stumbles down the first three steps when I jab my fist into his right rib. After regaining his footing, he salutes me with two middle fingers before galloping down the stairs. His hearty chuckle is still bellowing up the stairwell when I amble back to my apartment.

My eyes lift from the tiled floor in my kitchen when a creak sounds through my ears. I adjust my grip on the mug of coffee I've been nursing for the past thirty minutes when Clara saunters down the staircase and floats across the room wearing nothing but my navy-blue shirt she left crumpled on my floor last night. Her face is creased from where it was pressed against my chest, her hair is a mess, and her face is void of any of the makeup she typically wears, but she still looks one hundred percent appetizing.

"This is even more embarrassing than the walk of shame." She tugs down the hem of my shirt. "Where are my clothes?"

I crack a smile. "They're in the wash." I nudge my head to the laundry room attached to my kitchen. "They should be ready in around forty minutes." *Or eighty, since I'm close to extending the wash cycle.* Seeing her in nothing but my shirt is a cock-twitching visual I want to retain as long as possible.

Clara's eyes drop to the coffee mug in my hand as she slips onto a barstool.

"Coffee?"

She smiles. "Yes, please."

After filling a second mug with coffee, I place it in front of her before moving to the refrigerator to grab a carton of milk. Unlike me, Clara has her coffee with cream.

I tilt my torso out of the refrigerator when she quietly mutters, "I'm sorry about last night."

Grabbing the carton of milk, I stand in front of her. "It's all good." I set the milk down in front of her. "Are you okay?"

Her eyes lift from the speckled black counter to me before she nods.

"Then we are all good."

Taking a step backward, I brace my back on the kitchen counter. The next few minutes are filled with quiet as we stand across from each other enjoying the pick-me-up only a healthy dose of caffeine can give. Although Clara doesn't look as tired as she did last night, she still appears restless. That probably has something to do with the little whimpers that escaped her lips while she slept.

Once her mug is empty, Clara sets it on the countertop and lifts her eyes to me. "How come you didn't take advantage of the situation last night?" she queries with her brows scrunched tightly.

After placing my mug in the sink, I cross my arms in front of my bare chest. "Because under this *beastly* exterior is a man whose grandma raised him right."

Clara smiles softly. "You were raised by your grandma?"

I nod. "Yeah. My momma died when I was little. I have no clue about my dad."

A flash of remorse passes Clara's eyes, but she remains quiet.

"You?" I query, hoping since I've shared personal information, she may as well.

Her face cringes. "I was raised by a handful of nannies." She straightens her spine and sits higher in her chair. "My mom had been unwell for a long time, and my dad was always busy."

"I'm sorry to hear that."

Clara shrugs. "I guess it's all part and parcel of being born with a silver spoon in your mouth. Not something you would have ever had to worry about."

She balks as her pupils widen. Even though I can see she wishes she could ram her words back down her throat, it doesn't stop my anger from rising.

"No, it's not something I could ever say concerned me." I try to keep the sneer out of my tone, but I fail miserably. "Can I ask you a question?" Even though I'm asking a question, I continue speaking, not giving her a chance to reply, "Where was that silver spoon when your car got towed and you were served an eviction notice? Where was it when you moved into a rat-infested dump? And where the fuck was it when you got jumped in the alley while working on the side of town you should have *never* stepped foot in?"

Clara locks her soul-burning gaze with mine. "You, *of all people*, are going to judge me?"

"Yeah, I fuckin' am," I reply, ignoring the way her little snipe dented my ego. "Because if you didn't have the crew of Inked and me stepping up to the plate, you'd be out there swinging the bat on your fucking own."

My words are callous, but now that they're unleashed, I have no chance of reeling it in. My mind is spiraling, incapable of grasping how Clara can sit before me declaring she has a glamorous life when all I've witnessed the past several months is her taking blow after blow after fucking blow.

Ignoring the anger blemishing her skin with a pink hue, I ask the question I've wanted to know for weeks, "Where's this Isaac guy you wanted to mark your skin with? You cared enough about him that you were going to permanently bear his name on your hip, but he's nowhere to be found the instant your life starts circling the toilet bowl."

Clara pushes back from the kitchen counter, sending the barstool toppling over. She glares at me with nothing but disdain tainting her arctic eyes. Her lips twitch, dying to fight back, but not a single word spills from her mouth.

"He was your daddy replacement, wasn't he? A strong, dominant man you wanted to swoop in and look after you the way your father should have."

Her nostrils flare as anger envelops her entire body. "You don't know what you're talking about." Her words fly from her mouth like daggers.

"Fucking bullshit, Princess." My voice is as vicious as my words. "You're the classic story of a poor, unloved little rich girl. When you failed to secure the love of your daddy, you went hunting for the next best thing... a man just like him."

With her fists clenched at her side, Clara charges into the laundry room. The washing machine beeps, announcing it has been opened, when she yanks the door so hard, it indents the drywall.

Ignoring the fact her dress is still wet, she throws my shirt over the top of her head before dragging her dripping wet dress up her quivering thighs. You'd think her absurd overreaction would surprise me. It doesn't. The only thing I'm shocked about is that she doesn't attempt to refute my claim.

No bitchy reply.

No snarky remark.

Nothing.

"Come on, Princess. Where's your fighting spirit? What happened to the feisty little temptress who has told me time and time again how she can look after herself? Where the fuck has that Clara gone?"

"I *can* take care of myself," she hisses, her angry words unable to hide the sob sitting at the back of her throat, dying to break free.

"Yeah, you can. So fight me. Prove what I'm saying is wrong."

She angrily shakes her head while striding across the room. My eyes track her as she makes her way through my residence searching for her belongings, the water dripping off her dress leaving puddles in her wake.

When she snatches her purse off the coffee table in my living room, I push off my feet and race to the door. I only just make it to the entryway before her.

When she lifts her eyes from the floor, the heaviness weighing down my chest since last night grows. Fresh tears leak from her overfilled eyes as the same broken look she was wearing last night returns full force.

She won't fight as she believes every word I'm speaking is true.

"Look around, Princess." I wave my hand in the air. "There's no white horse, and I sure as hell can't see Prince-Fucking-Charming, but you're still breathing, you've got clothes on your back, food in your belly, and a roof over your head. Who gave you that, Clara?" Her face crunches as she battles to settle the heavy flow of tears streaming down her face. "You did. Not your daddy. Not Isaac. You did it. You're not a damsel who needs saving. You and only you crawled yourself out of the pit that was trying to swallow your life whole four months ago."

"If I don't need saving, then why am I here? Why are you helping me?" she stutters through a barrage of hiccups.

"Because it is what a man does for the woman he's falling in love with," I reply before my brain has the chance to object. "Last night scared the shit out of me. The thought of losing you... *Fuck!* I couldn't handle that. I can't handle that." I lock my eyes with her. "Don't *ever* make me handle that."

More tears spill from her eyes. "If you knew the things I've done, the people I've hurt, you wouldn't be saying that, Brax. You would leave me to fend for myself like every other member of my family and friends have. I'm not a nice person. I am not who you think I am."

"I don't care about your past, Princess. None of it matters to me—"

"It should," she interrupts as her glistening eyes bounce between mine. "No one should get away with what I did."

"You don't think you've already been punished? You got mugged at gunpoint in an alleyway, for fuck's sake. I think your dues have been paid."

"That's nothing compared to the hurt I've caused people," she replies, her voice switching from a medium volume to a faint whisper. "Not even close."

"Then tell me what you did. Let me make my own decision."

She balks before shaking her head.

"Then I guess I'll keep running with my own opinion." I move to stand in front of her. The closer I get to her, the more she retreats. Her fleeing steps only stop when her back is plastered against a wall in my apartment, and my body is splayed to her front.

"And my opinion is one hundred percent certain that I need to taste your lips again." I lift my eyes from her thrusting chest to her face. "So unless you tell me something shocking within the next five seconds, I'm going to kiss you. And since I'm planning on kissing you until you can't speak, you better speak now while you have the chance."

Lifting my hands, I cup her jaw. "Five."

I run my thumbs over her cheeks to gather her tears. "Four."

I drop my thumb to brush the mouth I'm dying to taste again. "Three."

I adjust the angle of my head to align our lips better. "Two."

I tilt my head closer to hers. "One—"

"I snuck into a taken man's bed while he was heavily intoxicated so I could pretend we slept together," she blubbers out, her hot breath fanning my hungry lips.

Although shocked a woman of Clara's standards would need to stoop to those levels, it isn't the first time I've heard of women running those types of tricks.

It also isn't enough to stop me from tasting the lips I've been dying to become reacquainted with for the past three weeks.

"I was also the reason my brother lost the love of his life."

I pull back and peer into her eyes. They're shimmering with silent regret, undoubtedly proving what she's saying is true.

"Have you tried to fix the mistakes you made?"

A big, fat tear rolls down her cheek when she shakes her head. "Why not?"

She scoffs. "Because I'm not who you think I am." After flinging a tear off her cheek, she locks her remorseful eyes with mine. "That vindictive two-faced bitch you met at Inked months ago, that's the real Clara McGregor. I'm a spiteful cow who doesn't think twice about steamrolling anyone standing between me and the ultimate prize. I'm not the Clara you see, Brax. Not in the slightest."

With that, she slips under my arm and throws open my front door. A waft of warm air hits me in the face when I slam the door shut before she has the chance to exit.

"I'm not even half done with you, Princess," I growl into her ear.

CHAPTER SEVENTEEN

I stand so close to Clara, her wet dress creates a large watermark on my jeans. "If you were a vindictive bitch who didn't care, you wouldn't be crying right now," I mutter in her ear. "You also wouldn't have sold *all* your designer dresses and shoes to give the profits to the women's shelter three blocks over from Inked."

She intakes a ragged breath, seemingly unaware I knew she sold every designer outfit she owned and not the half she had sprawled on her bed the afternoon she moved into her apartment.

"You did that because—"

"Because that women's shelter was where I would have ended up if you hadn't given me a chance," she interrupts, her words croaky, hampered by a sob sitting at the back of her throat. "I was two seconds from living on the streets."

Even though her admission hits me fair in the guts, I continue my endeavor to show her she isn't the woman she thinks she is. "It's not just that. You did it because under the hard shell you've been wearing the past... I don't know how many years... is a woman with a massive heart. The Clara you spoke of earlier isn't you, Princess. It is the sheltered Clara who was hiding behind a pile of money. The instant you stepped away from the lifestyle that was no doubt slowly killing you, the *real* Clara was set free."

I tap my finger on her chest that is furiously pounding her ribcage. "This didn't just start beating when you walked through the doors of Inked. It's been beating since the day you took your first breath. Just no one was listening." I cup her jaw and tilt her head back to face me. "I'm listening," I declare into her tear-welling eyes. "And I'll never stop listening."

I'm hoping my admission will have her spinning around and sealing her mouth over mine. What I'm not expecting is for her to bury her head into the crook of my neck and shed enough tears to fill a river.

Riddled with guilt that I pushed her too far, I gather her into my arms and stride to one of the sofas in my living room. I draw her in close to my chest and run my hand down her back as I whisper assurances in her ear. I tell her everything will be okay and that I will always step up to the plate for her, undoubtedly proving the words I blurted out in the heat of the moment ring true.

I'm falling for Clara. Only now am I realizing she's the reason my cock went into hiatus and why I've been so lost the past few months. And while I'm being totally fucking honest, she's the cause of my biggest worry.

Imagine finally getting close enough to something you've always wanted that you can taste it on the tip of your tongue, only to discover it might be short-lived. Although I truly believe the Clara sitting before me is the real Clara, I can't one hundred percent testify that she will stay this way if her silver spoon ever finds its way back to her mouth. I hope she will, but there are no guarantees in life, let alone for a woman who is as complicated as Clara.

Any concerns about only having her in my life for a fleeting moment shift to the back of my mind when Clara lifts her head off my chest and locks her wide eyes with mine. Just from the way she's staring up at me, I don't care if she can only give me a second, I'll take every moment I can get.

I move my mouth, preparing to continue apologizing for the callous words fired off my vindictive tongue, but my words fall short when Clara's hand grips the back of my neck to pull my mouth to hers. The aroma of coffee filters through my nose, and the flavor of salty tears swamp my taste buds when she seals her lips over mine. Just like our first kiss, I open my mouth to accept her tongue, but if she wants this to go any further, she needs to make all the moves.

"Take what you want, Princess," I mumble against her mouth when she freezes with the tip of her tongue bracing the seam of my lips. "If you want to stop, stop. If you want to take it a little further, take it further. But you need to guide the pace."

Pulling back, she peers into my eyes. Shock and confusion are marring her face. "Don't you want me?"

A smirk curls on my lips. "Believe me, I fucking want you." I jerk my hips up so she can feel the effect her PG13 peck had on my cock. "I just want to make sure this is something you want. I'm not going down the denial road again. We've already walked down that path, and I'm not repeating it. If this is going to happen, then I'm all for it. But if you're planning on waking up tomorrow morning in my bed and pretending it was all a dream, it ain't happening. You got me?"

My brow arches when Clara bites on the inside of her cheek, struggling to hold in her giggle.

What the fuck is she laughing about? I didn't hear anything humorous in my speech.

Spotting my furious scowl, she asks, "You do realize it is only ten o'clock? So the whole statement about waking up tomorrow morning in your bed was a little overboard."

"You don't think I'm up for the challenge?"

Heat creeps across her cheeks. "Well... no... it's not that."

"Then what is it?"

She mumbles something under her breath, but she's so quiet I miss what she said.

"Speak up, Princess."

Her eyes snap to mine. "From the conversations I've overheard at Inked, you don't wake up with anyone in your bed." Her voice is surprisingly strong considering the number of tears she just shed.

I arch my brow. "Did you not wake up in my bed this morning?"

She scoffs. "Yeah, but that's different. We didn't *do* anything."

"Only because I stopped you."

Her eyes roll as she huffs. "Thanks for the reminder. I would have hated for the sting of rejection to heal too quickly," she snarls, shifting her eyes sideways.

I grip her chin and force her eyes back to me. "How bad would that sting have been if I'd taken advantage of you last night? Was it not better for me to deny you than hurt your feelings?"

"Ah, you just called me out for having a daddy complex. My feelings were still hurt, rejection or not."

"Yet here you are sitting in the lap of a guy who's far from a father figure. Maybe I was wrong?"

I'm braced and prepared for her to either flee from my lap or unleash a scathing tirade. She shocks me for the second time in under five minutes by remaining quiet.

I don't know how many minutes pass with me holding her in

my arms as she stares out into space. I'm too entranced by her beautiful face to keep track of time. The silent void isn't awkward, and it doesn't feel uncomfortable. It just appears as if she needs a few minutes to gather her thoughts.

While she does that, I run my hand down her shiny locks, smoothing the frazzled pieces into place while relishing being the man she can find a moment of peace with.

After a stretch of silence, Clara mumbles, "I wasn't always like that."

I quirk my lips, pretending I don't know what she's referring to.

"I wasn't always attracted to men who could take care of me," she elaborates as the glazed-over look in her eyes fades. "I can't recall the exact moment it happened, but I'm fairly certain the switch was flicked on not long after my eighteenth birthday."

"That would make sense. The jump from adolescent to adulthood is pretty daunting."

"It wasn't that." Her words are barely audible over the mad beat of her heart. "It was so much more than that."

I hold my breath, hoping she'll open up to me.

My wish isn't granted when she leaps off my lap and declares, "I *really* need a shower."

I only just stifle the groan her sudden loss of contact spurred from my cock. He was as happy as a fish in water nestled against the soft curves of her ass.

There's no chance of holding back my second groan when Clara drops her eyes to mine. "Care to join me?"

I try to speak, but words fail me when I spot an unrecognizable glint in her eyes. Although her stance is strong and determined, something about her body language is off. I'd like to say I've witnessed a wide variety of her personalities over the past four months, but this one is leaving me wholly stumped. I can't tell if she's petrified or excited. And while I'm being entirely forthright, not being able to read her scares the fucking shit out of me. I've got enough obstacles to jump over. I don't need any more things added.

The unidentifiable sparkle brightening Clara's eyes fades by the moment, no doubt snuffed by my delay in replying. It isn't that I don't want to join her for a shower—believe me, I want that more than anything—but I want to make sure this is what she wants and she isn't acting impulsively from the mass surge of adrenaline pumping through her blood after her brush with death last night. I only denied her advances ten hours ago. *Is ten hours truly enough time to overcome shock?*

I scrub my hand over the stubble on my chin. "Are you sure this is what you want, Princess? I can't guarantee once I've had you, I'll ever stop. So if you're hoping your adventure on this side of town will be a short one, you need to step back and consider your options more thoroughly."

Any concerns clutching my throat loosen when a flash of excitement flares in Clara's eyes. "Who said my visit was going to be a short one?"

I shrug. "Just an assumption."

"A *wrong* assumption." Her words crack out of her mouth like a whip. Spreading her hand on her cocked hip, she stares me straight in the eyes. "Are you going to show me where everything is? Or am I going to figure it out on my own?" she asks, quoting the exact thing she said the first day she arrived at Inked for her two-week trial.

I slant my head to the side and return her fervent stare. It takes a massive effort to keep my feet planted on the floor when a glint I can identify ignites in her heavy-lidded gaze before my very eyes. Even a blind man would recognize it. She doesn't just want to be ravished, she wants a man to help her get back the confidence she lost last night.

So, that leaves me with two choices. I either back away and let another man step up to the plate or continue wielding the bat I've been holding the past four months. Since there's no chance in hell I'll ever let another man take care of Clara, let alone touch her, it looks like there's really only one option. I'd be lying if I said I wasn't as happy as a pig in mud to be awarded the challenge.

CHAPTER EIGHTEEN

The soft pants of Clara's breath increase the further we step toward the bathroom. A crackling of energy fires the air between us, inciting a prickling of goosebumps to form on her arms. When I swing open the thick black door and switch on the light, she inhales a ragged breath before her eyes absorb the grandeur of the bathroom.

Other than my bedroom, this is my favorite room in my apartment. It is roomy, dark, and incredibly manly. Although it took a good chunk of the money I had left after downgrading from a two-bedroom apartment and a solid forty hours of my weekend, I'm glad I put the effort in. Even more so now since it's managed to shock Clara into silence.

I watch the excitement in her eyes grow when I unfasten the button on my jeans and lower the zipper. Her eyes blaze when I glide them down my thighs and kick them to the side. She tries to hold my gaze when my Calvin Kleins follow the path my jeans just made. She fails.

I'm hard in an instant, jutted and firm when she gasps in a

wild breath. The heat scorching my blood turns potent when she murmurs, "Jesus," under her breath as her eyes drink in the effect her avid gaze has on my cock.

She drags her eyes away from the lower half of my body when I take a step toward her. "Your turn," I mutter, my voice laced with smugness, proud as a peacock about her slack-jawed reaction. "Wait," I instruct when her hands move to the hem of her dress. "I want to undress you."

Her eyes brighten with anticipation before she nods. The tips of my fingers float over the skin high on her thighs when I move them to grip the hem of her dress. My movements are hurried since I'm more than eager to see the skin after its scent kept me awake half the night.

A rich floral aroma floats into the air when I whip off her dress in one quick motion. Discarding it to the floor next to my jeans, I rake my eyes up Clara's body, gliding them past the velvety smoothness of her cock-teasing legs, over the flat planes of her stomach, and across the generous swell of her breasts. Her perfect body sends a jolting spasm straight to my balls.

"Fucking beautiful," I mutter more to myself than Clara.

My devoted gaze over her body only stops when I catch sight of her lust-riddled eyes. The unidentifiable glint her eyes were wearing earlier has been replaced with a gleam I know all too well. It's the shimmer of a woman preparing to be claimed. Taken. Utterly consumed.

And I know just the man to do it.

Now I just need to work out where to begin.

Should I start at her heaving breasts that are thrusting up and down with every breath she takes? Or at the glistening slit her sheer panties barely cover. If we weren't in the confines of a bathroom, I would have started with her pretty little mouth. Considering its fiery tongue was the main reason for my cock's extended stint of abstinence, it has a lot of making up to do.

When Clara drops her eyes to my lengthened rod and licks her lips, I wonder if she can read my thoughts.

"Although I'd love nothing more than to have your lips wrapped around my cock, that's not happening."

Her eyes rocket to mine as her face fills with confusion. "Why not?"

When I drift my gaze around the bathroom, her eyes track mine.

"Do you see a suitable location to host such an event?"

Clara's eyes instantly stop floating around the room and snap down to the tiled floor at my feet.

Ignoring my twitching cock, I shake my head. "Nope. Not happening."

Her eyes dart back to mine. The shocked expression on her face has increased tenfold.

"Princesses don't kneel for anyone," I mutter, answering the silent question her eyes are relaying. "When you suck my cock, it won't be while you're on your knees."

My balls tighten when a soft moan ripples from her mouth. She looks both shell-shocked by my admission and turned on. Her astonishment is about to increase.

"Beasts, on the other hand..." Her breathing turns excited when I fall to my knees in front of her. "They have no problems kneeling before princesses."

She stares down at me with her mouth hanging wide and the scent of her arousal lingering in the air. Other than her rapid breaths, she stays quiet, which makes me even harder. It's not every day a mere man can silence a fire-breathing princess.

"Do something," Clara eventually mutters when the stint of silence stretching between us becomes too great for her to ignore.

"I will when you tell me what you want."

"I want you," she immediately replies, her voice husky and ball-tingling sweet.

I don't have a chance in hell of holding in my smug smirk, so I just let it go. "You're going to need to be more specific than that."

"Why? Don't act like you don't know what you're doing, Brax. I had the unfortunate displeasure of witnessing your abilities first-hand. I can assure you that you've got this covered." Her brows scrunch together as a deadpan look slips over her face. "Please don't tell me you're one of those guys who act all macho until they step into the bedroom."

The smirk on my face morphs into a full-toothed smile. Not only has the silky softness of her voice been replaced with the tone she regularly uses, but the fiery spark that makes my cock ache is beaming from her narrowed gaze.

There's a brief flicker of the feisty temptress my cock is infatuated with.

If I weren't loving her renewed feistiness, I wouldn't hesitate to assure her my handing over of the reins is a one-time-only deal. But not wanting to snuff the impish gleam her eyes lost last night, I keep my mouth shut.

I lean back until my backside is resting on the balls of my feet before lifting my eyes to Clara. "Were you told what to do your entire life? How to sit, eat, act?"

She balks as her pupils widen, confirming my suspicion.

"That's not happening tonight. So, unless you tell me what you want, nothing is going to happen."

My attempt to boost Clara's confidence strengthens when her yearning eyes leer into mine. The heavy pants of her breaths quicken before she murmurs, "How specific do I need to be?"

My lips tug into a lewd smirk, pleased she isn't backing down without a fight. I shouldn't have expected any less. Although rattled from her encounter last night, Clara is one of the strongest and most opinionated women I've ever met, so I have faith she's got this.

"I only need to know three simple things. Where you want it, how fast, and how long."

She blinks three times in a row before she replies, "In the shower, hard and fast until my legs give out."

Ignoring my cock jumping from the hankering look beaming from her eyes, I ask, "No foreplay?"

Clara inhales a quick breath before she shakes her head. "Not yet."

The grittiness of her voice travels all the way to the base of my cock, puffing my chest high. I'm smug as hell she's considering round two when we haven't even begun round one yet.

More than eager to get this party started, I rise from the floor and band my arms around Clara's waist. A jagged growl tears from my throat when she asserts a small snippet of control I'm handing her by sealing her lips over mine and spearing my mouth with her tongue. She grunts a long, purring moan like my mouth is the most delicious thing she's ever tasted. She explores my mouth with slow, tantalizing strokes as her nails scratch my back. Her kiss is mind-hazing and lush, a promise of the greatness about to be unleashed.

Cupping her ass, I encourage her to wrap her legs around my waist. My cock hardens to the point it is almost painful when it is seared by the heat of her scorching pussy. While my tongue becomes reacquainted with every inch of her delicious mouth, I step toward the shower recess. I rock my hips along the way, ensuring she can feel the effect her kiss has on me.

Not removing my lips from hers, I lean in and turn on the shower before reaching up to bat the showerhead out of the way. I don't want anything impeding my view of her in the midst of ecstasy. I've been waiting for this moment for months, and I don't want anything between us, not even something as simple as a stream of water.

Steam curls around us as I walk through the double-size shower to the only sturdy wall. When I reach our destination, I pin Clara to the dark gray tiled wall with my body before dragging my lips away from her.

"Here?" My breathless word exposes my wavering constraint.

"Yes." She rubs her clit against my shaft. "Here. There. Fucking anywhere. Just do it already."

A ghost of a smile spreads across my face. This is the first time I've heard her say a proper cuss word.

I drop my eyes to her hot pink lace panties. "Expensive?"

Clara leans back and slithers her hand down the smooth planes of her stomach. An animalistic groan rumbles up my chest when she grips her sheer panties in her hand and tears them off her body before muttering, "Not anymore," exposing her patience is wearing thin.

She isn't the only one.

I secure a better grip on her hip with one hand while the other one guides my stiffened shaft to the entrance of her pussy. She purrs a ball-clenching moan when I rub the crown of my cock through the folds of her wet pussy, coating myself in her slick wetness. Her pussy grows wetter and warmer with every second that ticks by.

Happy she's wet enough to ease the friction she will feel from the lack of foreplay, I lift and lock my eyes with her heavy, hooded gaze. "You sure?" I ask, giving her one final chance to flee. If she agrees now, there will be no turning back. "Because my cock has a slight fascination with you that will most likely get worse once he has you."

"Your cock or you?" Although her words are breathless, I can't miss the cheekiness in her tone.

I sweep my cock across her clit, wiping the glint of cheek right out of her eyes and replacing it with the vibrant spark of lust.

"Does it matter either way?"

"No." She drawls out the short word in a long, breathless moan.

"Then let me ask you again. Are you sure?"

My cock twitches when she replies, "Yes, I'm sure."

"Then let's do this."

Clara throws her head back when I push the first inch of my cock inside her. Her pussy ripples around me, greedily sucking me in, begging for more.

I clench my teeth, vying to ignore how good it feels to have her snug slit wrapped around me. Even though I haven't climaxed in months, I want this to last as long as possible.

I've notched in another three inches when reality dawns.

Fuck!

Ignoring the begging protests of my cock, I withdraw from Clara in one swift motion, place her onto her feet, then head out of the shower.

"Where are you going?" Clara's voice is as shaky as her thighs.

"Need a condom." My words are gruff, spurred on by my stupidity of forgetting something as critical as protection. This is the furthest I've ever gone without a condom. Normally my cock wouldn't get within sniffing distance of its target without being wrapped.

Only a woman as captivating as Clara would force me to lose my rational head.

Snagging my jeans off the floor, I check the back pocket for my wallet. Even beyond annoyed with the delay, my cock is as hard as stone. The memories of Clara's heat wrapped around it is enough to hold its focus.

Failing to find my wallet in my jeans, I make my way to my

bedroom. My steps are as fast as the string of illicit curse words streaming through my head.

I stare at the top of my dresser for several seconds, shocked and confused. My bike key is in its rightful place, but my wallet is nowhere to be seen. I always house my wallet and key in the same location, so where the fuck is it? Only when the events of last night run through my head does another reality dawn on me. I left my wallet on my desk at Inked.

Goddammit!

I scrub my hand down my tired face as I stride back into the bathroom, mumbling incoherently under my breath. My steps are no longer eager, weighed down by my rapidly deflating cock. Because I've never brought a girl back to my apartment, and most of the bunnies I've played with bring their own supplies, I don't have a single condom in my entire place. Not a goddamn one!

When I enter the shower, my stupidity hits me fair in the guts. Even concealed behind a thick sheet of steam, nothing can take away from the entrancing beauty of a saturated and completely naked Clara. Her body is pure perfection. Graceful and lean but designed to be fucked with mouthwatering pert breasts, long toned legs, and just the right number of curves to set my heart racing.

Her body is a promise of many restless nights and mind-shattering orgasms. And I've gone and fucked up the opportunity by not doing something as basic as stocking my bathroom vanity with condoms.

I'm a fucking idiot.

When Clara notices me entering the shower, her lips part, and her breathing turns excited. Her chest thrusts up and down as she steps deeper into the flow of water. A steady stream of water rolls down her face, removing any tearstains left clinging to her cheeks. Her inviting eyes sweet talk me into joining her without a single word seeping from her lips. When I fail to step forward, she crooks her finger and gestures for me to move closer.

"I can't." My words come out strangled since I have to fight my mouth to release them.

Clara's eyes drop to my once-again jutted and primed-to-go cock, its new bout of stiffness stirred by the ravishing visual of her naked in my shower.

"I'm pretty sure you're good to go." The soft purr of her voice makes me even harder.

I shake my head. "Can't. Don't have a condom."

She flinches, her eyes widening. "Are you serious?"

"Unfortunately, yes." A brief chuckle escapes my lips which is full of torment and despair.

"Oh my God," she mumbles, her words muffled by her hand, which shoots up to slap over her mouth.

Her eyes bounce between mine for several heart-clenching seconds before she murmurs, "Are you clean?"

"No," I mutter, my response short and swift.

The width of her eyes grows as she gasps in a ragged breath.

I stare at her, utterly confused by her shocked reaction.

"Yes, I'm fucking clean. I work with needles, for crying out loud. We get checked regularly. I meant no to your suggestion of going bareback," I growl when it dawns on me why she's looking at me in disgust. "I'm not fucking you without a condom."

In an instant, a mask of anger slips over Clara's face. "Why? Are you worried I'll try to pin a pregnancy on you or something?"

"What? No! Don't be fucking ridiculous."

She crosses her arms under her mouthwatering breasts. "Then what's the problem?" The longer I delay in replying, the redder her face lines with anger. She stares at me with her eyes glaring and nostrils flaring. "If I'm clean and you're clean, I don't see what the problem is."

"Because I don't fuck without a condom. Period." My angry voice shrills off the tiled wall and jingles into my ears.

I'm not angry at Clara. I'm furious with myself. I've wanted this for months, and now I'm the one putting up barriers. But this is a rule I'm not willing to break. Clara has already forced me to break many rules I said I never would, and I'm not willing to back down on another.

Clara reinforces her firm stance. "You don't fuck without a condom?"

I nod.

"Just like you don't mess with members of your crew? And you don't bring girls back to your apartment?"

"Exactly," I reply, nodding.

My eyes follow Clara's hand as she runs it down her naked body. "Member of your crew, and the last time I checked, I was still a girl."

"That you are," I mutter while dropping my heavy-lidded gaze to her glistening slit.

Just like its owner, Clara's pussy is prim and proper. If it weren't for the small strip of light-colored hair running down the middle, it would be entirely bare. It is pink and smooth, and I have no doubt it tastes even better than it looks.

Dragging my eyes away from the pussy I'm dying to be immersed in, I lock them with a pair of eyes I haven't seen in months. Clara's gaze has the same determined look they had when she fought for her position at Inked. They show her mind is made up, and she isn't leaving this shower until she gets what she came here for.

So I guess I'm going to have to give it to her.

Clara's throat works hard to swallow when I push off my feet and slowly stalk toward her. For every step I take, the anger raging in her eyes dulls from a fierce storm to a faint mist.

"Do you want to come, Princess?" My words are gravelly and deep as excitement thickens my blood.

She stares me straight in the eyes before unashamedly nodding.

"I don't need a condom to make you come."

Any protests spilling from her lips muffle into an erotic moan when I fall to my knees in front of her, hoist her leg over my shoulder, and suck her throbbing clit into my mouth. Her thighs clamp around my head as my tongue is swamped by the most delicious thing I've ever tasted.

"Oh, Jesus," Clara moans, gripping the back of my head with her hand to draw me in even closer. "Don't stop."

"No chance of that happening." Especially since I've now had a taste of her, there's no chance I'll give this up.

Clara's back arches, her hips thrusting forward as my tongue runs the length of her silky-smooth slit. I gather every drop of the arousal slicking her pussy with more wetness than the water pumping from the showerhead.

When I spear my tongue inside her, she grows wetter, and her groans become more feral.

"Brax," she purrs, her voice husky and strained as she writhes against me. "It feels so good..."

I suck her, lick her, devour every fucking inch of her until she screams my name in a startled cry. I growl, and my cock throbs when my tongue is coated with evidence of her climax. She quivers against my mouth as her ear-piercing cries slowly simmer to a husky moan. Hearing my name torn from her throat during ecstasy is the most thrilling thing I've ever heard. It was just how I anticipated—throaty, breathless, and ball-tighteningly sweet.

I slow down the lashings of my tongue, trying to gently bring her back from the earth-shattering climax surging through her body. Once her violent convulsions weaken, I place a final lick on her pulsating clit before standing, meeting her eye to eye. Her heavy-hooded gaze is blazing, but unlike before we entered the bathroom, her eyes are fired with nothing but lust. Just seeing her sexually satiated look has me wanting to bang my chest like a caveman.

Maybe Clara was right. Maybe I am a beast?

"Are you ready for round two?"

Her eyes flash before she nods.

"Put your foot onto the step," I instruct while nudging my head to the tiled step on my right.

A grin tugs my lips high when she does as told without a protest. Although I said earlier Clara was going to control the pace of our exchange, now that I've tasted her, the dynamic has switched. Once my natural dominance is unleashed, there's no chance of reeling it back in. Thankfully, from the impish gleam in her eyes, I don't think she's concerned with the change of power.

I lift my eyes to Clara's flushed face. "Now I'm going to fuck you hard and fast in the shower as you requested."

Her breathing pants out as her eyes brighten with excitement.

"Only using these," I continue, wiggling my fingers in the air.

She sighs—it's a disappointed sigh.

Her disappointment shifts to exhilaration when I slip two fingers inside her. A tingle races along the length of my spine when her plush tightness clamps around them. She's tight, wet, and silky soft. When my fingertips brush the sweet spot inside her, her head falls back, and she sucks in a hasty breath. I keep my eyes fixed on her beautiful face as I rub my thumb over her clit and pump my fingers in and out of her at a speed I wish I were fucking her. My cock aches, begging to be immersed in her slick wetness, but I continue my mission, not willing to give into my desire until her legs give out.

A hiss parts my lips when Clara slithers her hand down the

ridges of my stomach and grips my throbbing cock. My balls clench when she matches the thrusts of my fingers stroke for stroke. With the warm water streaming out of the showerhead and the silky smoothness of her hand, I could pretend it is my cock plunging into her tight pussy, not my fingers.

Fighting the desire to replace my fingers with my stiffened shaft, I increase the speed of my pumps. I finger fuck her so furiously, her body jerks up and down with every thrust. My race to climax heightens when the generous swell of her breasts scrapes across my shirtless torso.

Her pussy's clutch on my fingers tightens as the whimpers from her mouth become more winded. "Please. Oh. God."

I stare into her eyes when her body tenses, wanting to watch her unravel in front of me, to see her quiver and shake her way through another orgasm I triggered.

"Give it to me, Princess," I hiss through clenched teeth as I battle to hold in my climax, which is rushing to the surface.

I grip her ass and pull her closer to me, aligning our bodies together so well, my cock brushes past her clit with every stroke she inflicts. Her groans become carnal, and her pussy ripples around my fingers as if she's milking my cock of the cum it's dying to give her.

"Come for me, Princess. Come for me now!" I demand.

Unlike her previous orgasm, this time she comes with a soft moan. Seeing the way her eyes flare during ecstasy sets me off. Hot cum rockets out of my engorged knob in rapid, quick-fired hits. When the spurts of my cum hit Clara's throbbing clit, the trembles of her pussy increase as do her pleasurable cries. I obtain a better grip around her waist when her knees give way to the violent convulsions racking through her body.

Once her vicious shudders slow, I pull my fingers out of her snug canal and draw her in close to my chest. The harsh pants of her breaths tickle my bare torso as she struggles to secure a full breath.

"God. That was—"

"Just the beginning," I interrupt, my throat hoarse.

A pleased grin curls on my lips when Clara briefly nods. Her throaty pants switch to a squeal when the water pumping out of the showerhead turns colder than a witch's tit.

"Jesus," she shrieks, leaping out of my arms and hightailing it to the other end of the shower.

The satisfied smirk on my face morphs to cocky when I notice her steps are shaky and slow as she has yet to regain full control of her quivering legs.

"It could have been worse."

Clara eyeballs me, blinking and confused.

"It could have switched to cold five minutes earlier." I lock my big-headed gaze with her twinkling eyes. "Before you came for the second time."

She rolls her eyes and crosses her arms in front of her chest, feigning annoyance. I'm not buying her act. Even if I could ignore the look of bliss on her face only two mind-shattering orgasms can produce, I can't miss the glimmer in her eyes I've wanted to put there for months.

Clara looks exactly how I want her to look.

Claimed.

CHAPTER NINETEEN

My head rockets to the side when someone knocking on my front door bellows into the bathroom. I consider ignoring the interruption until a raspy voice sounds through my ears, "Brax, are you home?"

Ryan.

I shift my eyes back to Clara. "I've got to get that," I inform her while nudging my head to the door. "There are clean towels under the vanity. Wait in here, and I'll bring you some clothes in a minute."

She huffs and crosses her arms in front of her naked chest, apparently annoyed by my request. Ignoring her white-hot glare, I rustle up my jeans from the floor, yank them up my thighs, and hightail it to the door.

Just before I open the door, I crank my head back to Clara. The lewd grin I've been wearing the last forty-five minutes turns massive when I catch her staring at my ass. My confidence hits an all-time high. Even annoyed at my request to stay put, she can't help but ogle my assets.

When she notices I've stopped walking, her gaze lifts and connects with mine. I arch my brow and stare into her gleaming eyes so she knows I didn't miss her lingering stare at my backside. A traffic-stopping grin stretches across her face, undoubtedly proving she isn't the slightest bit ashamed she was busted eyeballing me.

I cockily wink at her. She winks straight back.

After closing the bathroom door behind me, I make my way to Ryan.

"Hey," he greets me, his eyes shifting around my loft with the same amount of eagerness as Diesel's did earlier. When he fails to locate whatever he's searching for, he drifts his eyes back to me. "I heard from a reliable source you had an overnight visitor. Scare her off already?"

Like a perfectly timed skit, the vanity tap in the bathroom turns on.

Ryan's lips tug into a wry smirk, exposing two dimples that sit on his top lip. "Is that Clara?" he questions, waggling his brows.

From the smug look on his face, I know he already knows my reply, but since I'm still running on a high from my bathroom antics with Clara, I nod.

Ryan shoves a white paper bag under his arm before jabbing my mid-section with a set of rapid-fire hits. "Since when did Brax let girls into his bachelor pad?"

"About as long as you've been doing house calls," I fire back, my voice a mix of gruff and playfulness. "What the fuck do you want, Ryan? You're killing my mojo."

He freezes and studies my face. "Haven't you sealed the deal yet?"

I curse under my breath before yanking him into my apartment. "Keep your voice down. Clara wouldn't appreciate her business being shared with the neighborhood."

"There isn't anything to share if you haven't done the deed," Ryan mutters under his breath.

"Jesus Christ. Do I look like an asshole? She was in fucking shock," I reply, preferring to use the excuse of her shocked state than disclose my stupidity about not having any protection in my house.

Ryan glares at me in a sadistic, jeering type of way. "When has a little shock ever stopped you?"

"Whatever. Clara isn't a bunny, so the rules don't apply to her," I hiss through gritted teeth.

His brows hit his hairline. "Diesel said you were gone. Wouldn't have believed it if I didn't see it myself."

"Yeah, yeah, you've witnessed it. Now fuck off." I jerk my head to the hallway.

Ryan laughs. "You didn't even cite an objection. You're *way* past gone." He freezes and inhales a quick breath. "Holy fucking shit. Is Brax in love?"

His laughter simmers when I glare into his eyes, warning him I'm close to blowing my top. "You've got five seconds to tell me why you're interrupting an uninterruptable moment before I throw your ass out of my apartment."

He chuckles, knowing my warning doesn't hold any threat. Ryan and I have been friends for years, and not once have we come close to blows.

Suddenly, he stops laughing and stands a little straighter. "Shit. When I caught sight of the weird look on your face, I forgot the seriousness of my visit." The anger boiling my blood last night returns when he says, "Two of the men who mugged Clara were granted bail this morning."

"How the hell did they get bail so quickly?" My voice is smeared with anger. "It's Sunday."

Ryan combs his fingers through his hair before shrugging his shoulders. "Although I'm certain they have meddled in this activity before, they had no prior convictions." He locks his glistening blue eyes with mine. "The DA was also a little lenient on them since they spent a couple of hours at the hospital having a few nasty bruises and gashes taken care of."

"Could have been worse," I mumble under my breath.

Even though Ryan heard me, he pretends he didn't and continues speaking, "Do you want me to put a unit on Clara's apartment... or are you going to keep a close eye on her?" he asks, his eyes telling me he already knows my reply.

"You worried they're not done with her?"

His eyelid twitches. "I don't know. After the shakedown your crew gave them, they might seek revenge."

"Not if they're smart," I interrupt.

Ryan huffs. "Tell me one gangbanger who is?"

I cross my arms in front of my bare chest and glare into his eyes.

"You don't count. Your grandma and Ryder whipped that attitude right out of you."

"If only it were a few years earlier," I grumble.

"Better late than never," Ryan responds to my quiet musing. He sighs loudly. "I shouldn't be telling you this, but..." My gut twists from the cloud of worry brewing in his eyes. "The guys who mugged Clara are part of the Petretti crew."

My brows stitch. "I thought that crew disbanded when Col was killed?"

Col Petretti was a notorious mob boss running the streets of Hopeton for as long as I've been breathing air. He was killed in a joint FBI and Ravenshoe police sting late last year.

"Rumors are his son, Dimitri, is trying to raise his legacy from the ashes."

"By peddling petty crimes like mugging women in back

alleys?" My voice is rough as the events of last night filter back through my mind. Although Clara should have never gone into the back alley unaccompanied, it shouldn't be that way. Women should be able to walk wherever they want without fear of being harmed.

Before Ryan can answer, the creak of a door opening sounds through the room. My heart rate kicks up a gear when Clara saunters out of the bathroom with a dark gray towel twisted around her body and another wrapped around her drenched head. Her bare feet padding across the wooden floor as she makes her way from the bathroom to my bedroom can't drown out me backhanding Ryan, warning him to move his bugged-out eyes off Clara.

"What? Couldn't help but see what has your feathers ruffled," he mumbles, his words barely heard over his breathless chuckle. "I can understand your fascination."

His quiet chuckle turns to a full laugh when I whack him harder than I did the first time. Our little confrontation gains Clara's attention. She stops walking and cranks her neck to the side. My chest puffs higher when her eyes connect with mine. Even looking like a woman who's been taken to the brink and back, her eyes are still beaming with lust.

In a flash, the humorous expression on Ryan's face changes to regretful when Clara shifts her optimistic gaze to him and asks, "Did you find my necklace?"

Ryan reluctantly shakes his head. "No, not yet. I'm sorry, Clara."

The hope in her eyes vanishes. "That's okay. Thank you." With her shoulders sagging a little lower, she climbs the staircase to my bedroom and sinks deeper into the space.

I return my eyes to Ryan. "Do you have any leads on her jewelry?"

He once again shakes his head. "I don't like her chances of

recovering the tennis bracelet. It's probably already on the black market."

"She isn't worried about the bracelet. She just wants her necklace back. Seems to have a lot of sentimental value to her."

"She told you about the origin of the necklace?"

I shake my head. "No. I just have a feeling."

Ryan rubs a kink in the back of his neck. That's a sign he's holding something back.

"Why? What did you find out about it?"

"Nothing," he responds with a shake of his head.

I don't even need to look into his eyes to know he's lying. I can hear it in his voice.

I stare into his eyes, silently demanding him to spill the beans.

"I'm not saying anything, Brax. I learned the hard way to keep my mouth shut," he responds to my silent interrogation.

"Chris's death wasn't your fault. No one could have predicted he would go down that road," I reply, knowing him well enough to know what his brief statement is about.

Ryan connects his remorse-filled eyes with mine. "Do you think Noah would see it like that?"

I curtly nod. "If you'd ever give him a chance, yeah, I think he would. You've been carrying the burden of Chris's death for years. Don't you think it's time to let it go?"

A thick, cumbersome silence greets my suggestion. It is always this way when the guilt of our younger years is brought to the surface. Ryan, Chris, and I were the equivalent of the three musketeers back in our high school days. Although we had uniquely distinct personalities, we were thicker than thieves, inseparable until our last days of high school.

Always knowing the path he was going to walk, Ryan joined the police academy. Chris and I... we walked down a very different road. Those bottom feeders Diesel mentioned earlier, that was

Chris and me. I have no doubt my life would have mirrored Chris's if I hadn't gang-tagged the wrong man's building.

Young and stupid, I spray-painted a tag on the side of Inked. Like every young gangbanger, I thought I was invincible. I was cocky and full of attitude until Ryder tracked me down. He not only made me paint over the tag I left on his wall with the permission of my grandma, he also forced me to work at Inked for six months without paying me a dime. He said it was my penance for the injustice I did to the art world with my hideous graffiti.

Unable to knock the massive chip off my shoulder, I set out to prove him wrong. I started learning the craft. At first, I just traced pictures directly out of comic books. As the weeks went on, my drawing technique improved, closely followed by my attitude.

Although I never admitted it to Ryder, Inked became my life. I arrived hours before anyone else just to get in some sketching time, and I left hours later. I ate, slept, and breathed Inked. As the countdown to the end of my six-month sentence loomed, my devastation about leaving the Inked family grew. So you can imagine my excitement when on the final day of my punishment, Ryder offered for me to join his crew.

I was ecstatic... until he advised the stipulation his offer came with. I had to tattoo him. I'm not talking a small tat hidden away from view. He requested a highly complex tattoo to be placed on a prime chunk of real estate on his left shoulder. If he liked my tattoo, I'd become a member of his crew. If he hated it, I was out on my ass.

I'm not going to lie, I was fucking petrified. I guess I don't need to share the rest of my story with you. The fact I'm still working at Inked ten years later is a pretty clear indication of how that story panned out. Ryder loved his tattoo.

Ryder will never admit it, but he saved me. If someone had

done the same for Chris, I doubt he would have overdosed in his bathtub four years ago.

"You couldn't save Chris, Ryan, but you saved his brother from following in his footsteps," I say, breaking the silence between us.

An uneasy grin etches on Ryan's mouth before he briefly nods. The things Ryan has done for Noah over the past four years should by far outweigh any blame he harbors for what happened to Chris. Besides, if anyone should feel guilty, it should be me, not Ryan. With Ryder's help, I pulled myself out of the lifestyle that was going to kill me. Nobody helped Chris. Not even me.

"Clara will probably give me hell about it, but I'll keep her here with me until things calm down," I mutter, saying anything to move us away from our somber conversation. Nothing we can say will ever bring back Chris, so why dig up buried guilt?

Ryan cocks his brow and stares into my eyes. "If this is the Petretti crew, it could be weeks, possibly months, before this blows over. Are you willing to keep an eye on her that long?"

I try to hold in my smile. My efforts are fruitless.

All heaviness of our previous conversation vanishes when Ryan breaks into a childish song about Clara and me sitting in a tree. His hearty chuckle rumbles through my ears when I open the door of my apartment and shove him into the hallway.

I'm in the process of slamming my front door in his face when he mutters, "Think quick."

Before I have the chance to respond, the white paper bag he's been gripping the past twenty minutes sails across the corridor and smacks me in the chest. I only just grab ahold of it before it tumbles to the floor.

I shift my eyes between Ryan's snickering face and the bag as I pry it open. My cock twitches when I discover what is inside—a twelve-pack of magnum condoms. My eyes rocket back to Ryan. If

I weren't sporting major wood, I'd plant a massive sloppy kiss smack bang on his grinning mouth.

"Figured you might need them since you never bring girls back to your apartment."

With a cheeky wink, he strides down the corridor. "Call me if you need me," are the final words I hear before slamming the door shut and bolting to the staircase of my loft.

My steps are hurried as anticipation scorches through my veins. My cock braces against the zipper of my jeans as I take the steps two at a time. I don't care if a hurricane roars down the main street of Ravenshoe, nothing will stop me from claiming the ultimate prize. It is time for the *Beauty and the Beast* fairy tale to turn into reality.

"Well, nothing except that," I mutter to myself when I land on the top step of the staircase, and my eyes roam over Clara lying in my bed wearing nothing but one of my T-shirts. She's rolled on her side with her hands tucked under her cheek. Her eyes are snapped shut, and the soft pants of her breath clearly indicate she's asleep.

She looks like a real princess when she's sleeping.

My princess.

Quietly striding to the edge of the bed, I secure a grip on the duvet and pull it up to cover her. She stirs when I tuck the covers in tight but stays fast asleep. After brushing a few strands of her hair off her face, I press a kiss to her temple and walk out of the room. My cock screams in protest with every step I take.

CHAPTER TWENTY

"Hey," Clara greets me, her voice groggy from just waking up.

Just like this morning, she glides through my apartment wearing nothing but my short-sleeve tee she fell asleep in. Even without a speck of makeup, her face is fresh and vibrant. That might have something to do with the fact she just napped for two hours straight. I've been wondering the past week if she was getting enough sleep in her new apartment. It wasn't just the dark circles plaguing her eyes that had me guessing. It was the fact she couldn't stop yawning.

Anyone will tell you there's nothing more contagious than a vigorous yawn. I bet you're yawning right now, aren't you? Well, that's what it's been like at Inked the past week. Every time Clara yawned, it spread through the entire crew like an out-of-control fire.

Her brisk strides to the kitchen slow to a snail's pace when her eyes stray to a suitcase sitting at the entryway of my apartment. "Is that bag from my Tumi Alpha luggage set?" she queries, swinging her eyes back to me, her voice high and ear-piercing.

"If you're asking if that is your bag, yes, it is," I reply, having no clue what Tumi Alpha is.

I stand straighter, bracing for impact when I spot the fighting spark igniting in her eyes.

"Why is my bag sitting in your foyer?"

The confusion on her face escalates when her eyes bounce around my kitchen, absorbing her fruit bowl, smoothie blender, and a handful of cosmetics Charity rustled up from her apartment scattered across the countertops.

"Two orgasms don't equal a lifetime commitment," Clara mumbles, her concern growing by the minute.

Her eyes rocket to mine when I ask, "What about three?"

A grin curls on my lips when the concerned mask on her face momentarily slips, exposing a flare of excitement from my tease.

Quicker than I can snap my fingers, the excited gleam is replaced with anger when I mutter, "You got an itch you need scratched, Princess?"

My cock turns to stone when she replies, "You're lucky the kitchen counter is between us, or my knee would have become reacquainted with your crotch."

I smile a shit-eating grin. "Don't break it before you get the chance to use it."

Her breathing becomes excited when I nudge my head to the box of condoms sitting to my right. She tries to keep the expression on her face neutral. She miserably fails.

A smug grin curls on my lips. I've never seen her so muted. She usually spits her fiery words off her still sizzling tongue when we engage in a bit of friendly banter, whereas now, her lips twitch but not a word spills from her mouth.

I like this new look, and I can't wait to study it in greater detail when she's beneath me.

Clara's throat struggles to swallow before she mutters, "How long?" Although her question is short, her interrogating gaze adds to its length.

"As long as it takes for your shock to wear off—"

"Already gone," she interrupts, her eyes blazing with the spark our earlier union in the shower renewed.

"And..." One word is all it takes to secure her utter devotion. "Until the men responsible for your attack are held accountable."

Her brows tact together. "How long will that be?"

I lift my right shoulder into a shrug. "Could be days... or weeks."

Her eyes bug as her lips purse into a sexy pout. "Weeks?" she squeaks out. "You want me to stay here for weeks?" She gestures her hand around my apartment.

When I nod, her pupils enlarge to the size of dinner plates. She balls her hands before her eyes drift between me and the entry door of my apartment, no doubt calculating the most viable exit.

I arch my brow and glare into her eyes, warning her that if she attempts to flee, I won't hesitate to tie her to my bed. There's no chance of her leaving here before I've had my fill, and considering I've just spent the last two hours moving her belongings into my private abode, and I didn't freak out once, the chances of me getting my fill anytime soon are low. *Very fucking low.*

"Weeks of finding out how many ways you can scream my name." My voice is as wild as my desire to claim her. "Do you have a problem with that, Princess?" My words are crass, but I want to test her to see if she's only here because she's afraid of being alone or because she actually wants to be.

Clara snaps her eyes back to me. She doesn't say anything. She just stands across from me, wide-eyed and open-mouthed. I slant my head to the side and stare into her glistening eyes. The more I stare, the livelier the glint I identified last night becomes. Clara isn't here because she's afraid or lonely, she is here because she wants to be ravished. Consumed. Devoured.

And I know just the man for the job.

"If you keep leaving your mouth hanging open like that, I'll find something to fill it with."

Clara sucks in a deep breath and lets it out slowly before her eyes drop to my jeans. My cock—now hard—pulses against my zipper when she licks her lips before slowly raking her eyes up my body. Even though I'm wearing a pair of ripped jeans and a short-sleeve shirt, her eyes drink me in as if I'm standing before her as naked as the day I was born.

When her heavy-lidded gaze reaches my face, I jerk my head back and say, "Come here."

I push off the kitchen counter I'm leaning on, preparing to beat her race to the door if she attempts to bolt. She stuns me for the third time in under twenty-four hours by simply shrugging her shoulders before spanning the distance between us. I can tell by the look on her face that she wants to engage in a war of words, but since I've caught her in a moment of weakness—her libido over-riding her astuteness—she appears more willing to put our game of tit for tat on the backburner for a few hours so we can undertake more stimulating activities.

If I were a better man, I wouldn't use her weakness against her.

It's a pity I'm not a better man.

My cock firms as Clara steps toward me with her eyes blazing and hips swinging. Some men would feel intimidated by the deter-mination set in her eyes. Lucky for me, I don't have a problem with a woman who calls it as she sees it. Don't get me wrong, I can't wait to have her flushed and speechless beneath me, but I sure as hell won't cite an objection to her climbing onboard and taking herself for a ride.

Fuck! Just the thought has my cock wrangling the zipper in my jeans, dying to break free.

A jagged groan rumbles from deep in my gut when Clara slings her arms around my neck and seals her mouth over mine. Her tongue sweeps across my lips before plunging inside my mouth. I return her kiss by weaving my fingers through her silky hair and twirling my tongue around hers. The warm goodness of her mouth has my cock aching to be immersed inside her.

Curling my arms around the back of her slim thighs, I hoist her feet off the floor. She smiles against my lips when I place her on the kitchen counter on my right. Her backside dangles far enough off the edge, our crotches align.

The stubble on my chin scratches Clara's neckline as I place a succession of featherlike kisses along her jaw, making her purr like a kitten. My chest swells. There's no greater compliment to a man than being able to switch a strong, determined woman to a purring little kitty. Clara is a take-no-shit type of lady, and I love that about her, but when she loosens the tight reins she governs her life with, I feel invincible. *Like King-Fucking-Kong.*

After a few more nibbles on her jaw, I pull back and peer into her bright eyes, distracted by something rumbling louder than her erotic purrs—her stomach.

"Sorry," she mumbles, chewing on her lip. "I haven't eaten anything since the carrot last night."

I inwardly swear. I was so caught up in ravishing her, I didn't even consider she hasn't consumed a single nutrient in the past sixteen hours.

"Food first," I reply to her whimpering protest when I pull away and walk to the refrigerator. My tone relays my internal battle not to kiss her sexy pout right off her sinful little mouth.

I groan when I swing open the refrigerator. It is so empty, I can hear wind hollering through it.

Upon hearing my grunted response, Clara hops off the kitchen counter and saunters toward me. "What have you got?" she queries, bobbing her neck and peering into the refrigerator. The cutest little crinkle scrunches her nose when her eyes roam over the bare basics it is stocked with. "It isn't too bad," she mumbles under her breath, snagging the half-filled carton of eggs and a nearly empty bottle of milk.

Pushing the door closed with her hip, she steps to the cooktop. After leaning my back against the counter, I cross my arms in front of my chest, relishing the view of a princess preparing breakfast for a beast.

Clara moves along the main counter of my kitchen, swinging open each cupboard she drifts past. I tilt my head to the side and arch my brow when her search extends to the overhead cabinets. Her stretched position forces a small portion of her scrumptious naked backside into my view. I've never been one for going it alone, but with a visual that enticing, I'm fighting the urge to whip out my cock and give it a few strokes.

She grabs a glass mixing bowl I didn't even know I owned from the top cabinet before turning around to face me. "Are you going to show me where anything is? Or am I just going to work it out on my own?" She tries to keep her words sharp, but the cheeky grin tugging her lips high foils her attempt.

With a wink, she spins around and commences cracking the eggs into the glass bowl. I give my eyes a few more moments to drink in her long bare legs, sexy-as-sin body, and tousled hair before pushing off the counter and striding toward her.

I wrap my arm around her waist, pull her in snugly, and drop my head into the crook of her neck. "What do you need me to do?" The heat of my breath bounces off her skin and filters through my nose, engulfing my senses with her rich floral scent.

"Not distract me," she replies before slipping under my arm.

I try to hold back my groan. I fail.

"Do you have any paprika?" she asks after twisting her neck to peer at me.

My brows stitch. "What?"

Clara smiles before briefly shaking her head. "Do you have anything with a bit of heat I could add to the egg whites to give them flavor?"

I quirk my lips. "Chili sauce?"

She smiles a broad grin. I move to the pantry to gather the hot sauce while she pulls out a frying pan from the cupboard below the stove.

"In time, buddy, I promise," I mumble to my cock when the alluring image of Clara bending over has him springing to life.

Twenty minutes later, I'm sitting down to the most unmanly lunch I've ever eaten. Forever healthy, Clara divided the yolk from the eggs, removing all the hearty goodness a guy of my size loves. My ceramic plate is void of the regular crispy bacon and pancakes it is generally stacked with, replaced with slices of avocado and apple.

I push back from my four-seater dining table, causing a massive creak to sound through my apartment, then amble to the refrigerator. Clara's egg-white loaded fork stops halfway between her plate and her mouth when I stride back into the dining room with a chunk of cheddar cheese and a grater.

I drench every inch of my plate in the scrumptious goodness of cheese before lifting my eyes to Clara. "Cheese?" I angle my head to the side and arch my brow.

Clara chews on her lip before shaking her head.

"Are you sure?" I ask, noticing a flare of hesitation sparking in her eyes.

I scoop up a sizable chunk of cheese-covered egg whites and shovel it into my mouth. Clara squirms in her seat when my deep, throaty moan rumbles up my chest. "It is so good."

Her nose screws up as she pushes her plain egg whites around her plate.

After leaning in close to her side, I whisper, "What about if I guarantee you will burn off those calories within twenty minutes of eating them."

Her eyes snap to mine.

"There's no better cardio than sex, Princess."

I transfer some of the cheese piled up on my plate to hers. "Now eat up. You're going to need the energy."

A grin curls on my lips when she fails to sound a single protest to my demand. My grin turns into a full smile when she digs her fork into her now cheesy eggs and raises them to her mouth. Just as her fork disappears between her pouty lips, she locks her wintry eyes with mine. The huge smile etched on my mouth gets wiped right off when she releases the most provocative fucking moan I've ever heard when the eggs hit her taste buds.

I was wrong earlier. Sex isn't Clara's weakness. It is her ally.

I thought I had our whole dynamic worked out. She would be a strong and independent woman until we stepped into the bedroom—then, she'd happily hand the baton to me. But I was wrong. *Very fucking wrong.* Not only does Clara have me over a barrel outside the bedroom, but she also has me by the throat inside as well. All it took was hearing that one little moan topple from her lips, and I'm ready to do anything to hear those noises torn from her throat in the middle of ecstasy. *Anything at all.*

The last ten minutes have felt like I'm an inmate serving a life sentence with no chance of parole. It's been torturous. I devoured every scrap of food on my plate within thirty seconds, shamefully displaying that my patience to have Clara beneath me has worn thin. Clara, on the other hand, has taken her sweet-ass time enjoying her first meal in over sixteen hours.

If that isn't bad enough, she savored every last bite with soft little moans and slow, gentle chews. If I didn't want her to know her little ploy to unravel me was working, I would have dragged her across the table and force-fed her. And no, I'm not referring to food.

Once the last smidgen of avocado is smeared off Clara's plate and popped into her mouth, I seize her wrist and yank her across the table. A limited-edition hearty giggle topples from her mouth and jingles through my ears.

Her laughter transforms into a throaty moan when her new straddled position has her feeling the thickness of my cock. Any defiance her eyes have been wearing the past ten minutes fades into the horizon when I pull my shirt over her head and discard it on the floor. Her eyes grow darker, switching from an icy blue to the color of a dark ocean. I wait for her to speak, to put up a protest about me stripping her bare without first seeking permission. Not a word seeps from her lips.

The voluptuous swell of her chest is thrust into my face—as if she's offering them to me—when she slings her arms around my shoulders and draws in nearer. I connect my eyes with hers before taking one of her taut pink nipples into my mouth. A hiss parts her lips when I swirl my tongue around her tweaked bud.

"Brax..."

Fuck, I love the way she says my name.

As one of my hands moves to secure a handful of her curvy ass, the other cups her spare breast. The tightness of her nipples firms as my mouth and fingers work her at a chaotic pace, eliciting more purring moans. My cock stirs, loving her hearty moans but hating the constraint of my jeans.

Like she can hear the silent protests of my cock, Clara slides her hand underneath my shirt and fiddles with the button on my jeans. Her throaty moans turn into a feral groan when her fumbling movements are unable to unclasp the fastener. A chair scraping across the wooden floor thunders through the room when I abruptly push my chair away from the table. I feel her smile against my lips when I undo the button of my jeans and slide down the zipper. A deep growl vibrates through my mouth as she slips her hand inside my jeans to stroke my cock.

Clara pulls her lips away from mine and stares down at me, her eyes sparkling bright, her lips swollen from our kiss. For a woman who protects her heart with an iron fist, she's open, vulnerable, and utterly unguarded. She's exposing sides to her I've hoped to see but have never witnessed. She holds my gaze as she speeds up her strokes, her focus solely devoted to taking me to the brink of ecstasy.

Her affectionate—almost loving—gaze has my chase to climax strengthening and my heart swelling. Every minute I spend in her presence makes me more beguiled by her. And from the doting blaze sparking Clara's arctic-blue eyes, I'd say I'm not the only one becoming entranced.

When the shriek of my landline sounds into her ears, Clara's strokes halt, her head snapping to the side. I ignore the interruption, not willing to harness my desire to claim her any longer. I bite down on her nipple before jerking my hips upward, trying to recapture her devotion.

My plans go to shit when a deep voice sounds over my answering machine. "Brax, it is Daniel from Caramine Care. Don't panic, but your grandma took a turn this afternoon..."

CHAPTER TWENTY-ONE

The heavy stomps of my boots bounce off the walls and cluster in my ears as I stride down the narrow corridor of Caramine Care. My heart is thrashing in my chest, still panicked about my earlier phone call with Daniel. Although he downplayed the seriousness of the situation, I've still arrived at Caramine Care within twenty minutes of his call. My grandmother means the world to me. She's the woman who raised me, and the woman who owns a vast majority of my heart. *All but the little snippet enlarging to accommodate Clara.*

The instant Daniel's message sounded through Clara's ears, she slid off my lap and secured my shirt off the floor. She stood at my side biting her nails as I returned Daniel's call. I didn't need to speak for her to know the urgency of the situation. The concerned expression on my face told the whole story. I was gutted.

Although Daniel assured me my grandmother was comfortable and resting, I knew the twisted feeling in my stomach wouldn't settle until I saw it with my own eyes. That sick feeling spread from my stomach to my heart when I suggested that Clara come with me. I tried to smother the panic in her eyes by pretending it wasn't about her meeting my grandma, that it was just killing two birds with one stone. She could visit her friend while I checked on my grandmother's condition. The soulless gaze that filled Clara's eyes the night she was mugged returned stronger than ever.

She blinked back tears before mumbling, "Friend? What friend?"

Her chin quivered, exposing she knew exactly who I was referring to. Deciding to play stupid, I said, "The person you were visiting the day I bumped into you at Caramine Care."

Any walls I crumbled between Clara and me the past twenty-four hours reformed before my very eyes. She took a stumbling step backward, her retreating strides only stopping when she crashed into the kitchen counter.

"I can't visit her today," she mumbled, her voice the weakest I'd heard. "I can only visit her the first Sunday of the month. It's not the first Sunday of the month."

"Visiting hours are whenever you want them to be," I replied, my eyes drifting between her haunted ones. "You don't have to stick to a schedule."

Worry churns in my stomach when her pleading eyes stare into mine, begging for me to drop it. Her face is ashen, and her eyes are pained. I draw in a deep breath before briefly nodding my head. Relief fills Clara's eyes. Although I want her to open up to me, I know if I push her too much, her retreating steps will reach my front door. Willing to do anything to ensure she will still be at my apartment when I return from visiting my grandmother, I simply drop the conversation and act like I can't smell the fear oozing from her pores.

It is a fucking hard feat.

My grandma's rheumy eyes lift to the door when a creak announces my arrival. She sighs softly before shifting her gaze to the window illuminating her room with an orange hue from the afternoon sun beaming inside. My brows tack together when Penny—the nurse my grandma tried to set me up with—exits the bathroom adjoining my grandmother's room.

Penny smiles a greeting as she saunters to my grandmother's bedside. Any concerns about my grandma conjuring up a ruse to force Penny and me together dampen when my eyes zoom in on a bruise on my grandma's wrist while Penny carefully checks her pulse.

After completing a set of observations on my grandmother, Penny mutters something quietly into her ear before gesturing to talk to me in the corridor. I lift my index finger in the air, requesting a minute. When Penny enters the hallway, I walk to my grandma. The twisted, sick feeling in my stomach intensifies when my eyes zoom in on a bruise on her right cheek.

Being mindful not to touch her bruise, I press a quick kiss onto her cheek before muttering, "I'll be back in a minute."

When my grandma's gaze remains on the window, I spin on my heels and make my way into the hall. I cross my arms in front of my chest, hiding the shake of my hands before asking, "Is she okay? What exactly happened?"

Penny locks her green eyes on me. "We're not exactly sure. Your grandma is a very *spirited* woman—"

"Stubborn would be a more appropriate word," I interrupt, mumbling.

Penny smiles softly. "We believe she took a tumble in the bathroom a couple of hours ago."

My heart beats triple time. "Hours ago?" The shortness of my reply doesn't hide my anger.

Penny nods. "Yes. We only discovered the incident when another resident arrived at her room for an afternoon game of gin."

"I thought you had protocol for stuff like this? Isn't there an aide button installed in her bathroom?" I gesture my hand to my grandma's door.

"Yes, there is. Grace refused to use it."

I run my hand over the stubble on my chin. I shouldn't have expected a different reply. My grandmother is so determined not to grow old gracefully. She refuses to use any device with the stigma of age attached to it. Her phone? The latest fandangle device Hunter could design. Her watch? A brand spanking new Apple Watch. No, I'm not kidding. The day I see my grandma shuffling behind a walker will be the day I announce I'm never tattooing again. It will *never* have a chance of happening.

Penny brushes her hand across my forearm. "Go easy on her. She's still a little fragile after being informed her care is being upgraded from minimum to high." My personal bubble pops when she takes a step closer to me. "We would really appreciate it if you could talk to your grandma about the possibility of having some grab bars installed in her bathroom."

I jerk my chin up. "Yeah, I'll have a talk with her now." I shrug my shoulders. "I don't know what good it will do, but I'll give it my best shot. Thanks, Penny, for all your help."

"No worries," she replies, her voice low and throaty. "If you need anything, Brax, anything at all, don't hesitate to call me."

My brow arches. Even in the seriousness of my visit, there's no way in hell I could miss the sexual ambiguity hidden in her statement. It is like seeing a pair of tits on a bull—obvious and shocking. Although Penny is no doubt beautiful, my cock didn't stir the slightest from her offer. Not even a twinge. Twenty-four hours ago,

I would have been panicked my cock was broken, whereas now, I'm beyond ecstatic it wasn't riveted by Penny's offer.

My cock only has one blonde on its radar.

Penny isn't her.

After bidding farewell to Penny with a dip of my chin, I amble into my grandma's room. She tries to maintain an irritated attitude, but her composure slips the instant I sit in the reclining chair next to her bed. She quirks her vibrant, red-painted lips as her world-assessing eyes bore into mine. My brow cocks when she inhales a big, undignified whiff through her nostrils. Her eyes widen as they bounce between mine.

Before I can ask what her odd behavior is about, she blurts out, "Joy by Jean Patou."

I stare at her, shocked and confused.

"The smell of the perfume on your clothes. It is Joy by Jean Patou." She inhales a quick breath, her expression astounded. "The last time I smelled that scent was when you came to visit me months ago. When you were in my room with Clara McGregor."

I move my lips, preparing to speak. My words become trapped in my throat when my grandma cuts them off with a fierce glare.

"Don't think you're too big for me to take over my knee, young man. I may be half your size, but that won't stop me from punishing a liar."

I wave my hands in front of my body, calming the dragon. "I wasn't planning on lying," I mutter. I'm not that stupid. I have no doubt she'd spank my ass if I were ever caught lying to her. Seventy-eight or not.

"I was just going to say we aren't here to discuss why I smell like women's perfume..." I won't lie, I'm grinning like the Cheshire cat at the fact I smell like Clara, "... we are here about your turn."

"Turn, ha!" she says, spitting her words off her tongue in a malicious snarl. "The only thing that is going to have a turn is your backside when I give it a good walloping before marching you right out that door."

Her eyes snap to mine when I mumble, "Do I need to start scrutinizing your reading material? What's with your sudden fascination with spankings?"

She tries to keep her eyes stern, but the corners of her mouth tugging into a lewd smirk gives away her real composure. *There's the grandma I know and love.*

After releasing a deep sigh, she mutters, "I had a little tumble."

Scooting across the cool leather, I sit on the edge of my seat. "Have you been feeling unwell? Dizzy?"

A heavy line of worry indents her forehead before she mumbles, "A little."

I try to hold in my growl. I fail.

"Only a little bit. Nothing to worry anyone about. I'm fine. Look at me," she babbles, gesturing her hand down the front of her body.

In her head, she believes she's gesturing to a twenty-something-year-old female, but all I see is a little old lady who hates the idea of getting old. I'm all for enjoying every day life gives you, but that doesn't mean I want to see her getting hurt for being too stubborn to admit she isn't as young as she once was. Her fall could be the result of something life-threatening or as simple as a low blood-sugar count, but with her refusal to acknowledge she needs help, we'll never know.

Like she can read my thoughts, she says, "I'll have a blood test... on one condition." She connects her glistening baby blues with my eyes. "You have to tell me every detail as to why you have arrived at my room smelling like Clara McGregor."

I arch my brow. "Every detail?"

"Every. *Sordid.* Detail," she replies, her voice slow and calculated. "It couldn't be any worse than the books I've been reading," she adds on with a cheeky wink.

Forty-five minutes later, I'm leaving my grandmother's room with a less heavy heart but a more twisted stomach. Although I kept my half of our discussion on a clean and even playing field, my grandmother threw out curveball after curveball. It is lucky my grandfather passed away six years ago, or I would have never been able to look him in the eye. The only good thing about being told stories that will give a grown man nightmares is that my discussion not only has my grandmother agreeing to have the blood workup Penny requested, she will allow them to install a grab bar next to the toilet and in the shower. It isn't because she needs them. It is for any 'visitors' she may have. That statement had me vomiting in my mouth for the eleventh time in the past half an hour.

Slipping out of my grandma's room, I take a left instead of my usual right. I need to ask Daniel to have the railings installed in my grandmother's bathroom before she can change her mind. My quick strides slow to a snail's pace when I walk past the room I spotted Clara exiting nearly six months ago. I'm taken aback when my eyes zoom in on a young woman lying still in the bed. I was expecting to see someone close to my grandmother's age, not a lady in her early twenties.

My bewilderment grows when my eyes scan her room. From the technical equipment attached to the motionless female, I can easily derive she's on a life-support machine. And from her frail and withered body, I'd say she has been on it for a long time. My heart pains for the young woman. It is terrible to see someone who should be in the prime of their life more fragile than my grandmother.

My eyes drift away from the young brunette when my name is called from a deep voice on my left. Daniel is standing halfway between his office door and the corridor. Noticing my stunned expression, he pushes off his feet and heads my way.

"I was unaware you knew Sophia," he says, nudging his head to the door I'm standing next to.

"I don't," I reply with a brisk shake of my head.

Daniel seems surprised by my admission. I guess it would appear odd that I've stopped to gawk into Sophia's room without knowing who she is. The only reason I stopped was because I remembered Clara's rattled composure the day I bumped into her in this very hallway. Now her demeanor that day makes sense. I don't even know Sophia, and I hate that she's going through this. I can only imagine how hard it is for Clara.

I swing my eyes to Daniel. "Her last name isn't McGregor, is it?"

I'm filled with relief when he briefly shakes his head. "No. Her name is Sophia Remy."

My brows stitch as I try to recall the last time I heard that name.

When the reality slams into me, the twisting of my stomach extends to my heart.

CHAPTER TWENTY-TWO

"Sorry," I apologize when my thoughtlessness has me crashing into a gentleman exiting the foyer of my apartment building in a hurry.

A fit-looking man in his mid-thirties with a military-style haircut dips his chin—accepting my apology—before increasing his pace. His brisk speed from the awning of my apartment building to a steel gray Audi parked at the curb a few spots up from the underground garage exposes he's carrying a semi-automatic weapon. My brows scrunch when I notice the burly man sitting behind the steering wheel of the Audi also has the same style haircut and is wearing an identical suit.

I thought Ryan was holding off on putting an undercover unit on Clara?

Shrugging off my confusion, I adjust the bag of groceries I collected from the corner store and amble into the foyer. My mind has been working overtime since I left Caramine Care two hours ago. It could be a coincidence, but deep down in my soul, I know Sophia is somehow connected with Clara's necklace. It isn't only my intuition telling me this is the case, it is the fact Daniel advised me Sophia is Clara's age, and before she was transferred to Caramine Care, she lived in Hopeton, the town where Clara grew up.

Just remembering the bleak look in Clara's eyes when she asked about the possibility of her necklace being returned had me spending the last two hours scouring every pawn shop within a twenty-mile radius of Ravenshoe. Unfortunately, Clara's necklace hasn't been seen. Since the mugging was less than forty-eight hours ago, the local brokers believe it will be a few more weeks before it surfaces. I don't care if it takes me weeks, months, or years, I won't stop searching until I find it.

When I walk into my apartment, I'm confronted with silence.

I don't fucking like it.

I place the bag of groceries on the kitchen counter and climb the stairs to my loft. Although my room still smells like Clara, it is empty.

I don't fucking like it.

I check the laundry room, the bathroom, and the patio attached to my living area. Clara is nowhere to be seen.

I don't fucking like it.

I hated leaving her alone, but she assured me she could take care of herself and didn't need a babysitter. When I failed to see any untruth in her eyes, I left, expecting her to still be here when I returned.

Obviously, I can't read Clara as well as I thought I could.

I hate that more than anything.

The seething rage bubbling my blood simmers to a slow boil when I catch the quickest giggle. I stop frozen in my tracks and crank my neck. It is only faint, but there's no doubting who the laugh belongs to. *Clara.*

My eyes rocket to my bedroom when the soft babbling of a

conversation sounds above me. Once my eyes travel from the living room to the loft, I notice the door to my rooftop garden has been cranked open.

The quiet hum of dialogue between two female voices grows louder as I climb the staircase. From the high tone and limited vocabulary of the second voice, I can easily tell it belongs to a child.

I hit the stoop of the stairs when a female child's voice asks, "Are you staying here long?"

I round the corner to discover my eleven-year-old neighbor, Clementine, sitting next to Clara on the frayed double couch. They have two half-full wine glasses of soda and a bowl of plain chips sitting on a makeshift pallet coffee table.

Clara finishes twisting a piece of Clementine's thick wavy hair into a fancy braided design before she answers Clementine's question, "I don't know. Brax said it could be days or even weeks before I can go home." A grin curls on my lips when a mask of worry slips over Clara's face during the last half of her sentence.

Clementine huffs and crosses her arms over her chest. After placing a tie in Clementine's hair, Clara adjusts her position so she's facing the girl. "Don't you want me to stay? I thought we were having fun today?"

Clementine's shoulders hunch forward. "It isn't that. It's just... just... you shouldn't get comfortable. You won't be here for long."

"Oh," Clara breathes out heavily at the same time I mutter, "Are you trying to scare off my girl, Clementine?"

Clara and Clementine's heads snap to mine in sync. Clementine smiles a cheeky grin I've seen numerous times over the past six months. It's usually worn when she's creating mischief for Ms. Hartler who lives in apartment 2B.

After shaking her head, denying my claim, Clementine turns her eyes back to Clara. Clara slants her head to the side and stares at me like she's shocked to see me standing on my rooftop garden. Her pupils are wide, and her plump nude lips are parted.

I need those lips on me. Anywhere.

"Clementine, I think I hear your momma calling you."

Clementine springs up from the sofa. "Really?" She angles her head to the side and hoists her ear into the air. "I don't hear anything."

Like the stars aligning in the sky, the faint holler of Mrs. Daphne bellows up the stairwell. If I were a religious man, I'd send thanks to God. Since I'm not, I simply thank my lucky stars.

Clementine's eyes bug before she rushes to the door. Her brisk pace slows when I say, "Clementine."

When she cranks her neck back to peer at me, I hold out the packet of Mars bars I'm clutching in my hand for her. She smiles a broad grin before she crosses the space between us. Her steps are so fast, she reaches me in less than a heartbeat. I learned early on in life that candy is my best ally in keeping any female in my life happy.

If only Clara were a fan of sugar.

Still grinning, Clementine snatches the chocolates out of my hand and presses a quick kiss to my cheek. My brow cocks over her audacity. She's always been a little showy around her friends from school, but she's never taken it this far before.

She must be trying to impress Clara.

Clementine's girly giggle is only just heard over the stomping of her feet as she gallops down the stairwell. When the front door slams shut not even two seconds later, I drift my eyes back to Clara. Her expression is even more shocked than it was earlier.

In a nanosecond, she switches the appearance of her face, changing it from stunned to forthright. "How's your grandma?"

I smile. "She's good. A hurricane couldn't slow her down."

Clara releases a deep breath before a rare and genuine smile etches onto her mouth. I'm in trouble with this woman. I've only been away from her a little over three hours, and she hasn't left my mind. I knew the day she walked back into Inked she'd be trouble. I just had no clue the type of trouble she would cause.

Clara curls her feet under her bottom when I take the empty seat next to her. "Tread carefully with Clementine, Brax," she mumbles while brushing her hand over the sticky lip gloss stain Clementine left on my cheek. "She's too young to understand the repercussions of chasing an unattainable man." Her voice comes in barely a whisper. "I wish someone had given me the same warning."

"Isaac?" I ask, even knowing I could be throwing the first grenade in World War III.

Like I could be any more shocked the past twenty-four hours, Clara surprises me again by simply nodding. "Despite what everyone thinks, I did care for Isaac... a lot."

I nod. The fact she was going to get his name inked on her hip is a pretty compelling point.

"But I didn't care about him because of his money or power. I just thought if two people with half a heart joined, they could have one whole heart again." Her voice is so weak my ears strain to hear what she's saying. "I just never considered his heart would heal on its own."

Seizing her wrists, I pull her to sit side-saddle on my lap. I fight the desire to bang my chest like King Kong when she doesn't cite a single protest.

Now is not the time for cockiness.

Clara's pained eyes lift to mine when I say, "A broken heart never mends, but it can swell to accommodate more people in it. You don't have to live your life unloved because your heart was once broken. You just have to be willing to increase its size to include the new people in your life. The people who care for you. Guys like me."

Diesel and Ryan are right. I'm gone for this woman. Completely and utterly fucking done.

The hurt in Clara's eyes softens as she quietly mumbles, "Do you really think that's true?"

I nod without pause for consideration. My heart swells when she cups the edge of my jaw and smiles a knockout grin. Her eyes bounce between mine. She looks like she wants to say something but not a word spills from her lips.

After twisting a lock of hair behind her ear, I say, "I saw Sophia today."

Clara stiffens, and her eyes widen, but she tries to keep the expression on her face neutral. She fails. "How is she? Is she okay?"

"She's good. Daniel said they have had a couple of recent developments the past month he looks forward to discussing with you at your next visit."

Clara's pupils dilate more. "Recent developments?"

I smile before nodding. "She moved her toes last week."

She sucks in a deep breath as her eyes brim with tears.

"She has also been recorded taking unaided breaths."

Tears stream down Clara's cheeks as her hand clamps over her mouth.

"These are good signs, Princess."

"I know," she replies, her tone weak. "These are happy tears."

She takes a few moments to settle her composure before locking her red-rimmed eyes with mine. My heart rate kicks into overdrive, but I remain quiet, praying she will open up to me.

"Sophia is Remy's little sister. Remy was my first serious boyfriend. His real name was Victor Remy the Second, but everyone called him Remy. Although I was only a teen, I loved him. Truly I did."

Her eyes flare as a range of emotions flash through them.

"But my father hated Remy. Remy thought it was because his parents were divorced, but that wasn't the real reason my dad hated him. It was because he didn't have any money, and he lived on the wrong side of town. Remy begged me for months to leave my family and go live with him, but I couldn't. He could barely afford to live as it was, let alone take care of me, and since I was under eighteen, I had no way of supporting myself."

Her eyes gloss over. "Remy gave me my pendant the night of my eighteenth birthday party. The night was going surprisingly well. Although Remy looked slightly out of place in a pair of ripped jeans when all the other male attendees were wearing dress pants, but I didn't care. I loved him for who he was, not what he wore."

She takes a breath before continuing, "I don't know exactly how it started, but Remy got into a disagreement with my father. After they flung a string of hateful words at each other, Remy dragged me out of the party. I pleaded for him to wait until my guests had left, but nothing I said made a difference. He was furious I didn't stand up for him. I wanted to... truly, I did... I just couldn't get my mouth to cooperate. I was still six days away from officially turning eighteen, so I feared the repercussion of going against the wishes of my father. Remy broke up with me because I refused to leave with him. I was devastated."

She stops talking for a moment and stares out into space. "That devastation was nothing compared to being informed he was involved in a motorbike accident three weeks later. He was killed on impact. Sophia has been on life support ever since."

Fuck! No wonder she was so scared when I threw her on my bike.

"I'm sorry, Princess. If I had known, I wouldn't have forced you onto my bike—"

My words stop when Clara places her index finger on my lips. "It's okay. I know you'd never hurt me, Brax."

I strengthen my grip around her waist but remain quiet. Just like there were no words I could say to ease Hank's pain when Derrick was killed, I have no words to offer Clara to lessen the hurt brewing in her eyes.

After removing a tear tracking down her face, Clara lifts her tear-drenched eyes to me. "Sophia's parents couldn't afford Remy's funeral, let alone Sophia's extensive medical bills, so I made a deal with the devil to ensure she was taken care of. By becoming the daughter my father wanted... an upstanding member of society who never spoke unless spoken to and did exactly as demanded... Sophia's medical expenses were paid. As the years went on, I became more and more like my father, a vindictive and callous human being with an ice heart." A painful whizz of air parts her mouth. "I thought once my father died, his hold over me would vanish. It didn't. I was too far gone by then. My heart was beyond repair."

"I don't believe that," I reply, speaking for the first time in ten minutes. "If you didn't have a heart, you wouldn't have visited Sophia every month for the past eight years. You wouldn't have used seventy percent of your salary at Inked to put toward her care expenses, and you wouldn't have tears in your eyes right now. You have a heart, Princess. A very big one. Don't let a man with wrong values ever let you think any different."

I run the back of my hand down her cheeks, removing her tears before saying, "Besides, you can always hold onto the piece of my heart you've already stolen until yours fully thaws." I aim to keep my tone cheeky, but my words come out with more sentiment than I anticipated.

When the pain in Clara's eyes eases from my statement, I'm happy for her to take the meaning any way she sees fit.

"I have a piece of your heart?"

When I nod, a true and genuine smile etches onto her mouth.

"I like the sound of that," she murmurs before resting her cheek on my chest.

A stretch of silence passes between us. It isn't awkward. It is comforting and necessary, and I could stay like this for hours. I don't know why, but I've had an overwhelming desire to protect Clara since the day I met her. Finding out she has suffered a loss has strengthened my desire to protect her, but it isn't the only reason I'd happily sit here for hours with her in my arms. In some ways, this type of affection is more intimate than the moment we shared in the shower this morning.

Don't construe my statement the wrong way. Our time together this morning was out of this fucking world—better than I could have ever predicted—but it's during the quiet times like this that I get to see other sides of Clara, the ones not governed by her libido.

Her outward appearance gives the illusion that she's a woman with a frozen heart, but I realize now that isn't the case. She's protecting her heart so fiercely because she's afraid one more knock may shatter it completely, permanently disfiguring it. And although she puts on a brave front, even a woman as headstrong as Clara doesn't want to live her life unloved, no matter how much she pretends she does.

Enough time rolls by in complete silence that the sky changes from a vibrant blue coloring to midnight black. My eyes shift away from the stars scattering in the sky to Clara when she lifts her head off my chest.

The crazy beat of her heart pounds the nape of my neck when she curls her arms around my shoulders. "Kiss me, Brax," she mutters, fluttering my lips with her warm breath. "I've missed your lips on mine."

My lips tug high, loving that she's becoming so forthright with her desires.

"You wish is my command, Princess."

Her mouth tastes sweet and spicy. Sweet from the soda she was sharing with Clementine and spicy from the flavor of the potato chips they were consuming. Unlike our previous kisses, this time, I control the pace. I don't mind handing over the reins on an odd occasion, but I want to prove to Clara what I said was true. Loss, heartache, and betrayal are not something you simply get over. You just have no choice but to move on and live the best life you can. Although I hate the idea of another man holding a portion of Clara's heart, she isn't sitting in his lap, nibbling on his lips. She's here with me. And if I have it my way, that isn't going to change anytime soon.

After I'm happy I've sampled every portion of her mouth, I pull my lips away from Clara. I run my thumb over the curve of her top lip before locking my eyes with hers. My chest swells, beyond smug, her gaze is hazy and brimmed with lust. I tilt my head to the side and stare deeper when sparks of the unidentifiable glint she was wearing this morning resurfaces.

It brightens before she mutters, "Make love to me, Brax."

CHAPTER TWENTY-THREE

Keeping her entrancing eyes connected with mine, Clara tugs the hem of her shirt out of her skirt then pulls it over her head. My nostrils flare, relishing the rich scent of the floral smell floating in the air. The generous swell of her breasts falls gently to her chest when she slips her hand around her back and unfastens her bra.

I'm not a man who usually makes love. I fuck—*and I fuck hard*—but I am going to make love to this woman. Not only to prove what I said was true but also to show her what she means to me.

A husky purr escapes Clara's parted lips when I cup her breast and take her rosy-pink nipple into my mouth. The muscles in my stomach tense when she slips her hand under my shirt and runs her fingernails over the bumps of my abs. My cock throbs against my zipper, dying to be immersed in her silky softness. It's had an unquenchable desire to claim her as mine from the moment I laid my eyes on her, but his pleas must wait. Clara asked me to make love to her, and I'm a man who keeps my word.

I release her breast from my mouth with a little pop, the bud of her nipple hardening when I blow hot air onto it. My plans to take it slow go to shit when she rubs herself along the hardness in my jeans.

"Oh God, Brax, please touch me. I need you to touch me."

Her soft pleas strengthen when I slip my hand between our bodies. I groan when I feel how wet she is. She's saturated.

My rough moans are captured by Clara's mouth when she covers her lips over mine and kisses me. She kisses me with so much heat and passion that before I know it, she's lying beneath me on the two-seater couch, and I'm grinding up against her.

Slow, Brax. Slow.

Ignoring the protest of my cock, I pull back and rest my backside on the balls of my feet. Clara's skirt is bunched around her waist, and her chest is thrusting up and down as she stares up at me with wild, crazy eyes. Smiling a grin I've never seen, she slides down the zipper on her skirt and glides it down her thighs. It joins her shirt on the concrete floor not even two seconds later. My eyes drink in every inch of her glorious skin as I unbutton my jeans and discard them next to her clothes.

The full moon bounces off her smooth white skin, illuminating her in a silvery glow. If I didn't already know she was a princess, I would have sworn an angel had fallen from the sky. *My angel.* I drop to my knees and drag her ass to the edge of the couch. Her giggles trail off to a moan when I spread her open with my thumbs and run my tongue along the seam of her glistening pussy, absorbing the wetness shimmering on her pretty pink lips.

"Oh," Clara garbles when I wrap my lips around the swollen bud of her clit and suck softly.

Her thighs loosen as I devour her sweet pussy in slow and tantalizing licks and nips. I work her into a frenzy at a leisured pace, making love to her with my tongue instead of my cock. My slow speed is drawing out her race to climax, but I want her to feel every stroke of my tongue, every nip of my teeth, and every suck I inflict. I don't ever want her to forget the first time we made love, so if it takes me four hours to get there, it takes me four hours.

"Brax, yes. It feels so good. Oh, so, so good."

Clara's throaty moans have me dying to slide my fingers inside her and pump her until she comes screaming my name. The only thing stopping me is her writhing against me. She's rocking her hips in a similar rhythm as my tongue, proving she wants to go at a slow and controlled pace.

I delve my tongue in and out of her before sliding it up to her clit and sucking down. Any concerns about my moderate tempo lessening Clara's pleasure shifts to the back of my mind when a long, quivering orgasm shimmers through her body. Her back arches, and a cock-twitching moan spills from her O-formed lips as every fine hair on her body bristles. Pre-cum seeps into the material of my briefs when her juices gush onto my tongue.

God, she tastes good. So fucking good.

I'm rock hard, I swear my cock is about to burst out of my briefs. He'd even go at a leisured pace if it guaranteed him the opportunity to be wrapped in her warmth.

After guiding Clara down from her prolonged climax, I stand from my kneeled position. I scrape my hand over my mouth, removing the residual of her arousal before shoving my briefs down my thighs. My cock thickens as Clara inhales a sharp breath when it springs free from its tight restraints. I love the shocked reaction she gets every time she sees my cock.

While running my hand up and down my shaft, I lock my eyes with Clara. Even though her eyes are beaming with lust, I can't miss the glint they were wearing earlier. Except now, I can recognize that gleam. It isn't lust, feistiness, or a woman being ruled by her libido. It is the glint of a woman who wants to be loved—to be cherished.

I know just the man for the job.

The gleam in her eyes brightens when I nestle the crown of my cock between her wet heat. After lubing myself with her wetness, I slowly inch inside her.

Fuck! She feels so good.

Tight.

Wet.

Mine.

If I weren't set on ensuring the glint in her eyes never leaves, I could come right now. That is how good she feels. Instead, I grit my teeth and sink in deeper.

A curse word seeps from my lips when Clara scrambles backward, withdrawing my throbbing cock from her slicked pussy. "Condom," she mutters breathlessly. "You need a condom."

Placing my hands under her ass, I drag her back to me. "I don't need a condom." I push the first inch of my cock back inside her. "I don't mess with my crew, I don't bring girls to my apartment, I don't fuck without a condom, and I don't make love."

Clara's massively dilated eyes bounce between mine.

"With anyone *but* you," I mutter, inching further inside her.

I fight the urge to thrust into her in one quick motion when her pussy protests the intrusion.

"Open up for me, Princess. You've got to let me in, or I'll hurt you." *And there's no fucking chance of that happening.*

Clara nods before doing as asked. Her pussy ripples around me, sucking me in deeper as she swivels her hips to loosen their tight hold.

"That's it, Princess. Just like that."

Her teeth gnaw on her bottom lip when I take her to the root of my cock. I still my movements, waiting for her body to adjust to the intrusion before drawing back out. Clara's eyes pop open and lift to mine when I fully withdraw my cock. Before she can protest, I thrust back in at the same leisurely speed.

I rock in and out of her over and over again until her husky moans are heard over the mad beat of my heart shrilling in my ears. Although my speed is slow for a guy who is used to fucking, it isn't slow enough to stave off my desire to come. She feels too good to ever scare off that urge.

Her French-tipped nails dig into my ass when she adjusts the tilt of her hips so I can take her deeper. Her hips rock faster with every stroke I make. I try to hold back, to keep the slow pace she requested, but the fight becomes unwinnable when she mutters, "Please, Brax. More. I need more."

Banding my arms around her sweat-slicked waist, I roll us over so she's straddled on top of me. "Take what you need, Princess."

And she does.

Her nails dig into my chest as she rises and falls above me in a tempo not fast enough to be classed as fucking but a few notches faster than my previous speed. I slither my hand down her damp body to find her pulsating clit. Her pussy grows wetter when I roll the pad of my thumb over the throbbing bud.

"Oh God. You feel so good, Brax. I'm going to come," she purrs moments later.

"Give it to me, Princess. I want it all. Give me everything you have." I cup one of her bouncing breasts in my hand to tweak her nipple at the same speed I'm flicking her clit.

Her thighs quiver as her breaths come faster. She does another four rises and falls before she shatters like glass hitting a concrete floor. Her pussy milks my cock, my name spilling from her lips in a breathless, erotic scream.

"Brax. Oh..."

I wait for the shakes of her body to settle before gripping her hips with my hands and guiding her back up and down my thickened shaft. I jerk my hips to arouse her clit with my pubic bone as my cock consumes her clenching slit.

Dropping my eyes from her spent face, I lock them with an image I'll never forget. Her pussy is red and swollen, but nothing can take away from the sight of my cock pumping into her glistening mound in long, lengthened strokes.

The harsh pants of her pleasurable moans spur on my desire to come. My cock throbs as my race to climax intensifies.

"Give it to me, Brax," Clara quotes, her voice husky. "I want every drop."

Now I'm even harder.

Fuck, she's gorgeous.

Her tousled hair falling around her shoulders, her lips puffy and raw from our kisses, and her eyes sparked with so much life, I'm afraid she'll run out of room for anything else.

I thrust into her again, and again, and again until the walls of her pussy clench around my cock for a second time. She rides the intensity of her climax by slamming down on me so hard, her ass slapping my balls booms into my ears. Her legs shake, her words come out garbled, and her bucks turn wild.

"Fuck, Princess, you're strangling my cock with your greedy sucks," I roar, my words echoing into the quiet night. I jerk my hips up, my desire to come overwhelming me. "I'm going to come so fucking hard."

And I do.

I take my cock to the very base—giving her my all—before the hot thickness of my seed jets out of my throbbing crown.

"You feel that, Princess? Me inside you. Marking you. Claiming you with my cum."

Clara purrs like a little kitten as her pussy ripples around me, milking every drop of my cum while the wetness of her slit coats my balls. "I want it all. Give me all of it."

"You've got it all, Princess. Every fucking drop. Every fucking inch." I thrust in and out of her, smearing the walls of her pussy with my cum. "Not just my cum. You've got all of me. You hear me, Princess? I'm not ever giving this up. Tell me you understand what I'm saying?" I mutter, still pumping into her, my cock unable to stop now he has *finally* claimed the pussy he's been yearning for the past six months.

I come for the second time when Clara says, "I hear you, Brax. I hear every word you're saying."

CHAPTER TWENTY-FOUR

Propping myself on my arm, I adjust my eyes to the darkness of my bedroom. My eyes drop when the same pained murmur I heard thirty seconds ago sounds through my ears again. With the moonlight shining into my room from the rooftop window, I can only make out some of the features of Clara's face. Although disoriented from the darkness, I can't miss the heavy set of wrinkles lining her forehead. She looks scared and frightened.

When she whimpers again, reality smacks into me. She's having a nightmare.

I nudge her gently with my arm to wake her. As she claws her way through the dark pit of a nightmare, her skin is clammy and warm. Guilt riddles me, hating that her safety was compromised so much it is hindering her sleep. Her face contorts as she pulls her legs up into a tight ball. I put a little oomph into my next nudge. This time, she jerks awake, springing to a half-seated position.

Remorse and maybe a twinge of jealousy twist my stomach when she painfully whispers, "Remy."

I lean over and switch on the bedside lamp when the heavy pants of her breath increase. She's gasping for air so fiercely, I'm afraid she's about to hyperventilate.

"It's okay, Princess. You're okay," I soothe when her massively dilated eyes filter around my room. She looks both lost and confused. "You're in the bedroom of my loft."

Her head snaps to the side. Confusion and another look I can't work out mars her beautiful face. The jealousy squeezing my heart eases when she feebly mumbles, "Brax," under her breath before she throws her arms around my shoulders. I catch the remaining tears from her nightmare with my thumbs before drawing her into my chest.

Several minutes pass with me just holding her. She gathers her wits while I give into the fact that as much as I'm falling for Clara, I still have so much to learn about her. I was certain her nightmare was from her mugging. Now, I'm not so sure. It isn't just her mention of Remy that has me backpedaling on my initial assumption, it's the fact her eyes lost the glint I worked so hard to put in there the last forty-eight hours.

In all honesty, although Clara said she heard what I was saying last night, I was still expecting her to flee once she came down from cloud nine. I said what I did as I knew I had her in a moment of weakness, but she continues to shock me more and more every day. Not only did she not flee, we spent all day yesterday like a normal couple. We cooked breakfast together before making love in the shower. We ate lunch on the patio of my apartment before we fucked like rabbits on the couch in my living room, and we ordered takeout for dinner before we... yeah, you guessed it, we fooled around in my bed. My cock has spent the last twenty-four hours in heaven—Clara's sweeter-than-nectar pussy heaven.

Even though I've loved our vigorous sexual activities the past forty-eight hours, I also cherish moments like this. I love being the man Clara can find comfort with. And I'm as happy as a pig in mud that she trusts me enough to spill her deepest and darkest secrets without fear of rejection.

These are the moments that will tether us closer together, the moments that will see us growing into a strong, unbreakable couple, and the moments that have me falling in love with her even more.

S everal hours later, I wake up startled. It's not a nightmare waking me from my sleeping state, it is the alarm on my phone hollering loudly. Careful not to wake Clara, I slip out of bed, snag my phone off the drawers, and step onto the front patio of my apartment. I squint as my eyes adjust to the brightness of the mid-morning sun before dropping them to my phone. Reality smacks into me hard and fast when I realize why my phone was hollering. It is Tuesday. *Dammit!*

I was so wrapped up in Clara, it feels like months have passed instead of just two measly days. While scraping my hand over the stubble on my chin, I dial a number I know by heart.

Diesel answers on the first ring. "No closer to finding the third assailant yet, but we have our ears to the ground."

A car whizzing by sounds through the phone, proving he's already out looking.

"Ryan called yesterday. He got some grainy footage of the men leaving the alleyway from an ATM camera. He's going to see if Hunter can clean up the image enough to run it through facial recognition." My voice is gruff from just waking up. "Give Ryan a few days to see what he can come up with. If he doesn't get any closer, I'll call in a few favors."

Although Diesel doesn't reply, I can imagine him nodding.

"Talking about favors, I have one I need to ask."

"Anything," Diesel replies without a smidge of hesitation.

"Clara is doing well, but I don't think it'd be wise to throw her back into Inked so soon after her attack."

"That's understandable. We held down the fort months before she arrived, so I'm sure we can keep things going until she feels comfortable returning."

"I also don't want to leave her alone," I add on quickly.

Diesel is so quiet I can hear the smile etching onto his face.

"Do you think you could handle taking the reins at Inked for a couple of days?"

Diesel chuckles. "I hope so, considering I already rescheduled your appointments."

I smile. I shouldn't be surprised. He is always one step ahead of the pack.

"Call me if anything urgent comes up."

"Call me if you want a real man to show you how it's done," he replies, chuckling.

Laughing, I pull the phone away from my ear, but I return it when Diesel calls my name. "Yeah?"

"Give her an extra pound just for me," he adds, since his first tease didn't have the effect he was aiming for.

His hearty chuckle is barely audible over my furious growl. My attention is diverted from ways of seeking my revenge on him when a car honking shrieks through my ears, closely followed by crunching metal. When I walk to the end of my patio, I spot the cause of the commotion. A white sedan has run up the backside of a black truck.

I'm about to call for help when I notice a steel gray Audi parked at the curb. It is the same steel gray Audi I spotted two days ago when I returned from visiting my grandmother. A sense of dread washes over me when the occupants of the car fail to exit their vehicle to aid the people involved in the crash.

Shouldn't a police officer's priority always be helping civilians?

I stand out on my patio, watching the scene unfold for the next twenty minutes. Not once do the suit-clad men in the silver Audi step out of their vehicle. Not even when the female driver of the sedan stumbles out of her car with a massive gash on her forehead.

No longer able to restrain my curiosity, my finger slides across the screen of my phone before I punch in a well-used number.

"Ryan Carter."

"Ryan, it's Brax." My voice is gritty as concern strangles my vocal cords. "I thought you were holding off on putting a unit on Clara."

"I did," he replies with confusion in his tone. "You said you'd take care of her. Did something happen? Do you need a unit assigned?"

I grit my teeth. "No, Clara is fine. I need a favor."

Ryan delays in replying. He hates being asked a favor.

"I had my guys call you when they found two of the men who attacked Clara. That wouldn't have happened if you didn't ask me for a favor. Besides, if you can't do this, I'll call Hunter."

"Fine," he breathes out heavily, hating that I'm considering taking a non-legal approach. "What do you need?"

I adjust my position so the Audi is directly in my line of sight. "I need you to run a license plate for me…"

Two hours and thirty-nine minutes later, I'm pulling my bike into the curb of Destiny Records in Hopeton. Charity did a mighty fine job pretending she needed to speak to Clara alone for a one-on-one girl talk when she arrived at my apartment an hour ago. She was so convincing, she had Clara begging for me to give them some private time.

"Just for an hour or two," Clara pleaded, her begging eyes adding to the strength of her plea.

I acted disappointed before nodding. I'm not going to lie. A shit-eating grin etched on my face when I saw a petrified mask slip over Charity's face as Clara led her to my rooftop garden. Although I'll be kissing Charity's ass for the next six months, it will be worth it. The instant I discovered who the owner of the steel gray Audi was, there was no chance of ignoring my naturally ingrained protectiveness of Clara. And since she had a nightmare last night, I didn't want to leave her alone. Hence Charity's sudden desire for girl talk.

A pretty receptionist with unique yellowish-brown eyes greets me with a smile when I saunter deeper into the foyer of Destiny Records. She has a tight, fit body, luscious caramel skin, and dark, rich hair.

"Hello. Welcome to Destiny Records. How can I help you?" she greets me, her voice as absorbing as her eyes.

"I need to speak to Cormack McGregor."

The receptionist's eyes widen before she curtly nods. "I'll see if he's available."

She lifts the receiver of her phone to her ear as my eyes run around the space. Destiny Records' headquarters is an architectural wonder with large glass paneling and expensive features. The floors are inlaid with reclaimed wood, and I've spotted numerous expensive paintings lining the walls. The premise screams wealth.

Wealth Clara's brother is keeping to his greedy self.

My eyes return to the receptionist when she says, "I'm sorry, Mr. ..."

"Anderson," I fill in.

She smiles. "Anderson. Mr. McGregor is unavailable to speak with you at this time. If you'd like to make an appointment, I can check his calendar, or if you want to leave a CD, I can forward it to the creative artist team."

"I'm not a musician," I interrupt. "I'm here regarding his sister."

The receptionist's eyes bug. "Okay," she replies softly before lifting the receiver back to her ear. Her eyes shift between her desk and me as she speaks in hushed whispers. "I understand," she replies before disconnecting the call. "Is this regarding Cate or Clara?"

I arch my brow. "Does it fucking matter?"

She balks, shocked by my foul language. "Not to me, but to Mr. McGregor it does," she replies, her lips quivering.

Blood roars through my veins, thick and fast. Ignoring the security officer standing at the door of Destiny Records, I make my way down the corridor hidden behind the reception desk. The receptionist calls out for me, but I can't hear a word she's saying, too blinded by rage to hear anything.

My long strides have me walking the length of the hallway in two heart-thrashing seconds. I'm not at all surprised to spot a gold plaque with the name *Cormack McGregor* on a wide wooden door at the end of the hall.

The important people always make you come to them.

I swing open the door with brutal force at the same moment my shoulder is seized by a burly-looking security officer.

"You either leave of your own accord, or I'll throw your ass onto the curb."

"You have two seconds to get your hands off me before I show you that bad genetics won't be the cause of your ugliness. My fists will be."

Our little tousle is interrupted by a deep voice inside the office. "Let him in, Pablo."

The security officer loosens his grip on my shoulder, but he doesn't entirely remove his hand. I arch my brow and glare into his eyes. My stare is dark and brimmed with danger. When Pablo lifts his hand and takes a retreating step, I swing my eyes to my right. I don't need to see his identification to know the gentleman standing in front of me is Cormack McGregor. He's the spitting image of Clara, just a manlier version. Same wintry-blue eyes, same defined facial features, and same platinum-blond hair.

"When you look in the mirror every morning, do you feel remorse? Or are you too busy counting your millions to be worried about the safety of your little sister?"

Cormack cops my snide comment on the chin before gesturing for me to enter. I walk three steps into the room before stopping and crossing my arms in front of my chest. *I didn't come here to drink tea and eat cucumber sandwiches.*

"You have enough money that you can put a tail on your sister, but you don't care enough about her to make sure she's safe and well."

Cormack smiles. It is a pained and bitter smile. "I didn't put a tail on Clara. The men are there to ensure she is safe. I'm not a monster, Brax. I didn't send her out into the world completely alone."

I suck in a deep breath, surprised he knows my name, but my shock isn't great enough to leash my anger. "You're not a fucking monster? You're sitting in an overpriced leather chair in an office the size of most people's apartments while your little sister works at a tattoo parlor for minimum wage. You've got a fancy-ass mansion with a butler and a handful of maids while your sister is living in an apartment which is about as fancy as a crack house.

Your security team is getting around in a brand spanking new Audi for fuck's sake while your sister is driving a piece-of-shit car that is older than she is."

He attempts to interrupt me, but I continue speaking, foiling his attempts, "And while you're out eating meals worth hundreds of dollars a plate, your sister is getting jumped in a fucking alley by men wielding guns. Yeah, I guess you're right. That doesn't sound like a monster to me. It sounds like a coward."

Cormack balks as his face goes ashen. "Clara was mugged?"

I smile a conniving grin. "Yeah. All while your men probably stood by and watched it happen. What fucked-up game are you playing that you're willing to risk your sister's life?"

"It isn't a game. It is a lesson." His words come out weak like the man he is.

"A tough fucking lesson."

"I never wanted Clara to get hurt. I wanted to teach her not to take everything for granted. To be grateful for the life she was born into. I never wanted her to get injured. That is why I put the security detail on her. But every time they were about to step in, you were one step ahead of them. The night she took the bus, they were following her. They were about to react when the teenage boy approached her. You beat them. When she moved into the apartment, they were going to have security installed. You beat them again. I didn't want Clara hurt, but I wanted her to be taught a lesson. I wanted her to be grateful."

"Then where the fuck were they the night she got jumped?" I shout, my loud voice ricocheting off the pristine white walls and shrilling into my ears.

Cormack's face goes paler. "I don't know, but I *will* find out. I guarantee you I will find out." He locks his remorse-riddled eyes with mine. "Is Clara okay? Is she safe?"

"Maybe you should ask her that yourself." I spin on my heels and amble down the corridor, needing to leave before I break the promise I made to Ryan.

CHAPTER TWENTY-FIVE

My brisk strides down the hallway of my apartment building slows when the vibration of my cell phone shakes in my pocket. I'm not at all surprised when I see it is a call from Ryan. When he discovered who the Audi was registered to, he pleaded for me not to take the issue any further. My consideration of his plea only lasted as long as it took for me to remember the bleak look in Clara's eyes the night she was mugged.

Ryan's pleas settled when I promised I was only going to 'talk' to Cormack man to man, not have a 'word' with him. Considering I left without a single drop of blood being shed, I kept my word. I won't lie. It was hard. The only thing that stopped me from pounding some sense into Cormack was the look of repentance in his eyes. He was genuinely horrified that Clara had been assaulted. He was so upset, he looked physically ill.

I don't have any siblings, so I can't say I comprehend Cormack's logic of wanting to teach Clara a lesson. But even without siblings, I still think he has gone about it the wrong way. Clara's life was jeopardized. That is not something I'll ever be okay with.

Swiping my finger across my phone's screen, I press it to my ear before throwing open the front door of my apartment. "Not a drop of blood was shed," I mutter, not bothering to issue a greeting.

"Have you seen Damon?"

I throw the keys for my bike onto the entryway table before answering, "No. I was set to put a couple of hours into his back tattoo later this week, but I canceled my appointments to spend more time with Clara."

Ryan's deep sigh sounds down the line.

"Why? What's up?" My lips purse when my gaze locks in on Damon's ocean-blue eyes sitting across from Clara. "Ha. You won't believe this. He's here. Did you want to talk to him?"

"Damon is at your apartment?" Ryan's words come out in a hurry.

Even though he can't see me, I jerk up my chin. "Yeah. He's here with Clara."

Feet stomping bellows down the line before Ryan yells, "I'm on my way. Keep him calm," before he disconnects the call.

A sick feeling spreads across my stomach when I drift my eyes to Clara. She's nursing the same set of eyes she wore in the alleyway the night she was mugged. Her cheeks are stained with tears, and her face is as white as a ghost.

Hot anger boils my blood. "It was him, wasn't it? The third man in the alley."

My stomach winds all the way up to my throat when Clara nods, spilling fresh tears down her cheeks. Her confirmation means only one thing... I *am* going to kill Damon.

Clara squeals, and my quick charge to Damon comes to a dead stop when he lifts a gun I didn't notice he had until now and points it at Clara's head.

Clara freezes, her chest the only thing rising and falling as her massively dilated eyes lock with Damon's. When I take another step closer, Damon pulls back the hammer on the gun and curls his index finger around the trigger.

"I swear to God if you hurt her…" My words trail off as a wide range of ways I can kill him runs through my mind.

"I told them not to do it. I warned them your crew wouldn't stop until you found us, but they didn't listen. None of them listened to me! Why doesn't anyone listen to me?" His last sentence is only a whisper.

"I'm listening." I take a step closer. "But pointing a gun at someone to force them to listen won't get you heard. Put the gun down, then we'll talk."

Damon laughs a painful chuckle. "Like the *talking* your crew gave the other two men? They've pissed their pants the last two nights. That's how fucking scared they are that your crew will come back and finish what they started."

"This is different. You came to me. That changes everything."

"I came to see if you had any info on who the third man was. I didn't expect to have the door opened by the same face that haunts my dreams. Why is she here? You don't bring girls back to your place!"

"She's *my* girl, Damon. That is why she's here. And if you hurt her, we're going to have a problem. Is that what you want? Is that why you came back to Ravenshoe? To start trouble?"

Damon runs the back of his spare hand under his nose before using it to reinforce his brace on his gun. His hand is rattling so much, the gun is shaking like a leaf in a hot summer breeze. "I came here to get away from that life, but they followed me here. I didn't mean to hurt her. I don't want to hurt her."

"Then drop the gun." My voice hints at my wavering constraint. "Drop it before you make another mistake you can't take back."

It appears as if Damon didn't hear a word I spoke.

"How did you know it was me? I was wearing a mask," he asks with his gaze fixed on Clara.

Clara's lips quiver as she begins to speak, "I recognized your voice when you greeted Charity."

Fuck, Charity. I forgot she was here with Clara.

My heart rate climbs into dangerous territory, spurred on by the potent rage of fury blackening my blood. Just as I begin to ask about Charity's whereabouts, my eyes lock in on a pair of red leather boots sprawled on the floor between Damon and Clara. They're the same pair Charity has worn every day since she brought them two months ago.

I hold my hands out in front of my body, signaling to Damon that I mean him no harm as I slowly walk to Charity. Fury scorches my veins when I spot the welt on the top of her head. It looks like the mark a person would get when they're struck with the butt of a gun. I crouch down in front of her to check for a pulse. My heart starts beating again when I discover a pulse—it's faint, but it is there.

In a hazed blur, the front door of my apartment is kicked open at the same time Damon launches for Clara. He curls his arms around Clara's chest and plasters his body to her back. While holding his gun to Clara's right temple, he retreats deeper into my apartment. My fury hits a never-before-reached level when he uses her as a shield to protect himself from Ryan's gun.

Damon stares into his brother's eyes while declaring, "Drop your gun, or I'll shoot her." His voice is weak and pathetic like the man he is.

"If you don't let her go, I will shoot you," Ryan warns. "Don't make me shoot you, Damon. Don't put another death on my hands."

Clara's entire body shakes as her wide, horrified eyes drift between Ryan and me. New tears fill her eyes before spilling down her cheeks.

"Look at me, Princess. Keep your eyes on me," I request, my voice scratchy as a range of emotions surge through me. "You're okay. No one will hurt you."

I take a step closer to her as Ryan and Damon continue with their negotiations. I don't hear a word they're saying, I'm too fixated on calming Clara solely by using my eyes.

My ploy seems to be working as the shivers racking her body simmer to a dull vibration. She keeps her tear-filled eyes planted on me while Damon's remain glued on Ryan.

Using his distraction to my advantage, I charge for Damon. A gun being fired momentarily startles me, but it doesn't stop my pursuit. Ignoring the thick stench of fear plaguing the air surrounding me, I yank Clara out of Damon's grasp with one hand while striking his unprotected face with my other.

A bone cracking is barely audible over the deep "oomph" expelled from Clara's mouth when she lands on her backside with a sickening thud. Damon's eyes roll to the back of his head before he plummets to the concrete, his body crashing lifelessly to the floor, knocked out by one punch.

Bullets from the cylinder of his gun fall to my feet when I disarm it before sliding it into the back of my jeans. A massive surge of adrenaline pumps through my veins as I stoop down onto my knees to gather Clara into my arms. My pulse pounds into my ears as my eyes assess every inch of her. She's alarmed and highly distressed but uninjured. *Thank fuck.*

My gratefulness doesn't last long when Clara gasps, "Ryan!"

When I swing my eyes to the entryway of my apartment, a heaviness slams into my chest when I see a pool of blood seeping into Ryan's crisp white business shirt. His eyes lock with mine—they're lifeless and tormented. His gasps are wheezy and uncontrollable as he battles to secure a full breath. He mumbles the quickest apology, spraying his lips with droplets of vibrant red blood before he crumbles to the ground.

I scramble across the floor, ripping my shirt off in the process. Dropping to my knees, I wrap my shirt around my fist and apply pressure to the bullet wound in Ryan's stomach. "Stay with me, Ryan," I beg into his desolate eyes. He stares straight ahead, not blinking, not moving, not making a fucking sound. "Don't you fucking quit, Ryan. Don't you give up."

After using my cell phone I left on the floor to call for an ambulance, Clara falls to her knees next to Ryan. "What can I do?" she asks, her voice breaking into a sob.

"Hold this."

I release my hands from applying pressure to Ryan's wound and replace them with Clara's. The rattle of her hands is felt all the way up her arms, but she maintains enough pressure to slow the gushes of blood pouring from Ryan's stomach.

Fear grips my heart when I move my hand to Ryan's neck to check for a pulse and fail to find one. Acting purely on instinct, I begin the CPR resuscitation technique Ryder made all the Inked employees train in last year. I've never been more grateful for Ryder's analness for protocol as I am right now.

I continue to pump Ryan's chest when a brunette female wearing a sleek pantsuit enters my apartment. She has a government-issued gun drawn in front of her chest, and her dark brown eyes are scanning the room. When she discovers Damon sprawled unconscious on the floor, she balks and takes a step backward. "Ryan?"

"That is his brother, Damon." My words come out garbled as a range of emotions smack into me. "He shot Ryan. He shot his own fucking brother."

The brunette's eyes snap down to mine. She takes a few

seconds to absorb the scene before she calls in a command over the police radio strapped to her shoulder. "We have a 10-71 at 1314 Coulson Avenue. Officer down. I repeat, officer down."

She moves over to check on Charity, who is slowly coming to while I continue pumping Ryan's chest. My heart is smashing my ribs, and tears are swamping my eyes, but I don't stop. I can't.

After helping Charity sit on one of my couches, the brunette drops to the floor next to me. "How long has he been unresponsive?"

"Five minutes," Clara responds on my behalf.

The brunette's eyes rocket to Clara, the shock on her face intensifying.

"Can you call Isaac? He will get the surgical team at Ravenshoe Private on standby," Clara requests to the unnamed police officer. "They may be Ryan's only chance."

The brunette curtly nods as her hand delves into the pocket of her black pants to retrieve her phone. Just as she begins talking into her cell, feet stomping booms through my ears, closely followed by the sight of two first responders.

"Thanks, we can take it from here," one officer advises me, replacing my hands pumping Ryan's chest with his own.

I take a stumbling step backward, landing on my ass a foot from Ryan. As the paramedics work on his lifeless body, the realization of why Ryan feels guilt for Chris's death smashes into me. Ryan was the one who discovered Chris. He worked on him for over thirty minutes while waiting for the paramedics to arrive. Even after they officially pronounced Chris deceased, Ryan wouldn't give up. He only stopped pounding his chest when I dragged him away kicking and screaming. He didn't want to give up on Chris just like I don't want to give up on him.

Crawling across the small space between us, I bang my enclosed fist on Ryan's chest. "Come on, Ryan, fucking fight!" I roar, pounding on his chest over and over again. "You've never given up before, so don't start now!"

I pound, and pound, and pound his chest until I have nothing left to give. The stranglehold on my heart is crippling me, and my lungs refuse to secure an entire breath.

Feeling defeated, I slump to the floor, my heart beyond broken, my eyes full of tears.

I gave it my all, and I still failed.

Just as the first lot of tears escape my eyes, a ragged gasp booms through my ears. I run the back of my hand across my cheeks before lifting my eyes. Ryan's blue eyes are open and staring directly at me. They're haunted and brimmed with worry, but they're open, and that is the only thing that fucking matters.

CHAPTER TWENTY-SIX

Clara and I have spent the last two hours sitting in a little blue room at the Ravenshoe Private Hospital waiting for an update on Ryan's condition. Other than the nurse who came in to complete a set of observations on Clara, the room has been void of any other visitors.

Although Clara is clearly in shock, she refused to take the sedative offered by the nurse. Understandably, she wants to remain lucid until we receive an update on Ryan. Charity received four stitches to the welt on her head. With a prescription for a heavy sedative and pain medication, Diesel and Johnny took her home. Although she was adamant she was fine, I didn't feel comfortable leaving her alone.

Plain-clothed detectives and police officers have lined the corridor throughout the past two hours, but surprisingly, none have requested statements from Clara or me. Their priorities also remain focused on Ryan and not police protocol.

When another shiver racks through Clara's body, I sling my arm around her shoulders and pull her into my lap.

Twenty minutes later, our heads lift in sync when a creak of a door sounds through the quiet passing between us. The beat of my heart turns crazy when a small Asian doctor with a crisp white coat enters the room. Her inky black hair is pulled off her face in a twisted design, and her lovely green eyes are issuing silent sympathies.

I stand from my chair, taking Clara with me. We stare at the doctor, blinking and muted, but I release a deep sigh when she says, "He's okay." Clara squeezes my hand tightly while the doctor continues talking, "He was fortunate he had you both there. The amount of blood he was losing would have seen him hemorrhaging within minutes. By applying pressure to the wound and keeping his heart pumping, you saved his life." Her eyes drift between Clara and me. "Both of you. He has a long way to go, but he's doing remarkably well."

The doctor accepts my offer of a handshake before she runs her tiny hand down Clara's forearm. The instant she steps back into the corridor, Clara collapses to the floor. Tears roll down her cheeks as a devastating sob tears from her throat. "It's my fault. It's all my fault," she cries through a barrage of hiccups.

After gathering her in my arms, I stride to the chair I've been sitting on for the past two hours. Carefully, I pull her back and peer into her red-rimmed eyes. "This is not your fault."

"I should have taken off my jewelry. I should have listened to you."

"You shouldn't have had to listen to me. You should be able to wear anything you want. This is not your fault."

"But—"

"No, Princess. No buts. Damon pulled the trigger. Damon shot his brother. You did nothing wrong." I cup her cheeks in my hands and run my thumbs under her eyes, catching her tears. "This is not your fault."

She looks like she wants to push the issue further, but thankfully, she leaves it as is, nuzzling into the crook of my neck.

I don't know how long we stay huddled together, but it is long enough that the watermarks Clara's tears created on my shirt have dried, and she has fallen asleep nestled into my chest. Even though my ass is dead from the rock-hard chair, I refuse to move. Not just because I don't want to wake her but because comforting her is helping heal some of the cracks that chipped my heart tonight. Her touch soothes me in a way no words can.

My eyes lift from Clara when the main door of the waiting room swings open. I'm not surprised but more apprehensive when Cormack hesitantly enters the room. His eyes are restless, and his composure is distraught. The crisp dark blue suit he was wearing earlier today is disheveled, and his hair is messy like he has been running his fingers through it regularly.

The smell of expensive cologne filters through my nose when he crouches down in front of me. Sensing another presence in the room, Clara's head pops off my chest. She inhales a quick, jagged breath as her eyes glance at her brother's remorse-filled gaze.

Launching out of my lap, she wraps her arms around Cormack's neck. Cormack draws her in close before standing from his squatted position. He mutters into her ear, but he's so quiet, I can't hear a word spilling from his lips.

I give them a few moments of privacy by stepping into the corridor. Warmth spreads across my chest when I discover the number of off-duty police officers lining the walls of the ICU hallway. It is a sea of law enforcement officers for as far as my eyes can see.

I shouldn't have expected any different. Ryan is a much-loved member of the entire Ravenshoe community, let alone his law enforcement colleagues.

Ten minutes later, my neck cranks to the side when the

visiting room door opens, and Cormack strides through. Spotting me standing to the side, he raises his index finger to a gentleman wearing a three-piece suit standing at the end of the corridor. When the dark-haired man curtly nods, Cormack spans the distance between us.

"Thank you for taking care of Clara," he says, holding his hand out in offering. "I'll take it from here."

I keep my hands fisted at my side. It isn't that I'm ungrateful for his praise, but he said it like I was paid to take care of Clara instead of doing it of my own free will.

"I didn't take care of Clara because she's a member of my crew. I took care of her because I wanted to." My angry sneer gains us the attention of a handful of officers in the hallway.

"I understand," Cormack replies, gently nodding. "But she needs more care than you can give her right now. She's in shock. She needs to see a doctor, take a shower, and eat a warm meal."

"I can give her that. You don't need to step in."

Cormack's icy-blue eyes spear into mine. "Can you take care of Clara and Ryan at the same time?"

A dash of indecisiveness tinges my mind.

"That's what I thought," Cormack replies, reading my internal dialogue. "If you care for Clara like you say you do, you will encourage her to come with me. A hospital waiting room isn't the best place for her to be in her condition."

While scraping my hand along the scruff on my jaw, I turn my eyes to Clara. She's sitting on the hard plastic chairs that line the walls of the waiting room. Her posture is slumped, her face is gaunt, and she looks both physically and mentally exhausted.

I swallow the bile sitting at the back of my throat before muttering, "If I step back, will you call a truce with Clara? Stop this stupid *lesson* you were supposed to be teaching her?" I try to keep my tone neutral, but my words still come out in a vicious snarl.

Cormack's lips tug into an uneasy smirk before he nods. "Yes. You have my word."

"Your word don't mean shit to me." I take a step closer to him. "The fact you sat back and watched all the crap Clara went through the past four months and did nothing doesn't even make you a man in my eyes. Let alone a man of his word."

"Everything I did, I did for Clara. You may think it was cruel and unwarranted, but you should be thanking me. The Clara you see in there..." he points to his sister's slumped figure sitting in the waiting room, "... isn't the same Clara she was six months ago. My tactics may have been harsh, but they were necessary."

I hate to admit this, but part of what he's saying is true. Not the part about Clara not being the same Clara she was six months ago. To me, she will always be the same Clara. She just needed to be shown she deserves to be loved. My agreement is the part I should be thanking him for. If he hadn't forced Clara out of her comfort zone, she would have never walked back into my life.

For that, I will forever be in his debt.

Ignoring the twisting of my heart, I say, "Give me a few minutes to talk to her."

Not waiting for Cormack to reply, I walk into the waiting room. Clara's downcast head lifts from staring at the floor when the door gives out a slight creak.

"Is Ryan okay?" she asks, wrongly intuiting the forlorn look on my face as concern for Ryan. The tightness in her shoulders slackens when I nod.

"Do you have your purse with you?"

She nods while slipping her hand into the front pocket of her blood-stained jeans to produce her all-in-one cell phone purse. I've been so embroiled in everything happening, I didn't even notice we're both wearing blood-stained clothes. That just proves what Cormack said is true. I can barely take care of myself right now, let alone Clara.

"Do you want me to have your luggage dropped off, or will someone from Cormack's staff come and collect it?"

Clara's brows stitch as she stares at me, shocked and dazed.

"Cormack is going to take you home," I advise her baffled expression.

"To your apartment?" she queries, her voice high and laced with worry.

I shake my head. "He's taking you home, Princess. To the side of Ravenshoe where you belong."

"I thought... I thought you said I was staying with you until all this blew over?"

Her confusion intensifies when I shake my head. "I said you were staying with me until the men who mugged you were held accountable. That has happened, so there's no reason for you to stay with me anymore." My words come out strangled since I had to fight my mouth to relinquish them.

"You don't want me to stay with you?" Although she could mean staying with me at the hospital, her eyes aren't relaying that.

"No. I don't." Pain hits the middle of my chest the instant the words seep from my lips.

Clara glares into my eyes, searching for any untruth in them. The only reason she fails to detect any is because deep down, I knew this day would eventually come, I just never wanted to believe it. But by manning up and stepping away from the plate I've been guarding the past four months, Clara's silver spoon will find its way back into her mouth, and she won't have to keep fighting the struggle she's been battling the past four months.

I care enough about her that I'm willing to give her up to ensure she's safe and taken care of.

Clara's lips twitch, dying to speak, but not a word spills from her mouth. Her confused eyes dart to the door when it flings open and Cormack steps into the room.

Releasing a deep breath, she turns her eyes back to me. "Are you sure this is what you want?"

It kills me, but I nod.

She gives it her best fight to hold in her hurt, but a rogue tear rolls down her cheek before she mutters, "Okay. Goodbye, Brax," before making a beeline for the door, exiting without a backward glance.

CHAPTER TWENTY-SEVEN

It is a little after three in the morning before I'm striding toward the automatic double doors of the hospital. I'm beat —both mentally and physically. Ryan was in surgery for a little over three hours. After spending the next four hours in recovery, he was wheeled into a double private suite in the Intensive Care Unit. Although he was awake, he was barely lucid. But, thankfully, even with his words slurred worse than the weekend Chris and I spiked his cans of Coke with vodka, his doctor assured me he will have a full recovery.

Even being informed Ryan will have no long-term health issues from his bullet wound, the sick, twisted feeling in my stomach hasn't lessened in the slightest. I haven't been able to shake off the guilt I feel for hurting Clara. I spent the last forty-eight hours renewing the spark of life her eyes lost when she was mugged all to snuff it out by lying to her face. I know stepping back is the best thing I can do for her, but it doesn't make it any easier to do. It took all my strength—*and then some*—to keep my feet planted on the floor when she bolted out of the hospital waiting room. If it weren't for a uniformed officer arriving to take my statement, I have no doubt my fight would have been lost.

My brows become lost in my hairline when I stride out of the double doors of the hospital to discover my bike is still parked in the emergency vehicle only bay I had left it in hours ago. I already have my cell in my hand, prepared to call a taxi as I had expected it to be towed by now.

Shrugging off my confusion, I make my way to my bike.

I'm walking into my apartment twenty minutes later. The heaviness that has been sitting on my chest for the past eight hours amplifies when my eyes zoom in on the puddle of blood in my entryway. Just seeing how much blood Ryan lost makes the reality of the situation crash into me.

I nearly lost him today.

He almost died protecting the woman I love, and I thank him by pushing her away from me.

I'm a fucking idiot.

Call me a pussy, a soft-cock, or any other derogative name you like, but I'm not going to lie, tears are inundating my eyes and threatening to spill down my face at any moment. Ryan is the closest thing to a brother I have. He's my family. That is why it is even more devastating that his own brother shot him.

I don't know what is going on in Damon's life, but it must be pretty fucked-up if he thought his only way out was to harm his brother. And if all that wasn't already enough to have my mood hitting an all-time-low, knowing the gun that shot Ryan was pointed at Clara's head only seconds earlier utterly destroys me. Her frightened face when Damon held his gun to her head will forever haunt my dreams.

Ignoring the pit forming in my gut, I drag a bucket and mop out of my laundry room to clean up Ryan's blood that's soaking into my wooden floor. I run the back of my hand over my cheek, angrily removing a stupid tear that escaped my overfilled eyes before clearing away the mess.

Just as I've finished mopping up Ryan's blood, tiny feet padding down my staircase jingles through my ears. When I crank my neck to the stairs, I recoil and take a step backward.

"Princess?" I ask, certain I'm seeing things. I haven't slept, eaten, or had a clear thought in well over ten hours, so a stint of insanity could be surfacing.

Clara glides across the living area wearing nothing but one of my plain white short-sleeved T-shirts. Her hair is damp and hanging loosely, her eyes are brimming with tears, and her face is void of makeup. The only difference between the Clara who left the hospital hours ago and the one standing before me is this Clara's eyes are sparked with the gleam I thought I snuffed. They're bright, determined, and one hundred percent relaying she's not leaving this apartment until she gets what she came here for.

"What are you doing here, Princess?"

The smell of freshly shampooed hair overtakes the ghastly scent of blood when Clara stops to stand in front of me. "I wanted to clean that up before you came home, but, in all honesty, I didn't know how." Her nose screws up, and she looks genuinely mortified that she doesn't know how to use a mop and bucket.

The most inappropriately timed chuckle escapes from my lips. *Yes, I've definitely hit the insanity stage of my anguish.* I can't help it, though. Clara's statement abundantly proves she's a real-life princess. *No fucking doubt.*

Ignoring my erratic behavior, Clara removes the mop from my hand, places it into the bucket, and stores it back in the laundry room. Not speaking a peep, she encloses her hand over mine and guides me to the staircase to my loft bedroom.

"What are you doing here, Princess?" I ask again, my voice relaying my disbelief.

Clara continues walking while muttering, "You're in shock." She stops pacing when we reach the base of the stairs. "You're shaking and shit. So, unless you can give me the address of a family member or friend I can take you to, I'm staying with you. I'm going to take care of you."

I arch my brow. "You want to take care of me? That's why you're here?"

She nods without hesitation before locking her determined eyes with mine.

"Why?"

"Because that's what a woman does for the man she's falling in love with. You look out for them, even when they don't want you to," she answers, her truth-bearing eyes adding strength to her statement.

The massive weight sitting on my chest vanishes in an instant. She has no idea how much I needed to hear that right now. I was barely hanging on by a thread, and she just lassoed a rope around my waist and pulled me back in.

I knew I wasn't the only one falling.

"I want you here, Princess, more than anything, but what about your silver spoon?"

She shrugs. "What about it? I have food in my belly, a roof over my head, and clothes on my back. What more do I need than that?" She rakes her eyes over the length of my body. "Well, there's one other thing I need. But, lucky for me, it's free." Her arctic-blue eyes stare into mine as she climbs the spiral staircase. "And lucky for you, I don't have any concerns about messing with a member of my crew while they're in shock."

Keeping my eyes locked on her, I shadow her into my bedroom. My heart is beating a million miles an hour, but my mind is the clearest it's ever been.

Her gorgeous scent filters through my nose when her hands move to the hem of my blood-stained shirt to yank it over my head. She works on the belt of my jeans as she guides us across the room. Once the fastener has been unbuckled, she slides my jeans down my thighs. My cock twitches when she lifts her hankering gaze to me. Her eyes relay her intentions without a word needing to seep from her lips.

"Princesses don't kneel for no one," I mutter, my deep tone conveying my wavering constraint.

She sighs softly. "I want to take care of you, Brax, to make you forget the image you should have never seen."

Who the fuck is this woman? She just saw straight through me. Only one other woman has been able to do that. My grandma.

I cup the edge of Clara's jaw and peer into her shimmering eyes. "Just you being here is already doing that, Princess. You don't need to kneel before me."

My cock leaps in my briefs when I catch sight of the determination brewing in her gaze. "Get on the bed, Brax," she demands, her voice throaty and ball-tingling sweet.

I arch my brow, feigning shock, but in reality, I'm loving the feisty spark brightening her eyes. There's nothing as captivating as a princess in battle.

Clara watches my every move as I make my way to the bed and sit on top.

"Do you have any objections to me kneeling above you?"

The thickness of my cock grows as does the vibrancy in her gaze when I shake my head. My eyes drink her in as she slowly prances my way, her hips swinging, her chest panting. A brief chuckle rumbles from my mouth when she pushes on my bare torso, sending me toppling onto the mattress.

My laughter comes to a screaming halt when she climbs onto the bed and frees my cock from the tight restraints of my briefs in one quick motion like a woman starved of my taste, then time comes to a standstill when her lips hover over the glistening crown of my rock-hard cock.

After rolling her tongue over the crest of my stiffened shaft—gathering a drop of pre-cum beading on the end—she bores her full-of-life eyes into mine. Tonight, they're so readable. They not only expose fragments of her personality I've yet to witness they also reveal she isn't just offering me her body she's offering me her heart.

I'd be lying if I said I wasn't as happy as a pig in mud to accept her offer.

EPILOGUE

My head lifts from a sketch I've been working on for the past eight weeks when a set of knuckles rap on the wooden door of my office. Diesel props his shoulder onto the wall before locking his hazel eyes with me. "We have a client out front requesting to speak to the manager," he advises, his tone gruff.

I arch my brow and glare into his eyes.

"Don't even fucking ask," he mutters to my questioning expression.

I push back from my desk and stand from my chair. After gesturing to Diesel to lead the way, I shadow him down the corridor of Inked. Charity smiles a greeting before gesturing her head to the gang-related tattoo she's placing on some young punk's rake-thin bicep. I run my fingers over the top of my scalp and shake my head. Although we haven't had any more incidents occur at

Inked the past six months, we've noticed an increase in gang-related tattoos.

Doing our bit for society, my crew inks the tattoo as requested by the client, takes a copy of the design, then sends the client on their merry way. What our customers don't know is that once they sit in a chair at Inked, they relinquish the rights to their tattoo design.

Any tattoo we believe to be gang-related is uploaded to a private server Hunter created specifically for Inked. If a gang-related crime occurs within the vicinity of Ravenshoe, we can scan the tattoo references into our database. If a compelling match is found, our information is handed to the Ravenshoe Police Department.

Although it may seem deceitful to our clients, I don't give a flying fuck. Women like Clara should be able to enter a back alley without fear of being jumped. Until that happens, I will continue my endeavor to clean up the streets of Ravenshoe.

When I enter the foyer of Inked, I swing my eyes around the room. A broad grin stretches across my face when my eyes lock in on a feisty blonde going toe-to-toe with another attractive female.

My cock jumps, spurred on by Clara's strong stance.

I've always loved a woman who gives a bit of lip, let alone a fiery-tongued princess.

Things between Clara and I have been staggering this past six months. Although Cormack kept his word by giving Clara back her silver spoon, nothing between Clara and me changed in the slightest. She still lives with me in my loft apartment, she still works at Inked, and she still continues to shock me every single day. The only thing that has changed is that I'm no longer falling in love with Clara. I love her. No doubts. No limits. One hundred percent fucking gone.

So does my grandma.

Although if she keeps nagging Clara for grandbabies, she may see a side to Clara she has not yet had the pleasure of witnessing.

I've not yet found Clara's necklace, but I won't give up until I do. I keep in regular contact with the pawnbrokers servicing the Ravenshoe area, and I called in a few favors so I have ears close to the ground throughout the entire state. When it surfaces, I have no doubt I'll be the first to hear about it.

Ryan's recovery, although rocky, is complete. His relationship with his brother... well, that's a whole other story. Unfortunately, Sophia's recovery is still a slow process. She continues to make advancements, but it doesn't appear that her level of care will be changing anytime in the future.

After giving myself a few minutes to absorb the beauty of Clara in her element, I make my way across the room. Her rich floral scent stirs my cock when I stop to stand next to her. "I heard someone needed to speak to the manager."

The petite blonde with a pixie-style haircut and piercing blue eyes shifts her gaze to me. "Yes. Becau—"

Clara shoves her hand in front of the blonde's face, stopping her midsentence. "We don't need the manager. We just need someone to give this *idiot* a hearing test. No matter how many times I tell her she will *not* be served at Inked this evening, this *moron* doesn't seem to understand what I'm telling her."

I sling my arms around Clara's waist, being cautious not to touch the newly inked skin on her hip and pull her in close to my side. "What have I told you about insulting the customers?"

Clara's icy-blue eyes blaze into mine. "I wouldn't need to insult her if she weren't *stupid*," she says loud enough to ensure the blonde can hear.

The unnamed blonde's mouth hangs open. Shock is all over her face. My cock firms when Clara maintains her ground, not the slightest bit intimidated by the vicious snarl the blonde has bestowed upon her. Keeping her eyes locked with me, Clara hands me a sheet of paper. "If you tell me this isn't a design only a *stupid* person would have inked on their skin, I'll apologize."

I drop my eyes to the sheet of paper. A grin curls on my lips when the reasoning for Clara's fighting stance becomes apparent. Not only is this tattoo hideous and overly floral, but it also has a name in thick red ink smack bang in the middle of it.

"I've explained on numerous occasions the repercussion of having a person's name inked on your skin, but no matter how many times I spell it out to her, she isn't listening," Clara advises me. "There's no cure for idiocy."

She spent four hours earlier this week in my tattoo chair having her princess tattoo covered with a new tat I designed for her. I had been working on the design from the day she stormed out of Inked rambling that she would sue me for every penny I had. Although the design was finished before she started working at Inked, I never showed it to her, worried I was exposing my hand too early, but in all honesty, even if I had shown her the tattoo, it wouldn't have changed a thing. Clara has had me over a barrel from the day I met her. She knew it and so did my cock. It just took me a little longer to submit to the idea.

It was my tattoo design that brought us back together. It was the sole reason Clara was waiting for me at my apartment the night Ryan was shot. After nursing me through my shock by using only her body, Clara admitted she found it while packing her belongings through a haze of tears. I've never been more grateful for my inability to leave work at work as I was that night.

I give Clara a cocky wink before turning my eyes to the unnamed blonde. "Is this your father's name?"

The blonde places her tiny hands on her even smaller hips before shaking her head.

"Your grandfather? Brother? Deceased uncle? Any type of

male relation?" I query while staring into her squinted eyes. When she once again shakes her head, I say, "I'm sorry, sweetheart, I can't do your tattoo."

"Oh, come on. Not even for a family member?"

I chuckle a hearty laugh. "Nice try, but I don't have any siblings."

The blonde scrunches her brows together. "Not your sibling. Hers." She hooks her thumb to Clara.

I drift my eyes between Clara and the unnamed blonde. Now that I've managed to drag my eyes away from Clara's mouthwatering curves, I can notice a lot of similarities between them. Same wintry-blue eyes, platinum-blonde hair, and flawless skin. The only difference is their personalities. This blonde is a little firecracker about to explode at any moment, whereas Clara is full of class and elegance, even when she's dishing out insults like they're grenades.

"Cate-with-a-C McGregor," the blonde introduces, holding her hand out in offering. "This ice queen's baby sister."

Clara rolls her eyes at Cate's snide comment but surprisingly, doesn't react to her taunt.

I accept her handshake. "Brax."

"So you're the famous Brax I've been hearing about. The man who thawed Clara's heart. What do you have? A magic heart-thawing penis?" Cate replies while indecently raking her eyes over my body.

This time, Clara reacts. If I hadn't tightened my grip on her waist, I have no doubt she would have leaped over the counter and strangled her sister.

My cock hardens more. Fiery Clara is beautiful, but jealous Clara... she's downright out-of-this-mother-fucking-universe beautiful.

Since I have a firm hold on Clara's waist, she issues her retaliation in another form. "I think you should do her tattoo, Brax." Her tone is sugary sweet, a huge contradiction to her earlier one.

I gawk at her, shocked and confused.

Clara playfully winks before turning her eyes to Cate. "If you're willing to make a few changes to your tattoo design, I think I can convince Brax to do it."

Cate eagerly nods. "Sure. I'm happy to make any changes necessary." She connects her lively eyes with mine. "Do anything you need to make this happen."

"Great," Clara exclaims excitedly as she yanks a tattoo contract out of the top drawer in front of her. I bite the inside of my cheek, fighting my hardest battle to hold in my smile when Clara slaps the contract onto the glass counter, hands Cate a pen, then says, "Just sign here, here, and here."

The next book in the Enigma Series is about Enrique Popov, son of Vladimir Popov and brother of Isabelle. *I Married a Mob Boss* <u>is already published.</u>

Facebook: facebook.com/authorshandi

Instagram: instagram.com/authorshandi

Email: authorshandi@gmail.com

. . .

Reader's Group: bit.ly/ShandiBookBabes

Website: authorshandi.com

Newsletter: https://www.subscribepage.com/AuthorShandi

Hunter, Hugo, Cormack, Hawke, Ryan, Rico, Brax, Brandon, Regan, and all the other great characters of Ravenshoe have their stories, and all of them are published.

If you enjoyed this book, please leave a review.

ACKNOWLEDGMENTS

Thank you to the following individuals who, without their contributions and support, this book would not have been written.

First to my husband, Chris. When I said I wanted to write a book, he simply replied with, "Okay, great." No hesitation, not even a small amount of consideration, he just offered his full support. This is very much in tune with exactly how my husband has been our entire marriage. I have an idea, and he supports me one hundred percent. I'm so grateful to have him in my life, and I wouldn't want to have it any other way. He is my most valued gift in life. Second to my darling Mum. She reads the entire first draft of every novel I've penned while attempting to assist in editing. I have never been good with anything grammatical-related, but she assists me where she can. For this, I will be eternally grateful.

Third but not at all least, to my readers. I appreciate each and every one of you. You're the reason I write something every day. It might only be a paragraph, or it may be ten thousand words in a day, but it is your encouragement and support that keep me writing.

So THANK YOU!

Please remember to leave a review of my book.
Shandi xx

ALSO BY SHANDI BOYES

** Denotes Standalone Books*

<u>Perception Series</u>

<u>Saving Noah</u> *

<u>Fighting Jacob</u> *

<u>Taming Nick</u> *

<u>Redeeming Slater</u> *

<u>Saving Emily</u>

<u>Wrapped Up with Rise Up</u>

<u>Protecting Nicole</u> *

<u>Enigma</u>

<u>Enigma</u>

<u>Unraveling an Enigma</u>

<u>Enigma The Mystery Unmasked</u>

<u>Enigma: The Final Chapter</u>

<u>Beneath The Secrets</u>

<u>Beneath The Sheets</u>

<u>Spy Thy Neighbor</u> *

<u>The Opposite Effect</u> *

<u>I Married a Mob Boss</u> *

<u>Second Shot</u> *

The Way We Are

The Way We Were

Sugar and Spice *

Lady In Waiting

Man in Queue

Couple on Hold

Enigma: The Wedding

Silent Vigilante

Hushed Guardian

Quiet Protector

Enigma: An Isaac Retelling

Twisted Lies *

Bound Series

Chains

Links

Bound

Restrain

The Misfits *

Nanny Dispute *

Russian Mob Chronicles

Nikolai: A Mafia Prince Romance

Nikolai: Taking Back What's Mine

Nikolai: What's Left of Me

<u>Nikolai: Mine to Protect</u>

<u>Asher: My Russian Revenge</u> *

<u>Nikolai: Through the Devil's Eyes</u>

<u>Trey</u> *

<u>The Italian Cartel</u>

Dimitri

Roxanne

Reign

Mafia Ties (Novella)

Maddox

Demi

Ox

Rocco *

Clover *

Smith *

<u>RomCom Standalones</u>

Just Playin' *

<u>Ain't Happenin'</u> *

<u>The Drop Zone</u> *

Very Unlikely *

False Start *

<u>Short Stories - Newsletter Downloads</u>

Christmas Trio *

Falling For A Stranger *

<u>One Night Only Series</u>

Hotshot Boss *

Hotshot Neighbor *

<u>The Bobrov Bratva Series</u>

Wicked Intentions *

Sinful Intentions *

Devious Intentions *

Deadly Intentions *